# PRAISE FOR KEEP MOVING, KEEP SHOOTING

"Hang on! An edge-of-your-seat thriller that finishes with a major bombshell. Novak's action scenes are riveting, told with the precision and lethality that only a person who has pulled a trigger can accurately portray. This book moves fast and as the ending proves, the reader should make no assumptions. An exceptional first work."

—Retired Brigadier General Mark O'Donnell, US Army

"Retired Army officer Terry Davis heeds his training to keep moving, keep shooting as he enlists friends new and old to unravel a conspiracy that threatens his life, his lover's, and the country itself. A taut, well-told story that will keep you moving through surprising twists and turns toward its dramatic climax."

—Steve McKenna, author of *Fair Winds, Following Winds, and a Few Bolters: My Navy Years*

"An exciting read from one of our nation's most seasoned, battle-hardened veterans. I could not put it down."

—Retired Brigadier General Martin Schweitzer, US Army

"An outstanding story about a warrior protecting our nation, written by a warrior who spent his life protecting our nation. A must read."

—Retired Lieutenant General James Huggins, US Army

"One of the most powerful page-turners I have ever read. *Keep Moving, Keep Shooting* is a must, especially for those who have served in the military. As veterans ourselves, my wife and I couldn't put it down."

—Nathan Aguinaga, author of *Division: Life on Ardennes Street* and *Roster Number Five-Zero*

"In Terry Davis, Clay Novak has created a character that stays with you long after you are done reading about him. Novak's words create worlds as clear as photos—and his plots will suck you in and keep you turning the pages!"

—Nick Santora, writer and producer of the
Amazon series *Reacher*

"Engaging, tense, and well-paced, Clay Novak's *Keep Moving, Keep Shooting* is a fantastic read in the vein of early Tom Clancy. A fantastic read for anyone who is looking for a suspenseful tale."

—Tracy Salzgeber, author of *The Girl in the Gun Club: My Time as One of the Few Good Men*

"A superb thriller that keeps you on the edge of tension and excitement. You look forward to what every page will bring to the web of intrigue. *Keep Moving, Keep Shooting* is a great book that begs for more from this newly published author."

—Retired General David Rodriguez, US Army

*Keep Moving, Keep Shooting*
by Clay E. Novak

*© Copyright 2022 Clay E. Novak*

ISBN 978-1-64663-846-8

Published by
 köehlerbooks™

3705 Shore Drive
Virginia Beach, VA 23455
800-435-4811
www.koehlerbooks.com

A NOVEL

# KEEP MOVING, KEEP SHOOTING

## CLAY E. NOVAK

VIRGINIA BEACH
CAPE CHARLES

*Dedicated to those of us*
*that raised our hands and took an oath*
*to defend our country*
*" . . . against all enemies, foreign and domestic."*

*And to "the Boys" of 3-505 PIR, Afghanistan 2002.*

# CHAPTER 1

His eyes opened slowly as his hand searched for the alarm clock. It was one of those old-time ones with the two bells on top and the clacker between. He didn't know if the alarm function even worked, really. His body had been conditioned after twenty-five years in the Army to wake early, making an alarm clock a moot point. As his eyes gained some focus, he could see it was just past 0630. Another habit engrained from all those years—his brain still read all time as military time. He rolled slightly in the queen bed, reaching behind him. Nothing. Cold sheets. She was out of bed and had been for a while. He should have anticipated it, after she woke him in the middle of the night by climbing on top of him. Sex like that came because she was awake and needed to burn some energy. He certainly wasn't complaining. She was an early riser, too, like him, but there was something stirring in her brilliant mind. She called it a bee in her bonnet. He referred to it as something that had lit a fire under her ass. Regardless, she couldn't sit still when this happened. She went to bed late, barely slept, got up early, and was always moving. Now, he just had to find her.

Margaret "Peggy" Baron grew up in this house. It had been in the family for almost a hundred years, like the six hundred and forty acres of Nebraska prairie it sat on. The house started as plans from the Sears catalog and piles of lumber lying next to a foundation poured by a bunch of farmers. It never should have lasted this long, but the Baron family had taken good care of it. There were creaks in the floors and some of the door hinges squealed. He always felt like he was being loud as he moved through it. Peggy could navigate it like a cat, never making a noise. He was the combat veteran and should have been the stealthy one, not her. It was almost frustrating.

He made his way down the stairs to the kitchen, peeking in rooms as he went. No sign of her. There were cold scrambled eggs with some fatty bacon on the stove, still in cast iron skillets, along with a few biscuits wrapped in a dish towel on the counter. At least she had eaten something. He assumed she was out with the horses or somewhere in or around the barn. He grabbed a biscuit and shoved a few pieces of bacon into his mouth before he retreated upstairs to get dressed.

Terry Davis would never be a cowboy. There were aspects about living out here that he loved, but he would always choose a baseball cap over a Stetson and hiking boots over cowboy boots. He grew up hunting and shooting, camping and hiking, but he wasn't a farmer or rancher and didn't grow up with horses like Peggy had. Peggy Baron grew up here and knew every inch of the property, just like she did the house itself. She spent so much of her life on horseback, Terry said he could see saddle stitching imprinted on her ass when she walked around naked. She left home at eighteen, but not as part of some teenage, rebellious tantrum. Intellectually, she was well ahead of the rural school district she had been born into and everyone knew her future was far away from the Platte River valley. After running around the globe for most of her adult life, she had settled back here to take care of aging parents and the property she loved so much. Terry had only recently begun to hang his hat here, although they had known each other professionally for years.

Terry grabbed the pistol off the nightstand, holstering it as he walked out of the bedroom, down the stairs and straight out the back door, slinging his rifle across his chest once outside. This is why he liked being out here—he carried a gun everywhere he went, and no one flinched. As soon as he started walking toward the barn, he knew where she was and what she was doing. The sound of chopping wood was distinct as it echoed off the red painted wood that enclosed the barn. He couldn't see her, but he knew Peggy was at the wood pile splitting logs. He admired her as he came around the corner and she came into view. Her technique was terrible, and she wasn't very strong, although she was working hard. The axe was old, but she knew how to keep it sharp, another skill learned living out here, so she was letting it do most of the work. He could see sweat on her neck and the faint stains of perspiration on the back of her shirt.

She was tall, about five feet nine inches, and had curves where they should be. She didn't have the typical flat ass of most women who spent as much time as she had in a saddle. She was busty, but with narrow shoulders and hips. She definitely looked like a woman, even in jeans and a work shirt. Peggy was about ten years older than Terry. He didn't know exactly how much older because he didn't care, but he was in his mid-forties and she was in her early to mid-fifties. Wandering around the house, she rarely wore a bra, and never wore panties when she was in the saddle. He found himself wondering if there was anything under her jeans and white tank top at the moment. She reached for another piece of wood and noticed him there.

"You just going to stare or are you going to help?" she said as she stood the log on its end.

"Since when do you need my help?" he returned quickly. It was a tennis match and she served first.

"If I *needed* your help, I would have dragged you out of bed." The axe came down clumsily as she tried to speak and swing at the same time, "I was just hoping you would *want* to help." She was never into the touchy-feely woman mentality, but she knew talking like this made him uncomfortable, so she did it on purpose.

"The only thing I *want* is to know what is running around in that head of yours." He leaned the black rifle against the barn and walked over to take the axe from her. "Let me chop and you fill me in on what got you naked and horny in the middle of the night." She gave him the axe, half relieved and half out of frustration that he knew her tendencies so well. He laid his gun belt across the woodpile and began to chop as she spoke.

"I was sent an email yesterday. About a threat inside the US." She looked at him as he paused briefly. The axe came down. *Chop.* "It was from the team at Whiteman. They were alerted by DHS, and some others, that there was a legitimate threat assessed to be headed there." Peggy was referring to Whiteman Air Force Base in Missouri, the home of the B-2 Stealth Bomber.

"And the threat is Middle Eastern." *Chop.*

He swung the axe. "So, they called you to see what you might know from your contacts or to see what you could find out on their behalf." He could see she was irritated at how quickly his mind worked at times. He was exactly right. "Did they send this to you unclass?" The axe fell again. *Chop.* He knew she hadn't left the property yesterday, so she wouldn't have been able to access her classified email.

"The threat was described as imminent, so they took a risk and sent it to me." He stopped chopping completely and looked at her. Her auburn hair was up in a tiny ponytail, as she had been keeping it shorter over the last year or so. The loose wisps were blowing around in the breeze and he could see the concern in her green eyes. There was more, so he waited for her to tell him. "I hadn't heard anything from anyone I knew, so I started reaching out. Every contact I have across the whole region said the same thing: 'we don't have anything' or 'nothing here.' That's never happened before. Not to me." He knew what she was saying, but this is how things worked. He would help her work through the information in her head and piece it all together. It was a beautiful, and yet very functional, partnership.

"So, you reached out to all your contacts across the intelligence community in the Middle East and got nothing." It was a statement, not a question. He started swinging the axe again, building up a light sweat of his own. "Now you're trying to figure out why—in this instance, with a very specific threat—there is a vacuum of intel at the source." Again, another statement.

She stood there, arms folded with her thumbnail in her mouth, staring out into the prairie. Her mind was turning but he was giving her focus. He continued, "So, I would say it is either independent actors not associated with any country or major terror group *or*—" she looked up at him intently as he momentarily paused, the axe above his head. "—the whole fucking Muslim world is in on it and they are working together." The axe came down. *Chop*.

She reeled back for a half second. "Why would you think that?" Peggy Baron was a world-renowned expert in Middle East cultural affairs. The region was like a second home to her; she had been moving in and through there since her early twenties. Iraq, Iran, Syria, Saudi Arbia, Kuwait, Lebanon, Israel, all of it. She spoke Arabic and could read and write Hebrew. She knew the customs, the history, and the conflict. She was protective of the people and what she loved about the region. She took Terry's "the whole fucking Muslim world" remark as an insult.

"Peggy, there is no such thing as *no intel*. You know this. Especially from that part of the world." He felt like he was getting ahead of her in analysis, which meant he had to tread a little lightly. He could see she was upset, so he gave her the opportunity to take charge of the tennis match again. "What else did they tell you in the initial message? Anything?"

"Not much. The estimate was three to five individuals, coming from the southwest. I assumed the Mexican border. It came from DHS, so I also assumed there was involvement from other agencies. I should call down to El Paso." El Paso was Peggy's shorthand for the El Paso Intelligence Center, or EPIC, that resided on Fort Bliss. It was a joint multinational interagency organization that monitored all the traffic across every border of the United States. Based on the location, many people assumed it was just focused on the border with Mexico, but it monitored the Canadian border and all seaports as well.

"I think a call to El Paso is a good idea." Terry leaned the axe against the barn, grabbing the pistol belt and rifle.

"Where are you going?" she asked as he walked by her.

"You need to get to a secure phone if this is going to be worthwhile. That means an hour drive to the National Guard armory. We need to get moving." Terry knew the National Guard unit down the road was used to Peggy just popping by unannounced. When she showed up, the captain just vacated his office and gave her his computer and phone. It wasn't uncommon for her to be in regular contact with people around the world, from the Pentagon to Afghanistan. She had all the credentials and even her own classified email account. Frankly, she had more need for the classified systems in the armory than the unit did. Terry knew the hour drive would give them more opportunity to talk through this before she got on the phone and another hour to analyze together on the way back.

"You don't need to go," she said. "I can handle this on my own."

"I know you can," he said with a grin. "I just thought you'd *want* me to go with you." It was a soft counterpunch to her earlier comment. She frowned at him as he walked by her toward the house.

Terry hung the rifle in the wall rack once he came in the door. He built the rifle a few years ago, partly out of utility and partly out of nostalgia. It was an AR-15 built to be as close as he could get it to the various M4s he had carried over his five combat tours. He built it to the same specifications as a service rifle minus the barrel. The government issued M4 had a fourteen-and-a-half-inch barrel, but the ATF said a civilian couldn't own one under sixteen inches without paying a two-hundred-dollar tax, so his rifle had a sixteen-inch barrel. Terry spent the extra money to add a Trijicon Advanced Combat Optical Gunsight, commonly referred to as an ACOG. There were better scopes out there, but he was comfortable with the ACOG and he liked it. The Surefire Scoutlight flashlight and the PEQ-15 laser aiming device were probably excessive, but he didn't care. The farm was in the middle of nowhere and if things went bad, he was a firm believer it was better to have and not need. He left it loaded with a round in the chamber inside the house and Peggy never said a word.

Both of them were dressed for doing work around the farm and not a trip *into town* as Peggy called it. Terry stopped in the kitchen for another handful of bacon and then followed her upstairs to change clothes. He walked in the same spots she did, her not making a sound and him making so much noise, he felt like he was waking the dead. Once she cleared the bedroom door, she stripped as she walked, leaving a trail of clothes from the door to the dresser. His question was answered—black cotton panties and no bra. He smiled. She was in great shape regardless of her age. With a pile of clean clothes in her hand, she brushed past him and headed for the bathroom, giving him a quick kiss on the way. She got a pat on the ass for her effort. His OCD got the better of him and he started to clean up the clothes strewn across the old hardwood floor.

"You really don't have to go," she said from the bathroom doorway trying to dissuade him. He ignored the statement. "Well, get in here then. Water conservation, remember? Let's go." She was completely naked now, standing in full view. He didn't need any more of an invitation. In public, they were very different people. Peggy appeared in every sense as an intellectual, including how she dressed, when they weren't on the farm. She wore expensive suits, designer glasses, silk blouses, and nice shoes. She looked as smart as she was. Terry was still an infantryman. He dressed in utility clothing. Unless an event required a suit, he always asked himself *can I fight in it?* before he put it on. In private, they were very similar. While the hot shower was a great opportunity for another quick round of sex, Terry and Peggy were both focused. There was some kissing and some foreplay, but they both knew this was not the time.

She was out of the shower quickly and mostly dressed while he was still drying off. Clean black cotton panties and a bra this time hidden away under a pair of casual pants, dress shirt, and even a light blazer. This was about as dressed down as she got when they went to town. He jumped into clean jeans and a T-shirt and threw a button-down shirt over the top. He slid the Glock 19 into a Kydex holster and tucked it into his waistband. He got a rare sideways glance from her. Terry carried a pistol almost everywhere he went, for the same reasons he had a loaded rifle hanging on the wall.

"What?" he asked her.

"Just wondering if that is more necessary than I believed before now. I know the world, Terry. It's full of bad people, but I always thought this place was safe. Now, I'm not so sure." There was genuine concern in her eyes. And she used his first name. She almost never used his first name.

Now he was concerned too.

## CHAPTER 2

There were two vehicles in the garage and Terry moved to the driver door of his Jeep as a reflex. She stood there impatiently at the driver door of her Audi Q5. She didn't like the Jeep on the highway, it was too tall and loud. And it was dirty inside. Her Audi was immaculate on purpose and it was *her* car, so when they took it, *she* drove. Today, she felt like driving. Terry knew it wasn't time for an argument, so he just moved to the passenger side of the Audi and climbed in. His normal response to her driving was to fall asleep so he wouldn't put his foot through the floor or his hand through the dash. In all fairness, he didn't like it when anyone else drove, no matter who it was. He hadn't been comfortable in the passenger seat of a vehicle since his father had stopped driving a few years before he died, and that was almost ten years ago. Pop taught him to drive, so he was comfortable with him in the driver seat. Even when he was a field grade officer, he was notorious for firing his Humvee drivers over and over, eventually just taking on the duty himself. Peg wasn't a bad driver, really, but she did drive a little faster than he preferred, and followed too close, too. Today he would suffer through it.

The farm sat on the edge of the 640-acre plot of land, so after about thirty yards of dirt driveway, they were up on the blacktop and heading south toward the highway. She was abnormally quiet. He had once referred to her as chatty, which she took as an insult, and he had caught an earful as a result. To her, chatty meant she was just talking to talk, not for substance, and she took offense. After a shoulder massage and a half bottle of wine, she finally settled down.

Terry told her that she never said anything simply. He had been trained not to use thirty-seven words when five would get the same message across. Their communication styles were different, that was all. She was satisfied with that but made him promise never to refer to her as *chatty* ever again.

Once they hit the state highway, Terry reached for the volume on the radio. Another sideways look. She was still processing, thinking. She clearly didn't want the radio on, so Terry sat back in the passenger seat and looked out the window. It was late August and he could see the Platte River off in the distance. In the silence, his mind turned to the duck season coming in a few months and he started making a list of all the things he needed to get done between now and then. Decoys needed some touch up paint and he needed to service the outboard on the boat for sure. Probably needed to inventory his ammo to make sure he had enough for the early teal season. It was all a mental distraction to keep her driving from scaring the shit out of him.

"Are you listening to me?" she said to him. He hadn't heard a word.

"Not even going to pretend I did. Start over," he said very plainly. Terry had been married twice before and swore he would never apologize for who he was ever again.

"Do you really think these guys are headed to Whiteman? In Missouri? Why would they do that?" she was moving forward based on what she knew and trying to form the questions she would ask to the folks at EPIC.

"Up front, no. I don't think they are headed to Whiteman. That's a suicide mission. Thousands of miles across the US, trying to avoid any and all intelligence gathering systems and every state, county, and local cop along the way. Then, once they get there, if they get there, they have to get through base security to even get on the Air Force base," he said, articulating what was in her head. "Once they are on the base, then what? Blow up a B-2 bomber? No way."

"But what if they *are* headed to Whiteman?" she asked, looking for confirmation of her other theory. "It has to be a publicity thing, right? 'We can strike you in the heart of America, at the most secure Air Force base, where your most lethal weapon is housed.' It isn't about the nuclear weapons. No way that is their goal." Terry felt like she needed him to confirm her theory.

"Then it's a publicity stunt. No impact on the war on terror, no impact on much of anything except the American feeling of security," he said in a very offhanded manor. He could see she instantly felt better.

"So, if not Whiteman, then where? Offutt Air Force Base? Some non-military target? Those are too many to name. So, where?" He could see the lightbulb come on. "I know what question to ask first."

"Tell me what you think it is," he prodded her along. He had his own idea and was willing to bet it matched hers. There was a grin forming on her face. She found a hole in the story and it should have been caught before she even got the original email from the team at Whiteman, but everyone was acting so quickly, no one stopped to think. No one noticed.

"What makes anyone think they are headed to Whiteman? None of my contacts anywhere have any indication of this, but somewhere along the line, something indicated they were headed to Whiteman. What is that *specific* piece of intel?" The grin was bigger now. "That's the first question."

He had come to the same conclusion, just with different words. He knew there was no way an operation like that could be executed without a solid support backbone including funding, transportation, a plan to buy or steal munitions, and a litany of other facets that five or six dudes couldn't orchestrate on their own. So, why would anyone think Whiteman was a legitimate target?

"Exactly. So, what is the second question?" he kept prodding her along. She thought for a minute but realized she had already asked that question out loud.

"If not Whiteman, then where?" The smile left her face. There were too many targets to name. The two of them had been brainstorming so intently, Peg didn't realize the speedometer had topped 90 mph until the county sheriff's deputy was behind her with his lights on. "Shit." Terry looked in the side view mirror and saw the lights. They were still on the two-lane state highway and there wasn't much of a shoulder to pull onto.

"There is an old lot up here by the next intersection. Just pull over there so we aren't blocking the road," he stated very calmly. She gave him an incredulous look.

"You mean the spot where the Tastee Freeze was? And then the used car lot after that? And now the spot where the salt trucks stage before a snowstorm? Yeah, I know the spot." The sarcasm was heavy. She was clearly stressed, and this traffic stop wasn't helping. Terry sat there quietly. No use in throwing gas on the fire. They came to a stop in the old lot with the deputy's car pulling up behind them. "That's new," she said.

"What's new?" he asked. The hairs on the back of his neck were starting to stand up. Every instinct he had was screaming that something wasn't right.

"The deputies around here always ride alone. There are never enough to put two in one car," she said. Terry looked in the mirror. There was a deputy getting out of the passenger side of the police car. He could see them both approaching slowly. Terry's hand moved to the Glock on his hip.

"If anything happens, just hit the gas and go," Terry said without taking his eyes from the mirror. The second deputy stopped before he got to the back of the Audi. His hand resting on his pistol. Peg rolled down her window and Terry heard the deputy on Peggy's side of the Audi.

"Ma'am, are you Margaret Baron? Can you please step out of the vehicle." It wasn't a question; it was a command.

"How do they know me? What is going on?" she wondered out loud in a hushed tone.

"Of course," he said under his breath. "Five combat tours and I'm going to get killed by Barney-fucking-Fife." She snapped a look at him. She didn't think that was funny. At all. That type of gallows humor among those that had *been there* was extremely common. Terry had spent his adult life as one of those men, and around others like him, and his sense of humor had become skewed because of it. With Peggy's grounding in the horrors of the Middle East, she normally shared the same style of humor, but in their current situation it wasn't appreciated.

Then a captain, Terry was in command of an Airborne Infantry company on 9/11. The whole world, including his, changed. He would spend the next dozen years or so in and out of Afghanistan and Iraq—five tours in all. He walked away from that life with a chest full of medals, two ex-wives, and a list of disabilities the medical folks in the Veterans Administration added up to qualify him as 100 percent disabled. Really, he walked away with a pension and a disability check that allowed him not to work if he didn't want to, and a perspective on life that made living a lot more interesting. Right now, it seemed that could all potentially come to an end because of some twenty-something deputy who barely shaved and had an itchy trigger finger. *Fuck.*

"Ma'am," the deputy said again, "please step out of the vehicle." Peggy looked at Terry and opened the door, slowly stepping out onto the cracked blacktop. Terry was cringing as he tried to keep one eye on her and the other on the deputy standing in the mirror. She stepped out of his field of view. "Ma'am, are you Margaret Baron? Or Peggy Baron?"

"Yes," she replied. "That's me. I'm sorry for speeding back there. We are on our way to the—"

"I know where you are heading, ma'am," he interrupted. "We were on our way to your place when you blew by us heading this direction." Terry was confused, but half exhaled in relief.

"Wait. You know? And you're supposed to escort us?" Terry

could hear the confusion in her voice. "I don't understand what you mean."

"Ms. Baron," he said very calmly, then lowered his voice. "Do you know the man in the car with you? Are you safe?"

"Of, of course. Yes, he is with me. Th-that is Terry Davis," she stuttered. "How do you know where we are going?"

"Ma'am, you're heading to the National Guard Armory, correct?" he asked. "The captain there is my brother-in-law. He said someone called for you and asked me to come get you and bring you there as soon as I could. He said it was important."

"A call for me?" Her confusion continued. Terry recognized quickly there was something else going on here.

"Peggy," he said from inside the car, "let's just get there and we will figure it out." With that, she nodded to the deputy and began to climb back into the Audi.

"We can take you from here and Mr. Davis can head home," the deputy offered.

"No," Terry said from inside the Audi. "If she is going, I am going." The deputy looked at her and she nodded.

"Just follow us, ma'am," the deputy told her with a shrug. "But we are going to keep it to the speed limit." Everyone piled back into the vehicles and the sheriff's car pulled in front, lights flashing but no sirens. Peggy followed closely behind.

The remaining five miles to the armory were uneventful, but there was a reception committee waiting for them. This was one of the newer armories, not one of the older ones that looked like a high-school gym from the 1950s. This building was a somewhat recent construction. Brick, steel, and glass but definitely modern. There were two uniformed soldiers who looked like they were standing guard by the front door and the parking lot had almost a dozen cars in it. Weird for a Tuesday. Terry's Spidey-senses started to kick in again. Something wasn't right.

"Those guys by the front door," he said as she pulled the Q5 into a parking space, "they're not wearing body armor, but they are armed. What the fuck is going on here?" He leaned forward in his seat, trying to get a better look. Peggy put the car in park, and they got out. The deputies didn't even stick around. They accomplished their escort mission and were already headed back out to patrol. As Terry and Peggy got closer to the front door, the guards closed ranks and blocked their path.

"I'm sorry, sir," the sergeant said, "only she is allowed inside." The two looked at each other as the door opened behind the guards. A captain came out and walked right up to Peggy.

"I'm sorry for all this, ma'am." This wasn't the first time they had met. Peggy had used the classified computer and phone here many times over the last couple of years. In fact, Captain Anderson was the third different company commander Peggy had dealt with since she moved back to the farm. "We obviously weren't expecting a phone call from the CENTCOM commander today." Terry looked at Peggy. "He wants you to call him back immediately. We had to secure the whole building since it isn't really cleared for this kind of phone call."

"Secured the whole building?" Terry asked. He had been around a lot of classified facilities, endured countless video and audio teleconferences, and read a lot of top-secret documents, but he had never seen anything like this. "Why the whole building?"

"Sir," Captain Anderson turned his attention to Terry, "this building is only cleared for secret communications, not TS." Anderson was using shorthand for top secret. "We don't have that kind of security and General Dawson said if we couldn't get her on a TS line, we had to clear the building." Again, Terry looked at Peggy. "That includes you, sir."

"The fuck it does," Terry snapped back. "I have a TS clearance, even now. I'm sure since I was General Dawson's aide when he was a three star, he'll be very happy to find out you kept me standing outside." Anderson was completely thrown by that and didn't know how to respond. A strong officer would have stuck to his guns and kept Terry out, no matter what. Terry could see that Anderson was not that guy and he planned to take advantage. The hesitation gave Peggy an opportunity to step in before Terry opened his mouth.

"I'm not calling anyone unless he is with me," she jumped in, throwing her thumb toward Terry. "So, you can tell General Dawson that, too." Terry was trying to hide his shock that she played that card. Frankly, he was impressed. Anderson melted where he stood.

"Um. Ma'am?" he was at a loss for words. She just stared at him. "Fuck. Pardon me, ma'am. Okay. I guess you're both going in then. Let them through. Please leave your phones out here. You can't have them inside the facility while you're on a secure line." They handed their phones to Captain Anderson. Peggy led the way and Terry followed, no longer hiding his grin. She would call it a shit-eating grin, one of the few terms her father had ever used with a curse word in it. They walked straight to the captain's office where the secret phone was. The big, bulky phone had a yellow post-it note stuck to it with a phone number. She reached for it and then hesitated.

"We came here to call the EPIC at Bliss. Now, the CENTCOM commander wants to talk to me." She picked up the post-it note. CENTCOM was short for Central Command. The headquarters resides in Tampa, Florida and is the joint headquarters responsible for all the operations in the Middle East. Peggy had done work for CENTCOM on multiple occasions in the past. Her expertise made her almost a regular when they were doing any deep-thinking projects related to the region. She had even briefed the commander there in the past, but he had never called *her*. With what she was told yesterday and the lack of any intel coming from her contacts, she was very confused.

"You okay?" he asked, breaking her concentration.

"Just trying to figure all this out," she said still staring at the phone number. She grabbed the phone and dialed. It rang twice and

Terry was surprised when Dawson picked up, expecting an aide or administrative assistant of some sort instead.

"Ms. Baron," the deep bass voice came through the phone loud and clear. Terry smiled. His old boss hadn't changed. "Is that you?"

"Yes, sir," she replied quickly. "I'm standing here with Terry Davis, sir. He says hello."

"Here it comes," Terry said quietly.

"Davis?" There was a pause. "Jesus," he feigned exasperation, "stay the hell away from that guy. Nothing but trouble." There was a chuckle. "I don't know what you two are doing together," the tone started to change, "but I am glad he is there. Did they clear the building like I told them to?"

"Yes, sir," she replied, still sounding nervous.

"I'm sure he is listening so you might as well put me on speaker so Terry can hear this too," there was a pause while Terry hit the speaker button on the phone base. "Can you both hear me now?"

"Hey, sir," Terry answered for them both. "It's Davis, sir. We can both hear you." Peggy stood there, arms folded with her thumbnail in her mouth just like when she was standing by the woodpile, staring at the speaker.

"Tell me what you know, Ms. Baron," Dawson said. Peggy recounted exactly what she told Terry that morning, almost word for word. She was halfway through their conversation in the Audi when Dawson broke in. "Peggy, listen to me very carefully. Terry, you too," Terry knew that tone and it wasn't good. Peggy continued to stare. "That message you received yesterday was sent from inside Whiteman Air Force Base, but it wasn't sent from the intel team. We don't know who sent it. Or how." Terry's mind started to spin. "All we know is it was sent to Peggy from Whiteman."

"Sir," Terry jumped in, "I've known you a long time and I'm calling bullshit." Peggy glared at him. "You wouldn't have called here if that was all you knew. What else is there?"

"Goddammit," Dawson said, impatience in his voice, "you were always too fucking smart for your own good Terry. We believe that someone is accessing our digital network and they are trying to get Peggy to expose her contacts in the intel world. Peggy did exactly what they wanted. She contacted all her people. All of them. Peggy, you said you contacted everyone you could yesterday?"

"She did, sir," Terry could see tears welling up in her eyes. "She contacted them all. They all told her they had no intel on the threat to Whiteman," he paused, "because there was no threat to Whiteman." It was all becoming clear to him now. Peggy had tears in her eyes. "What does this mean for those people, sir?"

"We don't know, Terry," Dawson responded softly. "And we don't know what this means for Peggy." Terry looked at her. She was still thinking about all the people she may have put at risk, never considering herself one of them. He knew what Dawson was hinting at though.

"Any chance for some help up here?" Terry was hinting at a security team.

"Right now, no," Dawson replied. "I know you, Davis. You'll do the right thing and keep her safe."

"Yes, sir." Terry meant that as a matter of course, not some gung-ho response. It was who he was, even before the Army. Even when he was a kid, he defended those who couldn't defend themselves, whether it was at school or in the suburban neighborhood he grew up in outside Chicago. He was in the first grade the very first time he punched someone in anger. Waiting in line outside the Catholic grade school, there was a fourth-grade boy picking on Terry's older sister and her friends. Other kids were standing around watching, too afraid to intervene, until Terry walked up to the bully and punched him in the chest so hard it knocked the bigger boy over. Just as that happened, the nun in charge of walking the children into the school came out and blew her whistle for everyone to get in line. The older boy never had a chance to retaliate and word spread quickly in the small school that Terry had "beat up" a fourth grader to protect his sister.

General Dawson disconnected, leaving Terry and Peggy quiet in the office. The room had gotten warm, quickly. Even with the air conditioner blasting, Terry had a bead of sweat running down his back. She exhaled deeply, as if to say *fuck.* She laid her glasses on the desk and leaned forward, rubbing her face with her hands. He knew she was thinking about the people she had contacted and now put at risk. Friends, both personal and professional. Some of them were relationships that had taken decades to cultivate. Now, she was being told she had ruined it all in one swift gesture.

Terry was thinking too, but in a different direction. Protect her. Keep her safe. Step one, get back to the farm. If it was him alone, he would never go back there, it would be too risky. He kept a go bag packed in his Jeep just in case, but they didn't have his Jeep. They had her Audi. She wasn't prepared for this, but that would be his focus for the next twenty-four hours or so. If it weren't for the horses, they could be gone in less than four hours. In the meantime, they would have to make arrangements for the animals, and he could use that time for some other prep work. His mind quickly assessed the risk—they were in rural Nebraska, they didn't know if there was a physical threat or not, and if they would have some early warning if there was. He was willing to assume this bit of risk until they could get moving.

"Now what?" she broke the silence, still with her face in her hands.

"First things first," he said. "We head back to the farm." That was comforting to her. Safe. Home. She may not realize yet that they would have to be leaving as soon as he could pry her away, but he would deal with that once they got there. She slipped off the desk and into his arms. It caught him off guard; he was already mission focused. The hug was brief, as if to say thank you. He smiled grimly a bit to himself because he knew that within the next few minutes she was going to be pissed. They turned and walked out of the office, him in front. She noticed he was no longer concealing the Glock under his shirt. Subtlety was over and he reflexively increased his readiness posture. She could see that, too, in the way he was moving.

The pair walked out the front doors of the National Guard Armory to find Captain Anderson and his people still milling around. The exposed pistol wasn't lost on Anderson either. Embarrassed neither he, nor any of his people, noticed it before they walked inside, he decided not to make an issue of it.

"Thank you, Captain," she said as she retrieved their phones from Anderson. Terry half cringed. Addressing someone in the Army solely by their rank, especially an officer, was culturally derogatory and usually reserved for an ass chewing. Peggy had never grasped this and meant nothing by it. Anderson probably didn't know any better and if he did, he certainly didn't show it. "We appreciate you letting us use your office." Terry threw him the obligatory head nod. Anderson just stared at him as the two turned and walked to the Audi in the parking lot.

## CHAPTER 3

As they got close to the SUV, she pulled the keys out of her bag and hit the remote unlock. He paused and looked at her. There was concern growing on her face.

"Hey, I got this," he said. "We will be fine. This is what I do." She paused, then nodded with an appreciative smile before she went to the driver's side door and climbed in. Terry gave Captain Anderson and his people a final wave as he got in the passenger side. Peggy whipped the Audi through the parking lot and back onto the highway. The pair were silent for the first few minutes until Terry spoke up.

"Hey," he said calmly. "Do me a favor and pull back into that lot where you got pulled over by the deputies." Peggy assumed he wanted to discuss what just happened in the armory. She couldn't have been more wrong.

As soon as the Audi came to a stop, Terry got out, walked to the back and popped the rear hatch. Peggy climbed out and followed him, curious.

"What are you doing?" she asked as he lifted the floor of the cargo area where the spare tire was stored. Thankfully, this was a model year 2016 and the last model year that actually had a spare tire in it, the newer versions had a repair kit and a jack instead of a spare. When she saw it, Terry got the reaction he knew was coming, although he didn't expect the cursing. "What the fuck is that?" Terry pulled a compact AR-15 pistol out of the spare tire compartment and extended the brace. The little rifle was in compliance with ATF guidelines, even though the barrel was shorter than his combat version at home. Because the barrel was only ten-and-a-half inches, it was equipped with what was classified as a brace instead of a stock, keeping it legal in the eyes of the government.

He kept going, the cat was out of the bag now. Reaching back into the compartment, he retrieved a magazine filled with thirty rounds of 5.56mm ammunition and inserted it into the magazine well of the rifle and turned away from Peggy. He pulled back the charging handle and released it, loading one round into the chamber. Turning back, he caught the incredulous look in her eyes as he reached inside to grab the two extra magazines. He knew silence was best right now. He closed the hatch and she spoke again. "This is *my car. You* put a gun in *my car,* and you didn't even tell me."

"Yes," he said simply. He wasn't arguing, he was agreeing with her statement. He knew she was mad because he did it without discussing it with her. If he asked, she would've said no, but he did it anyway. That's why she was pissed. The fact that he wasn't denying it and wasn't engaging in an argument about it could have made things worse, but Peggy wasn't stupid either. It was clear that he could throw out a huge *I told you so* argument because the time had come they may well need the rifle he had stashed in the car. She wasn't going to give him that opportunity, she just dropped it and walked away, climbing back into the driver seat. Terry threw the sling over his back, resting the small rifle against his chest and exhaled. "This ride home is going to suck," he said out loud to himself.

Not a word was spoken during the majority of the ride home. Terry rode shotgun on high alert for anything out of place. He knew while they were on the two-lane highway spotting a vehicle that seemed to be following them would be easy. He also knew that anyone who was capable of sending emails from a government network like Dawson said they had, didn't need to follow them. Whoever it was, they probably knew where Margaret Baron lived and could be waiting for them. Terry started planning contingencies in his head while they drove but knew that his earlier assessment of the risk was still valid; at this point, the threat was still low. He moved on while still multitasking, eyes moving from mirror to windshield to windows. He kept a three-hundred-sixty-degree scan going at all times. His mind started to build a list of the things he needed to get done when they got to the farm.

"You know we aren't staying long," he said plainly. He knew it wasn't the best way to break the long silence, but he wanted to make sure she knew before they pulled in the drive.

"What do you mean 'we aren't staying long'?" she said with a touch of residual anger.

"We can't stay long because if they can reach you by hacking government email, they know where you live," he said, purposely staying calm. "If they know where you live, whoever *they* are, they can get to you. You know how this works. We have to move." In the Army it had become a mantra to him when he found himself in dangerous situations. He had never had reason to question it. *Keep moving, keep shooting.*

"How long?" she replied quietly. His explanation made sense and she knew this wasn't a debate. She could dig her heels in, sure, but she didn't. "How long can we stay here? And what about the horses?"

"No more than twenty-four hours," he said. He was still working on the solution to the horses. "Can we just put them out in the pasture? Plenty of rain this year, the pond is full, so they will have grass and water. I fixed that hole in the fence, so they should be okay." He looked at her. Her face said she wasn't happy about it, but it was a decent short-term solution. "Does that work?"

"It's going to have to work, at least for a bit," she said, steeling herself a little. "If we are gone for a long time, I'll get Larry to come take care of them. He certainly doesn't look like either of us." Larry Deeter was an elderly Black gentleman who had been helping off and on at the farm for decades. Peggy actually had no idea how old he was, but he seemed old when she was in her twenties and that was thirty years ago. He lived nearby and was the closest thing to a cowboy or a ranch hand in the area. He knew horses, but he also knew *her* horses and that always made her feel a little better.

They pulled into the drive and she backed into the garage. She sat there for a moment before she reached for the handle. "I really fucked up, didn't I?" she said with a tear welling up. Twice in one day she'd said *fuck*. She almost never used that word. It struck him.

"No. You didn't," he looked at her. "I know more about fucking up than you ever will, and this isn't that. You did what you always do—you tried to help. Someone exploited that. It's not the same thing." She sniffed.

"Well," there was a little self-pity in her voice, "it sure feels like it." Another sniff. His body was screaming that there was work to be done, but his head told him to take the minute and let her breathe.

"I told you, we will be fine," he said, smiling at her. "I lived this life for a long time. I know what I am doing. Trust me." She nodded again and wiped her eyes, forcing a smile. Once they stepped out of the Audi, he had a feeling they wouldn't stop again for a while.

"What's first?" She was shaking a little, but he could hear her voice returning to normal.

"First, I need you to pack a bag," he said, shifting gears into mission focus. "Small. Something that *you* can carry. Not me, you. Probably a backpack. Underwear, T-shirts, socks. Maybe a spare pair of pants and another top. Minimal shave gear." She looked at him. He was talking to her like he would to a soldier. She knew what he meant, but the way he was treating her was new. "Leave some room because I'll probably have some stuff to add."

"Pack a bag. Okay." She was starting to focus. "Then what? What are you going to do?"

"I have some other stuff to focus on." He opened the door and started to get out. "You pack your bag. If we need other stuff, we will just buy it." She was looking at his back now as he closed the door. She sat for a half second, taking it all in, then opened the door and headed for the bedroom to pack. While she was upstairs, he went to the basement. Glock still on his hip, he laid the AR-15 on his workbench. He knew what was in the Jeep, so the trip to the basement was for only a few specific things. He unlocked the gun safe, exposing the plethora of weapons he kept in there. The Glock on his hip was perfect for concealed carry, but it was going into a hard-mounted holster in the Jeep and would be replaced on his hip by something with some heft.

The FNX-45 Tactical was exactly what the name lent to—a big bore pistol meant more for the battlefield than concealed carry. Throughout his career, he had mostly carried the Army's version of the Beretta 92 pistol, the M9, but when he was Dawson's aide de camp, he was assigned a Glock 19, like the one on his hip. The FNX he grabbed out of the safe encompassed everything he liked about those two pistols, but it was chambered in a good old American .45 Automatic Colt Pistol. Terry had added a red dot sight on top, a flashlight underneath, and a suppressor—all of it wrapped in a desert-sand color. He laid that pistol and three magazines on the bench next to the AR.

Back inside the safe, he grabbed the one pistol he knew Peggy could operate with her eyes closed. The old Smith and Wesson .357 Magnum her father had left her was immaculate. She had been shooting it since she was a teen and was accurate with it out to fifty yards consistently. He knew she wouldn't necessarily be happy about it, but it was going in her backpack along with a box of ammunition. The Smith was sitting next to the FNX on the bench when she came through the door. He kept working. There were three different scoped rifles in the safe for long-range shooting. He grabbed the very reliable Remington 700 from the back. He had bought it less than a year before, direct from Remington, but it was a used Army sniper rifle. Remington was selling them after they were refurbished for a somewhat hefty price, but it came with an Army kit, including the scope. Terry had only fired fifty or so rounds through the rifle, but he knew it was zeroed and he was as accurate with it as any of the other rifles in the safe. On the bench it went.

She was getting impatient. "Bag is packed, now what?" He reached over and handed her the revolver and the box of bullets.

"I told you to leave room," he said. "Load that and put it in the bag. If you have to leave something out to make it fit, then do that. The gun takes priority." With that, his head was back in the safe. She was standing there, holding the pistol, with a million questions that she knew he wouldn't answer because he neither had the time, nor the ability, to satisfy her need to know why. He grabbed the last gun he needed out of the safe. The Winchester Model 12 shotgun had been in his family for a long time. His grandmother bought it for his grandfather as a Christmas gift in 1948. For a number of years, it was the only gun Grandpa owned. Ducks, pheasants, squirrels, rabbits, and clay targets were all the victims of this particular Winchester. Inside the safe, it was one of four that looked generally the same, but this one Terry had been shooting since before puberty. Muscle memory from years of hunting and shooting clay targets had made the shotgun an extension of his body and he couldn't picture himself relying on any gun more than this one if the shit really hit the fan. He rested the shotgun against the bench, put the short AR from the Audi into the safe and closed the heavy door. She was still standing there.

"Is this really necessary?" she asked. "I mean, *all of this*. Do we really need it all?"

"Peggy," he responded calmly, "if there was ever a case of *I'd rather have it and not need it*, this is it." He began grabbing boxes of ammunition for the three guns still on the bench and jamming them into a backpack. "I hope to Christ this is nothing. I really do," for the first time, his voice started to get a little louder. "But, I will be *damned* if we are going to get caught shorthanded."

He slipped the backpack over both shoulders, with the FNX-45 inside, then slung the sniper rifle over his shoulder. He was running out of hands. He still needed to grab his M-4 clone with the ACOG he'd left upstairs. He grabbed the Winchester and with his one free hand, he grabbed her face and kissed her. "Go pack that pistol. And grab your holster off the table by the back door. Pack that too." He let go of her face and grabbed a green Army ammo can, brushing passed her as he headed for the stairs, again not looking back. She turned out the lights and headed upstairs to pack away the pistol as ordered.

Terry went straight out to the garage, snatching the M-4 with the ACOG as he moved, and unlocked the Jeep. He opened the swinging tailgate and the rear glass of the hard top, laying his small arsenal in the cargo space. Walking to the driver door, he slipped the Glock out of the hip holster and into the holster hard mounted under the steering wheel. The spare magazine from his pocket went into a magazine holder attached to the sun visor. He was moving quickly now. Ditching the concealment holster and tossing it into the cargo area of the Jeep, Terry grabbed the sniper rifle with three rounds and walked out the side door.

The big .308 caliber rounds were weighty in his hand as he loaded them into the action of the rifle. He knew the tree out beyond the barn was right at one hundred meters from the patio and planned to use it to verify the rifle hadn't lost its zero. Moving to the picnic table, he folded out the legs of the bipod and threw the rifle onto the tabletop. He hadn't grabbed his hearing protection before he came out, must have been moving too quickly. Oh, well. He looked through the scope at the tree, aiming for the center of the exposed wood where they had removed the remnants of a rotting branch that had fallen victim to a Nebraska windstorm. The rings in the wood were clear through the magnified scope. He took a deep breath . . . then squeezed. *BOOM.* He quickly cycled the bolt, sighted, and fired again. *BOOM.* He chambered the last round and looked through the scope. The first two rounds had both hit about an inch above his point of aim and were separated by less than one eighth of an inch, splintering the tree around them. He put the rifle on *safe* and carried it back to the garage.

She was standing there waiting for him, arms folded. This was going to come to a head and by the look on her face, it might be right now. He laid the rifle on the bipod in the cargo area of the Jeep and opened the bolt. The last live round popped out and Davis caught it in the air. He quickly grabbed four more rounds and loaded them into the rifle, closing the bolt with one round in the chamber. Checking to ensure it was still on safe, he slid the rifle into a green, nylon case and laid it back in the Jeep. Terry looked over his shoulder. Peggy was still standing there, now tapping her foot.

"Grab the brown cooler over there," he said, throwing a thumb to the back corner of the garage. "Put some ice and some drinks in it. Water, soda, whatever. And some food. Simple stuff. Cold is okay, but nothing frozen." He was loading shells into the Winchester and expecting a comment, a yell, another curse word, something to come back at him. He was surprised to hear her dragging the cooler back toward the kitchen to start packing it as directed. He didn't turn around, but merely slipped the shotgun under the backseat of the Jeep, leaving the chamber empty.

Terry had just slid the two full spare magazines into his back pocket, loaded the third into the big pistol, and racked the slide of the FNX-45 when he heard a crash from the kitchen. The sun was starting to set, and shadows were starting to creep into corners inside the house. Terry made his way quickly and cautiously toward the kitchen, clearing rooms and corners as he moved. Peggy was cleaning up a dropped dish that had shattered on the floor as Terry approached. He started to lower the pistol when he realized the two deputies from earlier in the day were standing in the kitchen. Something about this didn't feel right. He stopped out of their line of sight in the living room and listened.

## CHAPTER 4

Terry Davis knew he had a decision to make. He knew he could walk in and kill both the deputies before they could draw their pistols from the cumbersome gun belts around their waists. He knew that if he walked in, gun in hand, the situation could escalate rapidly and unnecessarily, putting Peggy in danger. He also knew that something was wrong and walking in empty handed wasn't an option either. He waited and listened, then his mind flashed.

He was back in Afghanistan ten years earlier, working as the aide de camp for then Lieutenant General Dawson. They were on a battlefield tour, visiting one of the combat units operating in the mountainous east on the border of the historic tribal areas that bled over into Pakistan. After the helos landed, they were ushered into a plywood building to attend a meeting with local Afghan tribal and governmental leaders. It wasn't anything they hadn't done before and, truthfully, Davis was distracted by the female intelligence officer that was trailing along in the crowd of people surrounding the general's party as they moved from the rock helipad to the building. He wasn't easily distracted, but in this case, it was hard to miss how her ass fit into her uniform pants.

As everyone got seated in the big conference room, Davis took to his normal routine of getting his boss settled. As Dawson sat down, Terry dropped a handful of fireball candies on the table in front of him and took a small foil packet from his sleeve pocket. He grabbed the preplaced bottle of water from the table, opened it, and dumped the powder from the foil packet into the water. He shook the bottle and placed it next to the candies in front of his boss. It wasn't great, but the peach tea flavoring was something his boss liked and that was Terry's job: keep the boss happy. He had the timing down perfect. As he stepped back against the wall behind Dawson, the colonel running the meeting began to speak.

Davis looked over his left shoulder to take a peek at the intel officer with the great rear end. She was standing against the back wall like Terry and the rest of the minions, and he was trying to determine if the face was a good as the ass with only her profile to judge from. Out of the corner of his eye, he saw an Afghan soldier in the corner of the room begin to move. Something wasn't right and Davis could see the guy was mumbling to himself as he moved. Terry watched, scanned, took in every detail and processed it all quickly. The man moved deliberately but Terry couldn't tell where he was going, what he was doing, or why. His hand fell to the Glock on his hip as a reflex.

Suddenly, the man vaulted the table to get to the center of the room, knocking over two elderly Afghan tribal leaders in the process. He had barely opened his mouth to shout "Allah hu Akbar" when Davis shot him in the face. *Bang.* The whole room scrambled. People dove under the tables or to the floor. Others with nowhere to go just ducked down. The dead Afghan soldier crumpled on the floor and Davis sprung over the table to the body. Now people started to clear the room as quickly as they could. Terry turned and looked back at his boss as he knelt, pistol still in hand, over the body. Dawson never moved, still sitting with his peach tea in his hand. Terry could see his hand was shaking.

There was a 9mm hole where the tear duct used to be and a big, bleeding hole in the back of his head where the round had exited. Terry could now see, for sure, the suicide vest that was concealed underneath the Afghan army uniform top worn by the would-be bomber.

Terry's mind flashed back to the present, standing in the living room. He came around the corner, slowly, peering into the kitchen.

The deputies were there, all smiles, guns still in their holsters and bending over to help Peggy with the broken glass.

"We are so sorry we startled you ma'am." It was the deputy that had ordered Peggy out of the car earlier in the day. "My brother-in-law asked us to stop by out here a couple of times tonight to check on y'all. We rang the bell, and no one answered—" His voice was louder than it should have been.

"You just came in!" Peggy interrupted him. "You just came into my house and scared the hell out of me. Who do you think you are?" Peggy threw the large chunks of broken dish into the trash can as she laid into him.

"Yes ma'am," the other deputy stepped in, quieter than his partner. "The glass by the front door was broken, so we came in to check to see if everything was okay."

Peggy froze and looked at the deputy. "What do you mean *broken?*"

Terry stepped into view for the first time. He leaned against the doorframe, concealing the pistol still in his hand. He startled the two deputies.

"Jesus, sir. You scared the shit out of me." It was the first deputy again, holding his chest. "Sorry for the language, ma'am."

"Answer her question," Terry said deliberately.

"Well, more like *gone* than broken," the younger man said. Terry's senses started to tingle. "The glass panel, you know in the frame around the door? The one next to the lock is gone."

Terry looked at Peggy. "Get to the garage." She nodded as he came fully into view, the big desert-colored pistol in his hand visible to the deputies for the first time. "You stay with her," Terry said to one of the deputies. "You come with me." Terry raised the pistol to start clearing rooms.

Not really knowing what he was doing, the deputy behind him followed his lead. Peggy and the other deputy flashed by them, moving to the garage. Terry decided that the two deputies were not the threat. Splitting up from Peggy wasn't optimal and neither was trusting the deputy to protect her, but he needed to take a look at the missing glass himself.

As he reached the front door, he could see the empty side window. Peggy was a lot of things, but an avid housekeeper wasn't one of them. The remaining panes all had a slight dingy film on the glass. The missing pane stood out without that gray, dirty tint. There was no pane inside or outside of the frame. It didn't fall out. There were no pieces of broken glass either. Terry knelt down to get a closer look. He could see the glass was cut, as there were remnants with flat edges still in the frame, not jagged like they would have been if it had been broken. This was professional. Someone wanted to get in and out without raising an alarm, but something else didn't seem right. Terry didn't have time to think through that; he had to get Peggy out of here. He stood, turned, and brushed past the deputy.

"Where are you going?" the young deputy called behind him. Terry didn't have the time or inclination to explain. He kept moving to the garage. Coming through the door to the garage, he could hear the deputy by the front door on his radio calling in a "suspected B and E at the Baron place." *Gotta love small town cops*, he thought. He expected to hear the echo of the radio call coming from the radio mounted on the other deputy's shoulder, the one who was supposed to be protecting Peggy. It took a half second to register that there was no echo. It wasn't being transmitted and broadcast like it should have been. It was being faked.

As he came around Peggy's Audi, he could see her standing over the deputy. He was sprawled on the ground, unconscious. She had her daddy's revolver in her hand and had clearly knocked him out.

"What the fuck?" he breathed quietly. She merely held her finger to her lips, indicating he needed to be quiet. She reached under his body and pulled out a small, red, metal object. A glass cutter. She would definitely have to explain this when she got the chance, but now was certainly not the time. He looked at her and moved to the body. He made a gun shape with his hand and pointed to the door. *Pull security.* Terry grabbed the deputy's cuffs off his belt and secured his wrist to the sidestep mounted on the Audi and then removed the Sig Sauer pistol from the cop's equipment belt. Terry looked up. Peggy was dutifully watching the door into the house, pistol in hand. He reached into the back of the Jeep, grabbing the suppressor for his FNX and threading it onto the barrel quickly. He gave her another hand signal, palm up and facing her. *Stay here.* She nodded.

Terry couldn't hear the other deputy anymore. He had stopped pretending to use his radio and gone silent. It was darker now and Terry knew the house itself would be his ally. If the deputy moved, the floor would give him away. He stopped inside the kitchen, leaning against the wall, feet flat on the linoleum floor. He listened. There was already a prisoner to interrogate, handcuffed to the Audi in the garage. He didn't need to keep this deputy alive. If the man gave him a reason to kill him, he wouldn't hesitate. He didn't want to kill him, but he would. *Creak.* It came from the dining room in front of him. He saw a shadow move. *Creak.* Getting closer. At the edge of the kitchen now, just outside the doorframe between kitchen and dining room. He saw the barrel of the officer's Sig before he saw the man himself. Terry knew the old walls were paper thin and wouldn't do anything to stop, or even slow, the .45 ACP rounds in his pistol. He purposely fired low, through the wall, striking the deputy in the thigh. The subsonic rounds, matched with the suppressed pistol, made hardly any sound at all. The deputy collapsed and screamed, dropping his pistol as he grabbed his leg. Terry came around the corner, shoving the suppressor into his face.

"I'll fucking end you right now," he said calmly. "What are you two doing here? Why did you break in?" The deputy he'd called Barney Fife earlier in the day was whimpering now, understanding that his pain was secondary to what may happen to him if he kept screaming.

"That, that National Guard guy . . . he called Jimmy . . . oh fuck this hurts . . ." Terry squeezed the man's bleeding thigh. He bit his lip, trying not to scream. "He said to come out here. Check on you guys."

"Bullshit," Terry squeezed again. "Why are you breaking in if you are just supposed to check on us? What's with the fucking glass cutter? And faking the radio call?" This time the deputy wailed in pain but there was genuine confusion in his eyes.

"We didn't break in. I swear," he was crying now. Real tears. "Jimmy told me to check out back. I just walked around. I, I came back, and he had the door open. He said he found it that way and we came in." None of this was making sense to Terry but he really didn't think the kid was lying.

"What about the radio?" Terry asked. "You never transmitted. It never came across the radio."

"I swear, I swear, I pushed the button," he replied. "I don't know man. I need a fucking doctor. Oh my God this hurts."

"Don't fucking move," Terry hissed at him. He picked up the officer's Sig and went to the garage. He knew Peggy was keyed up, so he took some precaution. "It's me. I'm coming in. Don't shoot," he said loud enough for her to hear. She came out from behind the Jeep, pistol still in hand. Officer Jimmy was still out like a light. "Why did you knock him out?"

"I'm fine, thank you," she responded with more than a hint of sarcasm. "And what do you mean, why did I knock him out?"

"What caused you to whack him over the head?" he responded trying to maintain his cool.

"Because of this," she snapped back, holding up a small black box. "Do you know what this is?" Frankly, he didn't. It was about the size of a garage door opener. There was a small red light on it. He stared blankly. "This is a fucking signal jammer. Cell phones, radios, everything." That was three times today she'd used that word now. *Might be a record*, he thought. She continued, "He had this in his hand. I checked my phone and it had no signal. That little x in the corner. Nothing."

"And that's why you whacked him?" he said incredulously.

"*No*," she was getting pissed. This wasn't a tennis match; it was a boxing match. "I hit him because he had this, he had the glass cutter—which means he snuck into my house— and because he tried to kill me." She pointed to a fixed-blade knife laying on the floor. It was the first time Terry noticed it. It was a knife not all that different from the Ek combat knife he'd carried on his kit. It was a knife designed for one thing: killing. This was a cheap knife, probably bought at a local gun show and made in China, but nonetheless, it was only meant for killing.

Terry was dumbfounded. Frankly, it was more about her reaction than it was the fact that the deputy had tried to kill her. She had put him down, knocked him out, and remained calm and quiet. He was both surprised and proud, a mix of emotions that was foreign to him.

His mind started to work. He needed to get back to the other deputy and see if that little shit was telling the truth or not. Was this Jimmy acting on his own or was he in on it? He grabbed the jammer from Peggy and went back into the house.

"Where are you going?" she called after him.

The deputy was still bleeding on the floor and was quickly losing consciousness.

"What is this? Have you seen this before?" Terry said to him, holding the jammer in front of his rapidly dilating eyes. "I'll call you a doctor, but you have to level with me. If you don't start talking, I'm going to let you bleed out and die."

He started to mumble "I've never seen that before. I don't know what it is." It was barely coherent. "I need a doctor."

"Terry!" Peggy yelled from the garage. He sprung to his feet. The deputy may die, but that was less of a concern right now. Moving quickly, he could hear her struggling. When he got into the garage, Officer Jimmy had Peggy by the leg with his one free arm. He was still groggy but was trying to drag her to the floor. Terry stepped in and calmly jabbed his thumb into the officer's eye. He squealed as he released Peggy.

"Alright fucker, you're going to tell me what is going on or I am going to blow your brains out," Terry said with a tone that was both calm and frightening. "Your partner is inside and dying. You can join him if you want, or you can tell me what you are doing with this." He held up the jammer. "And then you can explain why you tried to kill her." Peggy stood quietly and watched. She wasn't squeamish, but this was clearly Terry's show and she wasn't going to step in no matter how bad things got.

"Because she's a fucking terrorist," Jimmy spat back.

## CHAPTER 5

Terry and Peggy looked at each other. *A terrorist?* Terry was starting to replay all this in his head in shorthand, looking for anything he missed. *Cops show up. Come in through the front door. Scare Peggy. Say the glass was missing.*

"Wait a second," Terry said focusing on Jimmy. "You told us the glass was missing. And you have a glass cutter. Did you remove the glass?" Nothing. No response. Jimmy just stared at Peggy. "Did. You. Remove. The. Glass?"

"Yeah," he responded, turning to Terry. "I cut the glass."

"Why did you tell us it was missing if you did it?" Terry asked, trying to put all this together. "That doesn't make sense. Why give yourself away?"

"Because he knew you would investigate," Peggy was putting puzzle pieces together as well. "And that would allow them to separate us and deal with us individually."

"Except the other guy wasn't in on it, right?" Terry added. "That kid had no idea you were coming here to kill us, did he?" Peggy was behind in the analysis. Terry was outpacing her again. "Let me guess, you kill us and then you kill him. Make it look like we did it and you took down the terrorist lady. Big fucking hero." Peggy's eyes got wide.

"Wait," Peggy interjected. "Who told you I was a terrorist? Where did that come from?"

"Fuck you, lady," Jimmy said with hate in his eyes. "I'm not telling you shit. Muslim-loving bitch." Terry punched him in the face, breaking his nose. It exploded with blood.

"Let's try that again," Terry said as he grabbed the man by the hair. "Who sent you out here and who told you she was a terrorist?" The deputy was trying to shake the cobwebs out of his brain after the punch from Terry. "Who sent you? This is the last time I'm asking."

"Fuck you too, Army boy."

"Peggy," Terry reached out, handing her the Sig Sauer he had taken from the deputy inside the house. "Shoot this fucker in the face. That's his partner's gun. We can make up whatever story we like about these two after they're dead." Peggy took the gun. He didn't know if she could actually do it, but he hoped she was going to be smart enough to back his play. "Let me get out of the way first." Terry stood up and backed away. The deputy looked Peggy in the eye, and she sold it. Terry always said she needed to learn poker because she could convince anyone of anything, just with a look. He started to scramble, clawing at the cuff on his wrist. Terry added, "Don't hit your car."

"Stop! Wait!" he cried out. "Wait, wait, wait. It was my brother-in-law. After we escorted you, he sent us out here to put that thing in your house. Said it was national security." Terry and Peggy looked at each other. "He said you were a suspected terrorist. He told me not to tell Danny, just come out here and do it." Terry assumed Danny was the one dying on the floor in the house. "And, and then we put it in the house and, fuck, and I forgot to turn it on. So, we came back."

"Why the jammer?" Peggy asked.

It hit Terry like a sledgehammer. "We need to go, now." He grabbed the Sig from Peggy and threw it into the house. "Go get the cooler and get in the Jeep!" he was more urgent now. Peggy knew that tone and obeyed without questioning. The small-town deputy on the floor was confused.

"Where are you going? Hey! You can't just leave me!" the officer shouted as Terry closed all the doors on the Jeep and climbed in the driver seat.

"Someone is coming, right?" Peggy asked as he closed the door.

"That's what the jammer was for. So, no one, not even the police, can call for help." He reached past her and hit the garage door opener. He pushed in the clutch, started the engine, and put it into gear. The garage door couldn't open fast enough. Terry was only hoping whoever was coming had a hit time in the middle of the night and weren't waiting for them when the garage door opened.

While it was dark inside the house and the garage, there was still some of the orange glow on the horizon that lingers for about a half hour after sunset. Just enough light to drive for a while without lights on. Another one of those times that Terry was happy he disconnected the daytime running lights that came standard on the Jeep. The engine rumbled as they rolled out of the garage.

"Keep your head down," he told her closing the garage door behind them. He came out of the drive and headed north, the opposite direction they'd headed this morning. Not to the highway and not into town. Terry wanted to get some space between them and the farm. There was a blacktop road a mile north that headed west. The only traffic on that road was tractors and grain trucks. He would be able to see anyone coming from a long way out.

"Do you still have the jammer?" she asked.

"Yeah, it's in the backseat." He was focused on the road, but she made him curious. She started climbing into the backseat to find it. "Why?" He caught himself looking at her ass as she was digging around back there. She reemerged from between the seats with the jammer in her hand, red light still glowing. "We need to get rid of that thing," he said.

"So, here's the rub," she started, using a phrase she had learned from him. "There may be a tracker on the Jeep. The jammer should negate that, jamming the tracking signal. That's a good thing." She stopped. She was starting another tennis match and he wasn't in the mood.

"And?"

"And . . ." she was smiling because she couldn't see his frown in the waning light. "Well. It's more of a *but* than an *and*, really."

He snapped a little. "Peggy, just tell me." He reached down and turned on the headlights for the first time. She could see his face in the dash lights and decided it was best to cut to the chase.

"*But,* we are a rolling dead spot." He caught her meaning, but just let her talk. "Anyone who is experienced in electronic tracking may realize it and do a reverse track, looking for a lack of signal instead of the tracking signal. Not likely, but possible. And not easy."

"Well, the good news is," he chimed in, "we are in the middle of fucking nowhere Nebraska, so there is no cell coverage in most places here anyway. Finding a rolling dead spot out here will be even more difficult. We also won't be able to listen to the radio, so our situational awareness won't be great. If we hit the news, we won't know it."

Terry looked down at the clock and realized it had been just under an hour since the deputies scared the shit out of Peggy in the kitchen. It seemed like everything that transpired since then had taken a lifetime. He had been through this before. In his experience in Iraq and Afghanistan, firefights seem like they last forever but when he looked at his watch, they were over in minutes or even seconds. The adrenaline was wearing off already. He wasn't a kid anymore and knew events like this will wipe a person out. He knew at some point, the two of them would have to rest and recap what had happened and what their next move was going to be. He looked over at Peggy. In these few moments of silence, she'd crashed. She wasn't a kid either, and days like this weren't part of her DNA like they were his. She was asleep, holding the jammer in her hand, red light still on. Terry turned his eyes to the road and soon made the left turn onto the blacktop and headed west.

Terry tried to keep himself engaged to stay awake. He did whatever he could to keep his mind and body occupied while trying to let Peggy sleep. Keeping her safe included keeping her healthy, and that included sleep. He knew the rush out of the garage left all their gear a fucked-up mess in the back of the Jeep. There were guns everywhere and any cop that stopped him would probably drag him onto the pavement and put him in cuffs. He knew if he tried to analyze what had happened on his own, he would probably fall asleep. He needed that interaction with Peggy, both to make sure he didn't miss anything and to keep him awake, but she needed the sleep.

He checked what he could while switching hands on the steering wheel or even driving with his knees. He checked the Glock under the dash and the spare magazine on the visor. He pulled a Mt. Dew from the cooler and unscrewed the cap, hoping the fizz from the carbonation wouldn't wake her. The caffeine would help keep him awake. He reminded himself to get some Copenhagen dip whenever they stopped for gas. It was a thirty-year habit he'd started and stopped a half-dozen times. After his second divorce, he stopped trying to quit. Peggy tolerated it, never complaining, but usually turned up her nose when he tucked a pinch between his gums and his bottom lip. He had half a can left, so that would get him through the night and part of the next day.

He looked at Peggy again. They had met about twenty years before and the years had been kinder to her than to him. They looked about the same age, but the miles on his body and his soul had been rougher than hers. She was an academic and he was a grunt, and the physical impact of those two very different lives was apparent. The ten-year age difference wasn't noticeable to anyone unless they had known them in their younger days. She had been married once, a long time ago. Unsurprisingly, he was from the Middle East, where she had focused so much of her life. He was Syrian by birth, but his family left when he was a child and he was raised in a Muslim neighborhood in London. He could never embrace who she was and how widespread the respect for her was in the international community. Calls from international organizations, the US military, and Washington DC thinktanks to tap into her expertise always irked him. Her husband felt his wife should be prioritizing him over everything else. She would pack a bag and get on a plane in a moment's notice to go sit on a panel or participate in a planning group. Then she would come home to a dirty house, piles of laundry, and dishes in the sink. That started to grate on her as well.

She felt guilty that her first reaction to his untimely death was one of relief. He had been killed while driving recklessly, and just below the legal alcohol limit, on the George Washington Parkway one rainy night. Three days later, she was in a market in Baghdad when her cell phone rang with a call from his family in London. The DC Metro police had been to their house to notify her for two days straight, and when they couldn't get in touch with her, they tracked down his family. His traditional Muslim family was irate because she wasn't there, he hadn't been buried within twenty-four hours, as was the Muslim custom. They blamed her for all of it, especially his death. If she had been home, where they thought she should have been as a dutiful wife, this never would have happened. She saw his family once after he was buried and never spoke to them again.

She told Terry the relief she felt was reflexive, but it did always bother her. She knew she was no longer bound to him or their house or anything else. She was free to pursue whatever, or whoever, she wanted. Free to travel, to write, to do whatever she wanted. It was, in fact, a huge relief, but she still felt guilty that she felt that instead of sadness. She had even wondered if there might be something wrong with her.

Terry knew he was the only person she ever shared that with. It wasn't in some emotional outpouring, or even a drunken rambling, but sitting on the back porch of the farmhouse sipping a glass of bourbon on a summer night about a year ago. It had been ten years since he died, and she harbored that feeling until that evening. That was the first night Terry stayed until morning. He had been there ever since.

Terry turned his eyes back to the road. It was amazing he hadn't wrecked the Jeep on that blacktop. He had been looking over at Peggy for most of a minute while his thoughts wandered. Thank

God for Midwest roads that are dead straight and dead flat. He finished the bottle of Mountain Dew and put the empty bottle between his legs. He readjusted himself after fishing the carboard tin of Copenhagen out of the back-left pocket of his jeans. Tapping the can on the steering wheel he looked at Peggy again, conscious to make it a much shorter look. He knew when she woke up, she was going to be *full of piss and vinegar*, as his grandfather used to say. He was mentally preparing himself for it. The gas gauge was sitting just below half, and Terry knew he had a full five-gallon can strapped to the rear bumper. They could drive for quite a while longer if needed, but he hadn't determined exactly where they were headed—away from the farm was his only goal.

Making a decision on their next move without her input was probably more dangerous at this point than he could even imagine. He thought about the back of the Jeep being a fucking mess as his OCD was kicking in again. The clock said it was just before midnight, which his brain processed as 2357 hours, but he knew they were going to need to stop soon. They needed gas, he needed rest, and they needed a plan. His mind was spinning, and he needed to settle himself. He had a feeling this was going to be a marathon and not a sprint. He opened the tobacco can and put a pinch of snuff in his lower lip. He could hear Dawson's voice in his head: *"Keep her safe."*

He was thankful, without the use of the radio, that the old Jeep still had a CD player in it. He was even more thankful that the second Led Zeppelin album was already in the player. He turned up the volume loud enough to hear it but not loud enough to wake Peggy. The opening guitar riff of "Whole Lotta Love" came through the speakers as he spit into the bottle and stared into the darkness.

## CHAPTER 6

It was just getting light when the pickup truck pulled into the gas station. Terry sat awake in the driver's seat with the door open as the big white Chevy headed straight toward the Jeep. He reflexively put his hand on the Glock under the dash and watched the pickup slow as it got closer. The old man behind the wheel was cranking the window down by hand and it took a minute before he spoke.

"Nice Jeep," he said from underneath the beat-up trucker hat on his head. "You're parked in my spot."

"Damn, sir," Terry said. "I apologize. I'll move it so you can park." The gas station was an old one, definitely not a twenty-four-hour place with bright lights and some tattooed and pierced kid sucking on a vape pen behind the counter either. It had been closed when they pulled in. The pumps didn't even have the credit card scanners, not that Terry was going to use one and give anyone who was looking for them a clue to where they were. It was exactly what Terry was hoping to find when he pulled into this tiny Nebraska town at two o'clock that morning. Terry noticed the little lady in the passenger seat. It was safe to assume she was the old guy's wife. "Sorry for the language, ma'am."

The old man looked at his wife and returned with a grin. "Nah, leave it. I'll pull in over there." The window went up as slow as it came down and the old man pulled his truck to a spot about twenty feet away. Terry got out of the Jeep to meet the old man. He watched this sweet looking old couple slide out of the big pickup. He was in jeans and suspenders with a short-sleeve, snap-button shirt, work boots, his cap, and dirty eyeglasses. He couldn't have been more than five foot six inches and a hundred and five pounds. He shuffled when he walked. His wife was barely five feet. She was a round woman in a blue dress, with white hair and glasses on her nose. She moved better than he did and was around the tailgate quickly. When Terry got close, he reached out his hand.

"You ain't from 'round here," the old man shook Terry's hand. "I bet you need some gas. Let me get inside and turn the pumps on. I'm George and this here is Juanita." Terry smiled.

"Ma'am," Terry said as he reached his hand out to her. "Sorry about the language before. I didn't mean to offend." The old woman took his hand in a powerful grip.

"Son," she started, "I been married to a farmer and hanging around this gas station for almost sixty-five years. You can't say shit to offend me." She winked. Terry smiled. "That your wife in the Jeep? Lady-friend?" George disappeared around the front of the building.

"Let's go with 'lady-friend.'" Terry said, still smiling. He looked over his shoulder. Peggy was still asleep, but he knew that wouldn't last long. The sun was starting to peek over the horizon. "Do y'all have any food in there?" Terry was from Chicago but spent most of his career south of the Mason-Dixon. He could sound as Southern as he needed to, whenever he needed to.

"If'n you got some time, I'm gonna get the grill fired up and I can cook some breakfast for y'all," she said as the lights on the pumps came alive. "We only take cash, though."

"Well," Terry said trying not to lay on too much accent, "cash is all I got. And some real food sounds perfect." She turned and headed to the building. Terry turned back to the Jeep. Peggy was awake and climbing out the passenger door.

"Good morning, young lady," Terry started as did most mornings when he awoke before her. "How are we feeling?" He was tired and she could see it. She was willing to bet he hadn't slept a minute.

"Well, old man," she replied dryly. The tennis match was starting early. "I feel better. And you look like hell." She stretched and looked around. "Where are we?"

"One of those one-horse-towns in the middle of nowhere you always talk about," he quipped back. "I stopped a few hours ago. Those were the owners I was talking to—George and Juanita. She is going to cook up some breakfast. We will get some gas and figure out what our next move is." Peggy was freshening herself up as best she could, trying to brush the wrinkles out of her clothes with her hands and fixing her short ponytail in the sideview mirror. "One of us needs to stay close to the Jeep." Peggy had a panicked look on her face and started patting herself like a man who had just been pickpocketed.

"The jammer," she said with wide eyes. "Where is the jammer?"

"I thought that through before we pulled in," he said as he walked to unstrap the gas can on the bumper. "Those two cops didn't have time to hardwire a tracking device. We weren't gone that long. So, if there was a tracking device on the Jeep, it would have to be a hasty emplacement. I went over the exterior of the Jeep with a flashlight and a fine-tooth comb when we got here. I couldn't find anything, and I know this Jeep like the back of my hand." She knew that wasn't much of an exaggeration. He spent as many hours working on the Jeep as he did shooting—and that was a lot. She also knew from his stories that he knew what he was looking for. When Terry was in Baghdad, the US had initiated a classified program that was commonly referred to as TTL, which was short for tag, track, locate. His unit had been trained to install various tracking devices on vehicles to try to target terrorists. While they never did much of it in the city, Terry was a hands-on officer and went through all the training with his soldiers. If he couldn't find it on his own Jeep, it wasn't there.

"So, did you turn it off?" she asked reluctantly. "Not that anyone in this town would notice if they lost cell service."

"I haven't yet, for that exact reason." She felt better once he confirmed her conclusion. "We still need to dump and reorganize the inside of the Jeep. Once we do that, I will check all the nooks and crannies to make sure no one put one inside. I didn't think that digging through the arsenal in the back of this thing, out in the open, was the best idea." He was standing there with the gas can in his hand.

"Y'all want some food," Juanita called leaning around the corner of the building, now wearing an apron over her blue dress. "The grill is hot."

Terry waved to her. "Why don't you go in and order us some food. I'm sure they have a bathroom in there. I know I need to piss, and I'm sure you do, too." She pursed her lips at him. He was right, but she wasn't a soldier. He reached into his pocket and gave her some cash. "They only take cash." She turned and walked toward the building. "Hey . . . see if they have an old landline in there, too."

Terry went to the gas pump to top off the Army issue, five-gallon gas can. Peggy went into the small gas station and grill. It was an old building but very familiar to her. She frequented buildings like this in her hometown as a child, riding along with her daddy on the weekends. It was their time together, every Saturday. Gas stations, dime stores, hardware stores. Whatever errands he had needed to run, Margaret had gone with him. He was the only one who called her that. Even her mother called her Peggy.

Juanita was behind the counter, standing at the grill. George was sitting next to the cash register, newspaper spread out on the counter. Something told her they didn't get many visitors to their little business. Remnants of years gone by could be seen everywhere. It was almost cliché. There was a tear away calendar from the 1980s on the wall. Peggy left her glasses in the Jeep, but it looked like someone stopped keeping track in June of 1986. It wasn't cluttered like many of these old buildings were, but there were a few knickknacks strewn about. It was clean and orderly. There were still metal napkin dispensers on the counter, with glass salt and pepper shakers and glass ketchup bottles. In the cooler by the door there were cans of soda, probably bought in cases from the local grocery and resold individually. Her mind was wandering when she realized Juanita was speaking to her.

"What can I getcha, darlin'?" she said wiping her hands on the apron. This wasn't a place that had menus behind the counter. There was a chalkboard to let you know what was being cooked that day, take it or leave it. Peggy assumed they had the normal stuff like burgers and grilled cheese for lunch. Breakfast was probably the same.

"Um, can we get four breakfast sandwiches?" she asked. "To go?"

"Sausage or bacon on them sandwiches?" Juanita had already turned to start cooking. "Y'all want some coffee too? Ain't got any juice or anything. George says it goes bad fastern' we can sell it." George grunted at the mention of his name, never looking up from the paper.

"Two sausage and two bacon, please," Peggy responded. "And two black coffees. Do you have a restroom I can use?" George threw his thumb over his shoulder. He still never looked up from his paper. Peggy wandered into the back and found the only bathroom they had. No male and no female, just one bathroom. Peggy splashed some water on her face and even under her arms and then brushed her hair. Thankfully she wasn't one to wear or worry about make up. When she had finished, Juanita was almost done with the sandwiches and George was still buried in his paper. They reminded her of her parents. There was no physical resemblance of any kind. Her daddy was a big man, unlike George. He was every bit of six feet two and over two hundred pounds. Her mom was smaller than Peggy. She was five-and-a-half feet tall and thin. Juanita was a round little woman. What struck Peggy was how comfortable they were together. No need to talk, no bickering, just together all the time.

"Juanita," she spoke up. "Do you have a telephone here? For some reason I can't get cell phone reception."

George threw his thumb over his shoulder again. "There's a phone in the back," he said. "Never had any use for one of them cell phones. You callin' long distance?"

"Yes, sir," she said sheepishly. "We will pay for the call." She smiled at him and he warmed up. It was the first time he looked at her and there was a connection.

"That's fine little missy," he said softly. "That friend of yours outside. When did he get out?"

"Get out?" she assumed he meant out of the military but wanted to be sure.

"The military. He's a soldier if I ever seen one," he got quiet. "Reminds me of our boy Georgie after he got home from 'Nam." The mood had become instantly somber, so she didn't press.

"Um, he retired a couple of years ago," she said quietly. George was back into his newspaper when Juanita put the food on the counter. "How much?"

"Food'll be seven dollars," Juanita said with a smile. "Y'all getting any more gas?"

"I'm sure we are. How about I give you sixty. That will cover the sandwiches, the coffee, gas, and any calls we make," Peggy said holding out three twenties. "How'd that be?"

"That'd be just fine Missy," George said from his paper. Juanita took the money and Peggy turned to walk out. "What kinda trouble y'all in?" Peggy turned and looked at him, opening her mouth to speak. He cut her off. "Don't bullshit me young lady. I've seen this before and I ain't no stool pigeon. Me and Juanita here had our brushes with the law back in the day." Juanita walked up and stood next to him. "We used to run corn mash to folks 'round here when it wasn't so legal. 'Nita is the best goddamn getaway driver you ever saw." Juanita smiled at the surprised look on Peggy's face. "So, what kinda trouble is it?"

## CHAPTER 7

The four of them were standing around the hood of the Jeep. Peggy didn't know how to answer George's question about what kind of trouble they were in, so she brought them out to talk to Terry. She liked George and Juanita—probably too much—because they were her kind of people, but Terry would have to decide what they needed to know.

"I'm going to go in and try to call Larry," she whispered to him. The horses. Yesterday they had planned to put them in the pasture and only contact Larry if they were going to be gone a long time. They left in such a rush, they never took care of the horses. He just gave her a nod. She slipped into the gas station.

In the end, Terry told them what he thought they would understand which was more than Peggy thought he would. She walked out of the station about halfway through Terry's explanation to the couple. Now, they were standing there with George smoking a Pall Mall and Juanita cleaning her glasses. Terry was sipping coffee and reaching into the Jeep for his can of Cope.

"So, what kinda help y'all need?" Juanita asked. George looked at her sternly. "Don't you say a goddamn word to me George. I hauled your ass outta too much trouble over the years to give me shit over this." Terry was really beginning to like these two. George puffed on his cigarette while Peggy tried not to giggle.

"To be honest, ma'am," Terry started softly. "We just need about twenty-four hours of peace to figure out what is next. And then we will be on our way."

"We can muster that," George said as he knocked the orange coal out of the end of the unfiltered cigarette and mashed it with his work boot. "Some place where you can rest, think, and see anyone comin' from a long ways out. Sound about right?"

"Yessir, is surely does," Terry responded spitting onto the cement. "Got anyplace like that around here?"

"Mister," Juanita broke in, "we used to run shine. We got about ten places like that. George, I'll watch the store. Why don't you take these folks out to one of your spots," she looked at Terry. "And I don't want to know which one." She turned and looked at Peggy. "Goodbye, dear. You take care of that man and I guaran-damn-tee he will take care of you." Juanita turned and walked back into the store.

"Alright," George said, shaking another Pall Mall from the pack. "You two head east out of town. Seven miles. Exactly seven. There is a dirt road on the left." He lit the unfiltered beast with an old Zippo. "Git on that dirt road and drive to the crick. There's trees out there. Park in 'em trees and wait for me. I'll be out in a bit."

"Yessir, seven miles," Terry said. "I'll top this rig off with gas and we will head out. See you in a bit."

George shuffled over to his truck and headed west out of town. Terry moved the Jeep over and started filling her up with gas. Peggy was tempted to go inside and say thank you to Juanita but resisted. She just sat in the Jeep and waited for Terry to finish. She spotted the jammer, still with the glowing red light, sitting in the cup holder. He was done pumping gas and climbed into the driver seat, starting the engine. He put the Jeep in gear and smiled at her. She smiled back nervously.

"Seven miles," he said out loud. "Exactly seven miles."

## CHAPTER 8

"Boy," Terry said, "he wasn't fucking kidding. Seven miles, exactly." He turned the Jeep off the road and onto a tiny dirt track that hadn't had tires on it for a long time. The creek was about five hundred meters away by his estimation. They drove straight to the trees, both of them watching the mirrors behind them as they moved. They had been cautious from the moment they left the gas station. The Jeep hadn't moved in hours and if anyone had the ability to track them, they would be close by now. Convinced no one was following them, Terry focused on the trees to their front. He followed the dirt track that passed between two large hardwoods and turned left into a depression about eight feet deep, just wide enough, and deep enough, to hide the Jeep—or a pickup truck running shine—from anyone out on the main road. Terry smiled.

"I'm going to head down the creek bed about a hundred meters with the long gun." Peggy didn't know why exactly he called it that since they were all long guns to her, but she knew he meant the sniper rifle. She spent enough time around soldiers and heard enough war stories to know Terry was heading out to a position of advantage where he could watch—and shoot, if necessary—anyone approaching the Jeep.

"And what the fuck am I supposed to do?" she said to him with more venom than she intended. "Just sit here and wait?" She was nervous.

"That's four times," he said as he climbed out of the Jeep. "Four times in the last twenty-four hours you've said *fuck*. I'm clearly a bad influence on you. You should probably dump me." He smiled at her as he closed the door. She returned serve.

"I probably fucking should," she replied as she got out on her side. "That's five, since you're keeping score, and I know infantrymen are easily confused by math." She crossed her arms like a child not getting her way.

"Actually, if you wanted," he said from the back of the Jeep, "you could start straightening all this stuff up." He walked around to her side of the Jeep, rifle slung over his shoulder. He handed her the holster for her dad's pistol. "You should probably start wearing this. Pistol is under your seat."

She snatched it out of his hand and threw it on the seat, undoing her belt to thread it through the leather on the back of the holster. He grabbed a camouflage backpack as he closed the gate. Peggy had the holster on and fished for the pistol under the seat. She came out with it and slipped it into the holster.

"Check that," he said. "Make sure there are six in the cylinder." She pulled it out of the holster, pushing on the release on the left side of the frame. The cylinder rotated out showing five full chambers and one empty.

"There's five in here," she snapped it back closed. "Daddy always said carry it with the hammer on an empty chamber for safety," she said very matter-of-factly.

"Sweetie," he said very calmly, "no disrespect to Daddy, but he was never in a gunfight in his life. The best thing you can do for your own safety is make sure that thing has all the bullets it can carry." He produced a single .357 round and handed it to her.

Peggy rotated the cylinder out again and slid in the last round. She snapped it closed and slipped it into the holster. "You're slowing down, old man," she stated plainly. "Or maybe I am." He was thoroughly confused, which is what she wanted. "I had my belt undone and halfway off and you didn't say or do anything. Two days ago, that wouldn't have happened. You're slipping."

"No, baby," he said giving her a kiss, "I'm just saving it for later." He smiled and headed down the creek bed. He was twenty yards away when she called after him.

"If you're lucky!" she said with a half-hearted smile. He kept moving like he didn't hear her, but she knew he did. She'd won that match.

She turned back to the Jeep. He wasn't kidding, there was some serious work that needed to be done here. She knew that she couldn't unload everything and repack the whole Jeep in case they needed to make a quick getaway, but she did some general straightening in the cargo compartment, just making things neat and tidy. Next, she went to the back seat and pulled out the cooler. They should have gotten more ice from the gas station. They were going to need more food and drinks. They probably had enough for a day or so. She knew he had a stash of trail mix and jerky in the back somewhere, so she took that into account. Maybe a day and a half, then.

Peggy could see the butt end of the shotgun under the seat. An old family heirloom, she knew it meant a lot to Terry. She had shot it once because Terry asked her to, it kicked the hell out of her, and she hated it. She did know enough about shotguns to know that it was probably the best weapon she could have if someone came into that creek bed with her. She slid it out from under the seat and leaned it against the tire. She had finished up the rest of the housekeeping when she saw George's truck turn onto the dirt. She resisted the impulse to wave.

Terry moved out of his position down the creek bed when he was satisfied that George was alone in the truck and no one was following him. By the time he got back to the Jeep, George had made his way down into the gully with Peggy and the Jeep. The two of them had barely started a conversation when Terry emerged.

"Nobody followed me," the old man stated plainly. It had been about twenty-four hours since they were at the National Guard Armory speaking to General Dawson. In Terry's estimation, that was plenty of time for someone who knew what they were doing to track them down. He didn't excuse himself for being cautious. "How far down didja go?" George asked.

"I was down there about a hundred yards or so." Terry was setting the rifle in the back of the Jeep.

George lit another Pall Mall. "Well then, you saw the door?"

Terry was confused. He didn't see any structures of any kind. He gave George a quizzical look. The old man chuckled and dangerously flicked some ash into the dry grass. "Maybe you ain't as good as I thought. 'Bout fifty yards down that way, there is a door cut into the ground. We used to keep a still in there. C'mon, I'll show ya."

The three of them headed back in the direction Terry had come. The old man wasn't lying. About fifty yards down the creek bed, there was an old set of Bilco doors set into the ground. These were the same style doors on half the farmhouses in the country, but these were camouflaged with paint and overgrown brush. Terry had run right past them . . . twice. *Jesus*, he thought to himself. Maybe the old man was right; maybe he wasn't that good. Or maybe Peggy was right, and he was getting old. He was embarrassed and was trying to validate in his head why he had missed the two six-foot metal doors.

"Don't feel bad, son," George said as he grabbed the handle on the right door. "Coppers been looking for this spot longer'n you been alive." He pulled the door open and smiled, "They ain't never found it neither." It didn't make Terry feel any better, but he appreciated what the old man said. George led the trio down a flight of six steps built out of railroad ties. When they got to the bottom, George reached off to the right and turned an old-style light switch. Two bare lightbulbs came on and illuminated a ten-by-ten room with a dirt floor. There were more railroad ties holding up the ceiling. It reminded Terry of the mine shaft Rambo got trapped in running from the sheriff in *First Blood*. Peggy stood there quietly.

"You know, sir," Terry said as he spied a concrete pad in the corner, "I didn't know there were people runnin' shine in Nebraska.

I thought that was all North Carolina and Kentucky and that whole area."

"You like to drink, son?" George flicked his cigarette into the corner. "People 'round here do. And they don't always like to pay the government to do it. That ain't just local to Carolina." He was referring to the liquor taxes the government imposed. "We built this in fifty-eight, I think. Me and my brother and another guy. Tapped into the power a couple of years later. Poured that concrete over there in sixty-one." He put his hand on one of the support beams and pushed it to see if it was still sturdy. "We made batches out of here until right after Georgie came home from 'Nam in seventy-two. Y'all are welcome to it for as long as you need." The mention of Georgie made the old man somber again. He moved to the steps and hauled himself outside. Terry and Peggy just looked at each other then followed him out.

No one said a word until they got back to the Jeep. George went straight up to his truck with Terry on his heels. "I brought you a couple of things," he said as he dropped the tailgate. There was an old, forest green, metal Coleman cooler in the back. The latch was broken and replaced with a hasp like the kind on a shed door. George grabbed the hasp and opened the cooler. Inside was an eight-pound bag of ice, a loaf of bread, a jar of Skippy peanut butter, and a six pack of Coors Light. He called out to Peggy. "Hey, little missy. Why don't you come up here and grab this food and stuff?" He looked at Terry with a wink and whispered, "Women's work." Terry smiled. "I got some stuff in the cab, too." Terry followed him to the passenger door.

"You didn't have to do all this, sir," Terry said as he held the door open for the old man. George acted like he didn't hear him.

"I reckon, you're gonna need this," he handed Terry two cans of Copenhagen. "And you're probably gonna need this for medicinal purposes," he handed Terry an unmarked bottle of liquid. Terry could only assume it was some of the man's homemade liquor. "Go easy on that stuff. It burns a little." The old man reached under the seat and came out with a Colt 1911. At the initial glance, Terry knew this gun was old. It wasn't even a 1911A1, it was an original model. He handed it to Terry. "That's clean. No record of it and no serial number. Took that off with a grinder years ago." Terry turned it over in his hand and ran his finger over the worn metal where the serial number used to be. He saw Peggy making her second trip back to the Jeep, carrying the ice and bread as he slipped the pistol into his waistband in the small of his back. "One more thing for ya. This was Georgie's. Snuck it home from 'Nam in his duffle bag."

Terry almost shit his pants. "Goddamn," was the only word he could manage. The old man had pulled a worn, but clean, AK-47 from under the seat and handed it to him. Terry pulled the curved magazine from the bottom of the receiver. There were rounds in it. He pulled the bolt back and ejected the round that was in the chamber.

"I'm guessin' you know how to use that thing," George said. "I ain't got no more ammo for it, 'cept what's in that clip. It's full auto and it works. It's clean, too."

"Thank you, sir," Terry said. "This was your son's, you didn't—" The old man stopped him with a wave of his hand.

"You said you're just a grunt," he leaned on the truck. "Georgie was one of them LRRPs in 'Nam." He pronounced it 'Lurps.' It stood for long range reconnaissance patrol—small teams who operated all over Vietnam and sometimes ventured into Laos, Cambodia, and Thailand. It was dangerous work. Peggy wandered up to the truck. "You remind me of him. He milled around for a while, workin' odd jobs and such after he got home. Worked with me at the station for a while, too. Then in eighty-five, he says he is takin' a trip. Going to South America to do some work for a friend." He dropped his head for a second. "June of eighty-six, someone from the State Department shows up at the station and said he was dead. Died in Columbia. Mixed up with some drugs or somethin'. Hell, I don't know." The three stood silently for what seemed like an eternity. "Y'all take care of each other. Maybe when all this is over, me and 'Nita can have y'all over for Sunday dinner." He closed the passenger door of the truck and walked around to the driver's side. Before he climbed in, Peggy intercepted him and gave him a hug.

"Thank you," she said. She kissed his cheek. He blushed a little and grabbed her by the shoulders.

"Now don't you go telling 'Nita about that," he said referring to the kiss. "She'll get all jealous and make my life hell." Peggy handed him a small piece of paper.

"This man takes care of my horses when I'm not home," she said. "Can you please call him and ask him to take care of them until I get back?" George looked at the paper with a phone number and Larry's name written above it. He slipped it into his shirt pocket with the pack of Pall Malls.

Terry reached out and shook his hand. No words needed. George climbed into his truck and drove away. The pair stood there for a long second and watched him go. *There are still good people left in this world*, Terry thought.

"I thought you called Larry from the station," he said.

"He never answered," she replied as she headed back to the Jeep.

## CHAPTER 9

It took a few trips, but they got themselves settled into the little shelter. They didn't plan on staying more than a day, so they only brought the essentials. Terry wanted to be able to bug out quickly if they had to. Terry didn't want to leave any of the weapons in the Jeep and he wanted to inventory what they had, so it was now all laying on the concrete pad on the floor.

Peggy was sitting on the cooler, eating a peanut butter sandwich and sipping on a can of Coors Light. She sat quietly as he worked. It reminded her of those Saturday errands with her father. She always wanted to tag along but she knew when he was talking about tools with the man at the hardware store, or about brake pads at the auto shop, that she wasn't part of the conversation. "Children should be seen and not heard," he would tell her.

Terry had it all laid out so he could see it. The Remington sniper rifle was sitting on its bipod. There was a full box of twenty rounds with another partial box, thirty-eight rounds in all. The AR-15 built as an M-4 clone lay in front of that. Seven magazines with thirty rounds each and another full metal ammo can containing four hundred twenty additional rounds sat next to it. The AK-47 from George was off to the side. The forty-round magazine contained thirty-six rounds. No extra magazines and no extra ammo. The magazine had been stripped to count the rounds inside and then reloaded.

The Winchester Model 12, his grandfather's shotgun, was on the other side. It held six in the magazine under the barrel and one in the chamber. Terry had taken the plug out of the magazine a few years ago and never put it back in. That would have limited the gun to holding only three rounds, something required by game wardens for hunting. It wasn't a difficult process to remove it, but he was glad that was already done. He had three, twenty-five round boxes of shells filled with BB shot. It would be good for any human target at close range, especially with the full-choked barrel.

The pistols were in the center. His Glock had two magazines, both with a two-round extender so they could hold seventeen rounds each. They were both full and he had an additional fifty rounds of hollow points to go along. Her dad's .357 was there, six rounds in the cylinder and a partial box of forty-four rounds. The 1911 from George was next to it. Like the AK, there was no additional magazine. It held seven in the magazine and one in the chamber. Lastly, the bulky FNX-45 with the suppressor lay nearby; it was a bit unwieldy with the suppressor on, but it had already come in handy at the house. The big pistol had three fifteen-round magazines. The FNX and the 1911 both fired .45 ACP, so that helped. There were a hundred and forty-five rounds to feed the two pistols.

He had no idea what they were in for, but he felt confident they had enough to deal with whatever came. Two people with four pistols and four long guns. If they needed more firepower, he didn't know how they would carry it. He was satisfied with what they had, although a little more ammo for the AK would be nice. In his time at the farm, he had taught Peggy how to use everything that was in front of them, except the AK. He even had a 1911 in the safe she had fired a few magazines through, so she would be okay using that one as well. He exhaled loudly. He turned and looked at her. She was in mid-sip on the can of Coors Light.

"I need to teach you how to use the AK," he said.

"No, you don't," she said flatly. "I've been in and out of the Middle East for thirty years. I know how to use it." Evidently, she could still surprise him. His mouth was open. "Close your mouth. You'll catch flies."

"Alrighty, then," he turned away from her, trying to recover from his surprised expression. He had two backpacks he referred to as *assault packs*, using the military term. At this point in his life, every backpack was an assault pack, or a rucksack if it had a frame. He began to pack things up so they could grab and go. He handed her the revolver and she began to speak.

"It's been over twenty-four hours now," she set the can down next to the Yeti cooler she was sitting on. "We need to figure out how to get an update." He had been milling around the prospect of that since dawn, but he let her keep talking. "I got the email two days ago and started reaching out to my contacts. Then the call with Dawson. Then the deputies at the house." She was working in big chunks first, laying a framework for them to break down the activities of the last two days. "We left, met George and Juanita, then ended up here." He loaded a magazine into the AR and let the bolt go forward. It was loud in the confined space.

"Okay," he said. "Where do you want to start?" It was a loaded question. She seemed on the surface to be a somewhat scattered woman in the same way that most geniuses were slobs. She constantly lost track of her glasses and her clothes laid wherever she took them off until it was time to do laundry. Her purse was a pit where things were lost forever. He knew, after watching her, it was because her brain moved so quickly, she discarded things deemed trivial. She was either going to want to start at the beginning and move chronologically or she was going to want to start at the present and work backward in time. She worked laterally, in his assessment. Left to right or right to left. That is how he saw it in his brain.

He thought like an intelligence officer, trying to link major pieces together. He had an innate ability to find connections that others didn't. When he was in Baghdad, he was the operations officer for a battalion of paratroopers. The battalion intelligence officer would often ask him to come in and look at their analysis of the terror cell networks operating in the battalion sector to help them close some of the gaps. Terry chalked it up to him being a kid that ran the streets of Chicago without adult supervision gaining those street smarts. But there was more to it than that. Inside his head, he could overlay a Venn diagram with a network diagram and then add some common sense. The answers came quickly and easily, and he was rarely off the mark. That's why he and Peggy made a good team—they saw things differently and could communicate in a way to maximize their strengths.

"Let's start at the very beginning, a very good place to start," she singsonged. It was a reference to *The Sound of Music*. He only knew it because of his second wife. She had been a huge fan of musicals and he picked up on some of it through osmosis over the years they were together. Peggy knew it because as a child, if she wasn't riding horses, disappearing in a book, or out riding around with her father, she was with her mother watching and singing along to old movies. He paused at the quote, stopping his task of packing up to give her an exasperated look. She continued, "Fine. I got the email from Whiteman about the threat. Then—"

"Who sent it?" he broke in. "Or, since we think this was a cyber-related attack, who's email address did it come from?" He believed that words matter and being specific in what they were diving into could avoid some bad assumptions.

"Valid point," she said. "It came from Carrie Zukowski, the J-2." Terry had never met Air Force Colonel Zukowski, but she and Peggy had a long running relationship. Peggy would have no reason to suspect anything based on that. Zukowski was the head intelligence officer for Whiteman, so something like this would be in her purview. "She said they had received notification there was an imminent threat to Whiteman." He broke in again.

"Who notified them?" he was flashing back to their initial conversation. "You said 'DHS and others.' Who are the *others*?"

Peggy thought for a second, "DHS . . . NORTHCOM, um, ATF. That's it."

"Not State Department?" he asked. "Or CIA?"

"No, not specifically," she replied. "The message said the threat was imminent and it was from an unnamed group from the Middle East. She also said she was taking a risk by sending it over unclassified network, but it was an emergency. Then she asked me if I had heard anything or could find anything out."

"Okay." He was still packing things up but stopped to bounce all this back at her. He knew it was important for her to understand she acted appropriately based on what she received. There was a wave of guilt coming over the danger her contacts were likely enduring because of her actions. Some of them may be hurt or dead as a result, but he wanted her to understand it wasn't her fault. "So, a clean email from a known contact. There were minimal keywords in there that would generate a hit from any monitoring software." There were programs used by the military and law enforcement that detect certain key words, or combinations of words, setting off alarm bells. They were the same types of programs that alerted the FBI when some nutjob in his mom's basement sent messages containing the words *bomb*, *president*, and *kill*. Anything from Zukowski with *CIA*, and *threat* over an unclassified network probably would have set off similar alarms because of a potential security violation. Minimizing those types of keywords kept this off anyone's radar screen. "So, you started reaching out to your contacts."

"Yes," she said. He was waiting for the wave of guilt to hit her.

"Hey," he said softly but sternly. "Stick with me here. We need to work through this quickly. You can't undo what you did, so let's see if we can fix it. Okay?" She nodded her head. "How did you contact them? Phone? Email?"

"Some of both," she was regaining her composure. "It was the middle of the night there. I knew some wouldn't answer their phones anyway, so I sent emails."

"Well, we know phones can be tracked by the cell towers," he said. "Emails can be tracked by IP addresses being used when they open them. Any kind of virus software could provide that as soon as they open it. And everyone opened it or answered their phone?"

"Everyone," there was a bit of guilt creeping into her voice. "And they all said the same thing. They knew nothing about a major operation inside the US."

"Then *we* decided to go call EPIC," he was moving forward. "But we got intercepted on our way. We never got to call EPIC. Or anyone else . . ."

"Except Dawson," she broke in. "And he is the one that told us about the cyberattack."

"Yeah," Terry's heart sank, "but he was expecting *you*. He wasn't expecting *us*. He had them clear the building so no one else would hear. His aide didn't pick up the phone. He did. No one was supposed to hear or know about that call except you. He could tell you anything he wanted and there would be no witnesses. I was a fly in the ointment, but whatever he was up to, it was already in motion, so he couldn't very well stop."

"Do you think," she started, "do you think whatever this is, Dawson is part of it?"

"At this point we have to assume it is a possibility," he was drifting back to the dead suicide bomber and the fact that he saved Dawson's life. He shook himself back to reality. "Okay, what next?"

"No." She was backtracking. "The deputies. They intercepted us on the way. They said they were headed to the farm but we were already on our way."

"Right," he said. Good catch by Peggy. "So, the phone call was set up and they wanted *you* at the armory to talk to Dawson. And Deputy Jimmy asked if you knew me and if you were safe when he pulled us over. They were looking for a woman, not a woman and a man. They only knew it was you because of your car."

"They didn't think about you being out there. Or coming with me," she said plainly. "So, no one has been watching the house. I mean, you've been there for a year or so. If anyone was watching, they would have thought about that."

"That means this is new," he came to a conclusion. "This is very recent. Otherwise, they would have had time to set up some kind of intel gathering, either on the ground or from a drone or something. If this was something they have been planning for months, or even weeks, they would have known I was there."

"So," she was moving forward now, "did they want me at the armory or did they want me out of my house? I mean, they came to get me." He hadn't thought of that.

"Why would they want you out of your house? What reason would they have? To take something? To leave something? The jammer maybe?"

"I don't think so," she said referring to the jammer.

"We will come back to the jammer," he said. "So, let's take me out of this completely. Reset the board." She knew this is where he excelled, where his mind worked differently from hers. "You get the emails. You contact your people. The cops come to get you. They take you to the armory. Besides me, what changes in that scenario?"

"My car," she said with her thumbnail in her mouth. "I would have left my car at home and ridden with the deputies."

"Your car. Your car would have been at the house," he confirmed her conclusion. They were gaining traction and his mind was moving quickly. He was exhausted but this was important. "You leave your car and they come in to put a tracker on it. A good tracker. One that no one will find without really looking. It would give them plenty of time."

"But why?" she asked. "Why would they want to track me? Out in the middle of nowhere?" He was going to need some sleep to figure this one out. They still needed to figure out the deputies and the jammer, too. Most importantly, they needed to figure out what role Dawson was playing in all of this. Terry was fading quickly, and she could see it.

"Let's take a break," she said. "You need to eat and get some rest.

It's a marathon and not a sprint, remember?"

He got up and stretched. He looked at his watch—1742. He pushed open the Bilco doors and stepped outside for some air. He loved this part of the country. He stretched again and listened to the grasshoppers buzzing. She was right, he needed some food and some sleep. He went back in and closed the door behind him.

## CHAPTER 10

Peggy Baron sat in the dark for about forty minutes to see how asleep Terry really was. It was late summer and although it was after eight in the evening, there was still some light peeking in around the edges of the metal Bilco doors that concealed this little room from the world. He told her he hadn't slept well in years and after seeing him sleep, or sometimes not sleep, over the year or so they had been sharing a bed, she knew he wasn't exaggerating. Before he retired, he went through the long and drawn-out disability process where the military assessed not only how much damage they had done to his body, but how much financial responsibility they were willing to assume for it. Terry described it as "I have all of my parts, but not all of them work well." After fourteen appointments, three trips to the lab for bloodwork, and forty-three x-rays, he was qualified by the Veterans Administration as 100 percent disabled. Terry was never wounded in combat and there was no purple heart in his stack of medals, but he was certainly "broken," in his words. She hated it when he said that.

Peggy knew he was extremely tired. When he came back into the little dirt room, Terry grabbed some jerky and ate a peanut butter sandwich she made. After swigging down a bottle of water, he reached into one of the assault packs and produced a shooting mat and an Army issue poncho liner. He laid the shooting mat on the floor, it was something he carried in the pack for when he shot rifles from the prone and not designed for sleeping, but it was better than the dirt or concrete. The poncho liner was one of his favorite possessions. Like most soldiers, he referred to it as a *woobie*. It was a lightweight, nylon blanket with some sort of synthetic pile filling sewn into it. It was so old, the woodland camouflage pattern had almost worn off. He curled up on his side and she slid in front of him. When she wiggled her ass into his crotch and got no response from him, she knew how tired he was. He was softly snoring in less than a minute, his arm draped over her waist.

Now, she was waiting and hoping. Waiting for Terry to get into a deeper sleep and hoping he didn't wake when she tried to sneak out the Bilco doors. They were metal and the hinges squeaked, and she knew there was a chance that letting more light into the small room would wake Terry. She wanted to get back to the Jeep. The jammer was still in the cupholder and she couldn't stop thinking about it. They had pushed off thinking through the deputies until Terry got some rest, but she couldn't let it go. Terry wanted to leave it in the Jeep, at least until he could give it a final once over for any tracking devices. She knew they needed an update on what had happened since they left the farm. Were they on the news?

Peggy had seen devices like that one before, both jammers and trackers. Frighteningly, you could find them in various markets in Palestine. They weren't cheap by any means, but they were certainly available. She stood slowly, careful not to hit her head on the low beams supporting the earthen roof. Terry was sleeping with the Glock next to him, as he did most nights. She wasn't worried about him waking and shooting her, although the prospect of having the 9mm pointed at her was a very real. It had happened once in the past year. She hadn't heeded his warning not to shake him awake, in fact she forgot about it completely. The playful morning she'd had in mind went away quickly after she jumped into the bed next to him, startled him awake, and found herself looking down the barrel of his pistol. He was pissed at himself afterward, but it was certainly her fault for not remembering and she was embarrassed by it.

She moved carefully through the dark space and pushed slowly on the left door. The hinges squeaked quietly. Peggy looked over her shoulder to see Terry lying still, the poncho liner covering his head. Hopefully, that would keep the light from waking him. She stepped out and lightly closed the heavy door behind her, taking most of her strength to ease it back into place quietly. She had the .357 in the holster on her hip and realized she should have grabbed either the AR or the AK before she left, but quickly shook that off. There was no way she would have been able to manage one of the rifles and quietly open and close the door. She was risking it, but she assumed the risk was low and dismissed it quickly, as was her habit.

The light was fading in the late evening, so she made her way quickly down the dry creek bed. There clearly hadn't been water here in years. There was no mud and the entire bed was overgrown with long grass up both sides. Even their foot traffic wasn't stirring up any soft earth down in the bed; it was dry and packed hard like the farm fields above it. When she got to the Jeep, it was almost dark under the trees that provided both cover and concealment for the vehicle. Opening the passenger door, she could immediately see the red light on the jammer. She stood for a second, the jammer in her hand, and listened. No noise from the road. No traffic, no tractors, nothing mechanical. The only sound was the grasshoppers buzzing away.

She walked out from under the trees where there was still some light and stopped. The jammers in Palestine had a radius about the same as a wireless router. In the light, she got a better look at the device. It was black, had the red LED light on one side, and was smooth all the way around, and had the power switch on one side. No texture of any kind. And no markings. She exhaled loudly. The case was held together by four screws, she was relieved it wasn't sealed or even glued together. She knew Terry kept a myriad of tools in an old metal ammo can in the back of the Jeep, but she didn't know if there was a Phillips head screwdriver that small in the can. She wanted to see inside the device, especially since there were no markings on the outer casing. She was, by no means, a techie and knew she couldn't recognize whether the circuits inside were the right kind or not, but she still wanted to see it.

Peggy watched the road for almost a minute before she walked to the Jeep to find the ammo can of tools. Setting the jammer inside the cargo compartment, she dug through the darkness, feeling for the cold metal can.

"They wanted you on a government network." Terry's voice scared the shit out of her, and she jumped. Holding her chest with one hand, she turned and looked at him. "They wanted you out of your house and working on a government network where they could get into your computer. Whatever this cyberattack is, whoever is doing it, they want access to your computer, and they want you on a government network when they do it."

"When did you figure that out?" she asked, feeling the need to catch up.

"About thirty seconds after you closed the door," he said. She realized he was standing there with the AR slung across his chest. "Your car was only part of it. They can track your cell phone, so they don't need to track your car to track you. No one turns off their phones anymore, except to ride on airplanes. They wanted you to move, to leave the house to do your work," he continued as he filled his lower lip with Copenhagen, "and if this was as serious as you assumed, you would want to be on a government network to do it. You would have access on your phone, but you wouldn't do any serious work on your phone, you'd want your laptop for that."

"My laptop," it was a statement and not a question. "I left my laptop at the house."

"What's on it?" he asked quietly. "You already alerted all your contacts, so they don't need that. They got that when you made those calls and sent the emails. What else is on there? You're not working on anything classified, are you?" He rarely asked about her work. She was always working on something and almost always included him in the discussions surrounding whatever it was. He felt like he knew all the projects she was working on but wasn't positive.

"No," she said, staring off into the increasing darkness. "Nothing classified. Not now, and not on that computer. I know better than that." If she was caught doing classified work on a system that wasn't cleared for it, she would lose her clearance and, therefore, all her access to anything else classified.

"There has to be something," he said. He was trying to get her to focus. "Doesn't have to be recent. Anything. Any project you may have mentioned in passing to someone or—"

She cut him off, "They wanted to put something on there." He could see the lightbulb come on over her head. "There isn't anything on there, really. And if there isn't, that means they wanted to put something on there. Software. A program. Something."

It was almost completely dark now. He didn't like being out here like this. He suddenly realized all the things he didn't have with him. There were two sets of body armor in the basement, both set up to carry ammo and some other small essentials like first aid equipment. There was also a war belt set up in a similar fashion that could be worn with or without the body armor. His EK knife and his thigh holster for the FNX was attached to the belt. Lastly, he had left behind a bump helmet. It wasn't made of Kevlar, but of impact resistant plastic to keep from knocking himself out if he hit his head. More importantly, the AN/PVS-14-night vision monocular he had was attached to the helmet. In this ever-increasing darkness, he realized the need for the night vision device. They were all left behind in a rush to leave the farm. *Shit.*

"We need to get back inside," he said. "There is no way there is a tracker on the Jeep. Bring the jammer with you. We need to go back and think through the rest of this."

She closed the door of the Jeep and before they turned to head back to the dirt room, he saw the vehicle on the road. Just before the dirt track, it slowed and then sped up again. It wasn't George's truck, but a newer Chevy Suburban. Very out of place for this area.

"Get back to the shelter," he started. "Grab the AK, turn out the lights, and close the door. Stay there until I come for you. Someone is coming."

# CHAPTER 11

This location was too remote and there was too much going on for the Suburban to be a coincidence. The only person who knew where they were was George, and Terry seriously doubted George owned any vehicle beside the white pickup. The creek bed and the road ran parallel and the Suburban came from the same direction as the underground hideout and continued driving away from it. Terry moved in the direction of the Suburban, sending Peggy away from it. He stayed in the dry creek bed, watching for lights and pausing occasionally to listen for engine noises.

He was desperately wishing for the night vision monocular as he moved through the brush. Over the years of training and deployments, he had become very comfortable with using his weaker eye to look through the device while still allowing him to shoulder his rifle, even with the ACOG mounted on top. Using the PVS-14 over his right eye and shouldering his rifle would cause the two to bang into each other and probably result in a headache for him. He chuckled thinking about the dozens of young, inexperienced soldiers who got grabbed by their helmet and had their night vision forcefully swapped over to their weak eye by that grumpy officer with the Copenhagen in his lip.

Modern night vision devices pulled in all available ambient light to illuminate the landscape inside the device. While they weren't as awesome as the movies made them look, they could definitely help someone pick up parking lights or interior vehicle lights from a great distance. Terry was relying on the mostly full moon that was just coming over the treetops to move, while using his peripheral vision to pick up any movement or lights in the distance. They were only about forty yards away when he spotted them. Two men. No, three men.

He didn't hear the vehicle, but he assumed it wasn't far away. He was hoping it was just these three and they didn't have a fourth, or more, out there in the darkness. He peered over the grass and watched as they approached. He could make out at least one of them carrying a rifle. They were walking very close together and were talking in low tones as they moved. These weren't professionals—former soldiers or mercenary types. Or if they were, they were poorly trained, lazy, or cocky. Terry expected them to be spread out, maybe in a loose wedge, moving quietly and using hand signals instead of talking. They were walking through the bean field between the creek bed and the road, about fifteen yards into the leafy rows, heading toward the Jeep. Terry let them pass him and then followed quietly.

When they reached the gully surrounded by trees that concealed the Jeep, they stopped. Terry stopped, too, and listened. With the moon behind them, he could see all three were armed, one with an AR and the other two with submachine guns of some sort. He couldn't identify what they were in the dark but could see the tubular suppressors mounted to the barrels. Now he was wishing for his suppressed pistol, in addition to the night vision. The only silent weapon he had on him was a Benchmade mechanical knife he had been given on his first deployment. It was big and heavy for a folding knife but had never been used for much more than cutting nylon cord, opening an MRE, or other mundane tasks. Now Terry was going to be forced to use it to take down a grown man.

"Stay here," the man with the AR said, barely audible to Terry. "We are going to check out the vehicle. Once we clear it, we will come back and get you and then move to the bunker." Terry assumed that by *bunker* he meant the underground room that Peggy was holed up in. It was stupid for these guys to leave one man alone in the dark.

They should have all gone to clear the Jeep together. These were definitely not professionals. What was abundantly clear to Terry was that these men were a threat to him and Peggy. Three armed men, in the dark, in this very remote location, knowing about both the Jeep and the so-called bunker. This was not a coincidence.

Terry watched as the other two men disappeared into the darkness and quietly laid his AR down in the grass. He pulled the Benchmade out of his pocket and opened it slowly to avoid the metallic *snap* that came with activating the switchblade as designed. He was behind and below the man who was clearly outlined in the moonlight. He couldn't ask for a better position.

Terry had never killed a man with a knife before. He had been taught, years ago, how to take out a sentry with a long-bladed, fighting style knife. The Ek dagger sitting in the basement of the farm was designed for exactly this task, but he would have to manage this with the blade he had.

Terry went through US Army Ranger School in the mid-nineteen nineties, when the last few real Vietnam veterans were still in the Army. The students spent a number of hours in the first week beating the shit out of one another during hand-to-hand combat training. For the fourth and final session, each student was issued a rubber knife and they were taught some very basic principles of knife fighting. In the last hour, one of the first sergeants assigned to the school wandered over to the sawdust pit and assumed control of the training. He was old, a little overweight by Army standards, and didn't move quickly. The students picked up on the reverence showed this particular senior noncommissioned officer by the other instructors.

Terry was one of the few that recognized that First Sergeant Baer was wearing jungle fatigues from Vietnam. The camouflage pattern was similar to the woodland battle dress uniforms everyone else was wearing; they weren't the tiger-striped ones seen in the movies. They were cut different from the modern uniforms and fit the big man a little tight around the midsection. The uniform was adorned with badges and patches the Army didn't allow anymore: a Recondo badge on the left breast pocket, Vietnamese jump wings sewn above the right pocket, and a patch on the left shoulder in the shape of a black and red scroll with white writing. Baer had been a member of the long-range reconnaissance patrol designated as F Company, 51st Infantry. The same type of LURPs George's son, Georgie, had been part of.

The big bald man stood in front of the students that day and told them what it was *really* like to kill a man silently with a knife. It wasn't bluster. It wasn't a story of "no shit, there I was," with him trying to make himself sound tougher than he was. It was real-life experience. It was information that he had because he had done this, killed a man with a knife, and done it more than once. The image was burned into Terry's skull that day.

He knew before he left the ditch that he was going to have to move quickly. He knew that if he grabbed the man by the head or neck to expose his throat or cover his mouth, it was possible his slashing motion would be blocked by accident; the man would instinctively reach up for Terry's hand and likely block the knife in the process. He knew that men didn't die instantly from a stabbing; it normally took minutes to bleed out. He knew that a stab to the kidney or lungs would silence the man long enough to cut his throat, but he wasn't sure the Benchmade was long enough to puncture through skin, fat, and bone to get to those vital organs. He also didn't know if these men were wearing body armor, which certainly would make a stab to the torso a moot point. He decided that burying the knife into the side of the man's neck and slashing outward was his best bet. Risky still, but he had to decide before he left the creek bed, and not after.

Terry steadied himself and came out of the ditch quickly. He leapt at the man and did exactly what he planned, burying the knife into the side of the man's neck and slashing outward. The knife stuck and came out of Terry's hand as the man fell forward. The man wheezed and pulled the knife out of his neck, unable to scream or cry out. Terry lunged on top of him and felt the warm blood spray his face as the man's heart pumped. The man was trying to stop the blood from gushing, putting pressure on his neck with both hands. Terry rolled over, knowing that it wouldn't be long before the other two men returned, he punched the man in the face as hard as he could and knocked him out. The man's limp body would continue to bleed until he died in that very spot minutes later.

Terry found the suppressed submachine gun underneath the man's body. Pulling it free, he tried to determine what it was and where the safety was. The small weapon was an SMG 45 made by LWRC International. Thankfully, the little beast was designed and built in an era where most everything was modeled after the millions of AR-15s on the market. Although the magazine release was different, the safety selector lever was in the exact same spot and functioned the same as any AR-15. Terry was standing up as the two men approached.

"The vehicle is clear," the man with the AR said in a hushed tone, a little louder than a whisper. "They must be in the—"

He never got to finish his sentence. Terry fired two .45 ACP rounds into his chest then transitioned quickly and fired two more into the third man in the party. The little sub-gun was no louder than the FNX with the suppressor screwed onto the barrel. Terry knelt down on one knee and was silent, listening intently for any movement. Nothing. He had successfully taken down three men in the dark while barely making a sound. *Not too bad for an old fucking man.*

He knew his work wasn't finished. He needed to get all three of the bodies into the gully and then, eventually, into George's little dirt hideaway. He needed to find the Suburban, make sure there weren't any more men out there in the darkness, and he needed to get Peggy and get back on the move. The man with the AR was clearly in charge, so Terry dragged him to the Jeep first. He grabbed an old

Mini Maglite with a red lens from the glove compartment. Using the Jeep for cover, he began to search the man. No other weapons other than the AR-15 laying next to him. No body armor. The man was wearing active-style clothes, not tactical wear or camouflage of any kind. He had a cellphone, wallet, and keys in his pocket. Terry was hoping the keys were for the Suburban because that would reduce the possibility there was anyone else in the vehicle. There was no badge or law enforcement identification in the wallet or on his belt. Terry was thankful. He had likely killed at least one officer yesterday and didn't enjoy the thought of killing three more. No credit cards in the wallet and only twenty-three dollars cash. There was a Kansas driver's license under the name Jonathan Smith, which was likely a fake.

Terry brought the second shooter to the Jeep and searched him as well, with similar results. He found nothing that helped identify who these men were or who they were working for. The driver's license in the wallet was under the name William Smith. *Really fucking original.* Finally, Terry dragged the man he killed with the Benchmade into the gully. Thankfully, when he went to move the man, he kicked the knife in the dark. He had the knife on every combat operation he'd ever been on and he would hate to lose it now. Under the red glow of the flashlight, Terry could see the mess the man's throat had become. The Benchmade had cut through the man's right jugular vein and halfway through his windpipe. He looked like he had been attacked by a dog the way the meat was jagged and torn. No evidence on this man either. Another brother of the "Smith" clan; this one going by the name of Joseph Smith. The only man with a cellphone was the leader. That needed some looking into, but it would have to wait.

He hadn't heard anything from the underground location where Peggy was hiding. He knew he needed to check on her. For a second, he contemplated looking for the Suburban first, but discarded that idea quickly. He looked at his watch—2332 hours. It had been almost two hours since he parted ways with Peggy. Terry jogged one last time out to the place where he killed the three men. He used the red flashlight to check the ground quickly, ensuring nothing was missed. He recovered his own AR-15 and moved through the creek bed, and gully, pausing only long enough to grab one of the suppressed submachine guns, and back to the metal Bilco doors.

## CHAPTER 12

When Terry arrived, one of the Bilco doors was open. His heart stopped. *Was there another group of men out here?* he thought. *Did someone get to Peggy without me hearing?* He approached slowly, the sub-gun on his shoulder. The lights were off in the little room and he didn't want to peek his head around the corner for fear of having it blown off by Peggy or anyone else. He knelt outside the door.

"Peggy," he said in a low tone. He assumed it was loud enough for her or anyone else inside to hear him. He was louder this time, "Peggy". No answer. He rose slowly and froze when he heard that distinctive *Kalashnikov clack* of the selector lever moving from one position to another on an AK-47. Whoever it was, they were above him and outside the creek bed, the weapon close enough that accuracy wouldn't be important. He slowly held his hands out to his side.

"I almost shot you," she said plainly. "Good to know my ambush would have worked."

"Ambush?" he said with venom in his voice. "Have you lost your fucking mind? I told you to get in there and stay there. That was the safest place to be."

"There's nowhere to run in there, *asshole*," she answered. She didn't appreciate the way he was talking to her. "I was applying principles of war: surprise and maneuver." She walked past him and down the timber steps. He followed her and closed the door, turning on the lights. She turned and saw him covered in blood. There was terror on her face. "Oh my god!"

"What?" He looked down. "It's not mine. I'm fine. There were three of them. They are stacked by the Jeep. We need to pack up and go."

Peggy released the breath she was holding. "Dead?" she asked sheepishly.

"Yes, dead." He was moving to pack up their gear. "I killed all three of them. They were looking for us."

"Who were they?" She was following his lead and grabbing the cooler.

"I have no fucking idea." He threw an assault pack over his shoulders. "They had fake IDs and only one cell phone. We need to find their vehicle, stash their bodies, and then get moving."

It took a couple of trips, but they got everything down to the Jeep and got it loaded. Peggy saw the pile of bodies off to the side. Terry was quietly thankful she couldn't see the details of their injuries; it was bad enough she saw him looking like Sissy Spacek in *Carrie*. He picked up one of the bodies and threw it over his shoulder in a fireman's carry.

"What are you doing?" she asked. She assumed they were just getting into the Jeep and leaving.

"I am putting these guys into the room back there," he said feeling the weight of the man compressing his lower back. "Can't have them out here baking in the sun tomorrow." He turned and started walking toward the bunker, silently grunting under the weight. The third trip took much longer than the first. He could feel the adrenaline wearing off now. As much as he wanted to keep one of them, he had Peggy carry the AR and two sub-guns from the bad guys down and put them in the room with the bodies. He didn't need any evidence riding around in the Jeep with them. He knew he was taking a risk by keeping the Benchmade, but he wasn't parting with the knife.

They still needed to find the Suburban and then put some distance between themselves and this mess. He cringed at the thought of Peggy doing some of the driving, but he decided that may be inevitable. He pulled them slowly out of the gully without headlights. He knew he needed to turn left once they were on the pavement—that was both the direction the Suburban went before he lost sight of it and the direction the three men came from. It was a clear night and there was plenty of moonlight. They drove slowly along the paved road in the darkness, looking intently for the boxy outline of the big SUV.

"There," she pointed across his face. At first, he didn't see it, but he caught a shimmer of chrome trim in the moonlight and it became clear. The "Smiths" didn't even try to hide the truck. It was off the road, pulled up in a short driveway next to an old cattle pen. Obviously, this is where the truck was staged to load the cattle up for the sale barn. Terry didn't see headlights in either direction, so he pulled in next to the Suburban. Peggy had the keys in her hand and before he could say anything, she hit the key fob and unlocked the doors. Parking lights flashed, interior lights came on, and the horn honked. He stared at her.

"Sorry," she said. Terry opened the driver door and reached for the interior light switch. She could see again his face and shirt were covered with another man's blood. It looked terrible and she knew they were going to have to remedy that situation very soon. He switched off the lights. She reached in the glove compartment and the console and collected up all the papers in both places. This was clearly a rental based on how immaculate it was. She assumed the rental contract was somewhere in the pile of papers. Terry checked under and behind all the seats and in the rear cargo compartment. Nothing.

Taking the paperwork with them, they got back on the road and continued east, driving without headlights for about fifteen minutes. There was a lot to discuss, but neither one of them said a word. Peggy was worried about him. She knew he had killed people before, although she was never foolish or impulsive enough to ask how or how many. This had been up close and physical, judging by the blood covering his upper body. Things like this effected even men with a history like his. She knew she had to tread lightly. She felt bad about snapping and calling him an asshole earlier, not knowing what had just happened to him.

Peggy didn't realize that Terry had already moved on. He was mission focused and wasn't dwelling on what had happened. He knew they were about twenty-five miles north of the east-west road they had taken after they left the farm. Roads in Nebraska looked like graph paper when you saw them on a map. They had driven west just twenty-four hours before and ended up in that little town with George and Juanita. Now they were heading back east again. He hadn't told her yet, but they were heading back to the farm and then back to visit Captain Anderson at the National Guard Armory. He needed to sleep. He needed to clean up and change clothes. And he needed to fucking eat. He was starving.

They still hadn't solved the riddle of the laptop and what someone wanted to put on it. They didn't know what role General Dawson played in all this. They still didn't know what the hell happened with the deputies and why Deputy Jimmy tried to kill Peggy, other than his declaration of "she's a fucking terrorist!" And now they didn't know who the three corpses were and why they were looking for Terry and Peggy. Terry finally turned on the headlights.

"Not a word," she said. He realized that she had been talking and he hadn't been listening.

"Nope," he said. "Start again."

"I bet if I was offering you road head," she said sarcastically, "you damn sure would have heard that."

"Probably," he returned serve. "But I would have been wondering what the hell was wrong with you, since I'm covered in all this blood and shit."

"Anyway," she said, getting back on topic, "it looks like we are heading east. Just wondering what's next." She had never been great at directions, especially in the dark, but there was a faint light on the horizon. She was mistaking it for early evidence of the sun coming up when it was actually the lights from a bigger town off in the distance. He looked at the clock and then looked at her. He didn't ask how she came to her conclusion.

"Well, in the immediate future," he started, "I need to clean up, get out of these clothes, and get some chow." He paused. Those weren't the answers she was looking for. "Then, I need some more sleep. So, do you." She wasn't in the mood for his focus on the details.

"Then what?" she said, harsher than she intended. He was right, she did need some sleep. It was after two in the morning. "Where are we going?"

"Then we go to the farm."

She snapped a look at him.

"Then to see young Captain Anderson. Then we are headed to see Brian and Emma."

"You'll have to explain the purpose of each of those." She didn't know where his head was, but she knew he had specific reasons why he would put them at risk like that—and their dearest friends as well.

"All in good time, my dear," he said dryly. "All in good time. Any ideas on where I can clean up and get rid of these clothes?"

"Most of these old gas stations have water hoses, or if we can find a car wash somewhere." He knew the do-it-yourself kind she meant, where they had bays with pressure washer nozzles. He wasn't looking forward to that, but it would certainly get the blood off. As they drove, he started to fade. His eyes were getting heavy and he knew it was only a matter of time before he dozed off. The lights in the distance were getting closer. He promised himself if they could find a place to pull off and he could get cleaned up, he would find somewhere they could get some rack time. In his younger days, he would have powered through and probably made it well past sunrise before he needed to stop. These were not those days.

They got lucky. On the very west edge of town they found a car wash. It was just before three, so there was no one using any of the bays. Unfortunately, the bays were lit up like the Las Vegas strip and they all faced the road. Terry could only cross his fingers that a county sheriff or state trooper didn't drive by while he was cleaning himself up. He pulled behind the car wash and parked back against the trees, trying to use both darkness and the structure to hide the Jeep. He grabbed a little neoprene bag out of the console.

"Cute change purse," she said.

"Do me a favor and go stand out on the road, across the street by those hardwoods," she was going to pull security for him. "If you see headlights, use that whistle you have for the horses. That loud one that hurts my ears. I'll hide myself." They climbed out of the Jeep and she ran across the road and got back into the trees. There were six bays, three on each side of what looked like an office area of sorts. There was a door in front and back. Terry assumed they gave access to all the plumbing and to the backs of the change machines mounted in the front wall of the car wash.

He picked one of the two nearest the center and grabbed the pressure gun out of its tube mounted on the wall. He stripped off his T-shirt and dropped five quarters into the slot on the wall. He was just going to use water but decided some soap would help. Thankfully, the blood hadn't set into his denim jeans yet. The pressure gun with soap pushed the blood out of them like he was stripping paint. There was a pool of it on the floor when he was finished.

Terry was about to turn the spray gun on his upper body, something he was dreading, when he heard the whistle. Terry quickly put the sprayer in the tube and hid behind the building. He watched the headlights go by as he peered around the cinderblock corner. It was a tractor trailer and didn't slow down a bit as it rolled out of town. Terry resumed his duties. First, he tried to use the gun without full pressure, but he didn't see the pool of bloody water on the floor as he did with his pants and had to assume it wasn't working. He closed his eyes and held his breath, hitting himself directly in the chest and neck with the gun. It hurt like hell. He knew he was going to look like a fucking lobster after this. He looked down through the soapy water dripping from his face—yep, blood. *Good*, he thought. He sprayed off his face and felt like he was going to lose his beard and his eyelids in the process. He was working on his hands when the second whistle came from Peggy.

This time the headlights were on a pickup truck. Like most people in this area, the driver wasn't in a hurry to get anywhere. Terry assumed it was well after three before he looked at his watch. 0342. Either that guy was getting an early start or was heading home after a hell of a night. The driver flicked a cigarette butt out the window before he accelerated out of town. Terry was quickly back into the bay and finished up his hands and forearms. From what he could see of his skin, he had removed all the blood. He took an extra minute to spray the remaining soapy water and blood mixture into the drain in the floor, then he gave Peggy a wave to signal he was done. He couldn't see her back in the trees, so he hoped she was paying attention. He turned back toward the Jeep when he saw her silhouette emerge.

Peggy had been watching him intently from across the street, thankful she remembered her glasses. Whether he considered himself old or not, didn't matter to her. Whether he considered himself broken or not didn't matter either. He was attractive in a very rugged way. He wasn't the thirty-something she had met so long ago, and the years had been hard on him, but he was a good-looking man with the self confidence every woman quietly desires. He was as fit as a much younger man. Now there was a little less definition to his muscles, and he didn't move as quickly as he used to. He was still solid, strong. Terry had never spent much time lifting weights in the gym. He was a runner and soccer player growing up and wickedly fast by reputation. He gave that up when his knees quit on him near the end of his Army career. "Too many rough landings," he used to say. He spent over ten years of his career jumping out of planes and it took its toll.

Terry grew a beard after retirement, as many soldiers do. He was very surprised when it started to grow in. He had a good mix of red facial hair he inherited from his mother's Irish roots. As the beard grew, he realized all that red was coming in gray. After listening to him complain about gray hair on his head and in his beard, Peggy offered to help him color it if he wanted. He looked at her like she was insane. She never offered again. He was just complaining to complain.

He was handsome, but not what anyone would consider gorgeous. He wasn't very tall, barely an inch taller than her five foot nine inches. He had wrinkles around his eyes and more in his face, hidden under his beard. His skin was weathered like an old cowboy, but his came from stress along with years of exposure to wind, desert sun, and cold North Carolina rain. He was strong, but from honest work and probably a million pushups and sit-ups over his Army career. And he was smart. Damn was he smart.

When he was going through the litany of exams for his disability, the diagnosis for his traumatic brain injury led the neurologist to send Terry to a psychologist. After an initial interview, Dr. Podolski decided to dig deeper into the psyche of the combat veteran in front of her. She started by administering a neuropsychological evaluation and what she found was somewhat remarkable. Even with his already diagnosed traumatic brain injury, Terry registered an IQ in the mid-140s. She estimated that earlier in life, Terry may have tested as high as 160. He was literally a genius. He also became a favorite patient of Dr. Podolski and the rest of the all-female staff at the behavioral health clinic. Terry's charm, intellect, and subtle smile was the talk of the office after every one of his visits.

Peggy only knew that story because he told her himself. He left out a lot of detail, but she knew the results of his testing and the way he spoke about the "team of ladies" that took care of him. He wasn't ashamed and he wasn't bragging. When he told her about all of it, it was very matter of fact. He wasn't hiding anything from anyone. Peggy put the pieces together that one, or probably all, of the women that worked there had some level of attraction to him either for his brains or his charm. She knew he was attractive, not only to her, but to lots of women. She felt lucky he had chosen to stay with her for so many reasons, most of which he didn't even know.

## CHAPTER 13

Terry pulled a clean T-shirt from his go-bag in the back of the Jeep and was pulling it over his head when she walked up. She was breathing a little bit heavy from the two-hundred-yard jog she'd just made. He was about to say something to her when she kissed him. It was a deep kiss and he responded quickly. Had they been at the farm and not standing in the parking lot of a car wash, he would have been working to get her clothes off. There was hunger in her kiss.

"What brought that on?" he said as he paused between kisses.

"I've been watching you from across the street. You're sexy and I'm horny," she said with another kiss. "And I know you're not complaining."

"Not even a little," he said. It was tempting to get her into the Jeep and try to at least get some foreplay in. They weren't young and there wasn't much room in the Jeep to begin with, regardless of the gear they were hauling around, so sex wasn't much of an option.

"We can address this at a later date," she said with one last quick kiss. She pulled away from him and got into the driver's seat of the Jeep. He shook his head and moved to the passenger side. He could count on one hand how many times she had driven the beast, but he knew he was tired even after the impromptu shower and her getting him all worked up, so he figured her driving was probably the best option. She held her hand out as he climbed in. "Keys, please." He pulled the keys out of the pocket of his wet jeans and handed them to her.

"Let me get some food out of the cooler before we start moving," he reached into the backseat and opened the tan YETI as she started the engine. As much as he wanted it, he skipped the bottle of Mountain Dew and grabbed a blue Powerade. He doubted the high caffeine of the green soda would keep him awake at this point, but he didn't want to take a chance. He hadn't so much as looked inside the cooler since they left and had no idea what she had packed, he only knew what George had given them. He grabbed a Hostess cupcake, a foil pack of strawberry PopTarts, and a Snickers bar. As he sat back in his seat, she took stock of his breakfast.

"You eat like an infantryman," she said.

"That's because I *am* an infantryman," he said quickly.

"Not anymore, old man," she parried back. "Where are we headed?" she asked before he could counter. He was buckling the four-point harness he had installed with the suspension seats, replacing the factory set up.

"Go back west." He pointed back in the direction they came. "There was a north-south road about a mile or so out of town. Take that and head south. If it goes all the way through, it should get us back close to the farm."

"We aren't going back there, are we?" she asked as she put the Jeep into gear and gave it some gas.

"Yes," he was opening the PopTarts. "But not all the way to the farm. We are going to stop short and I am going to do a little recon on foot. If I fall asleep, wake me when you get to the two lane we headed west on yesterday." She stopped the Jeep at the edge of the car wash parking lot.

"You mean, Old Fifty Road?" she said. It was the same tone as when she was going on about the Tastee-Freeze that had become the used car lot where they pulled over for Deputy Jimmy on the way to the armory. He wasn't talking down to her. He knew she knew the area better than he ever would.

"Sure," he said through a mouth full of pseudo-pastry. "Old Fifty

Road. Whatever. Pull over there and wake me up." He was getting irritable. Definitely time for some sleep. He was out before he finished the first PopTart.

She began mumbling quietly to herself, going through the events of the day. "I told Terry the story about the email from Whiteman and that I contacted my people. And no one knew anything," she said as she found the north-south road he was talking about and turned left, heading south. "We went to the armory. Deputies stopped us. They were going to get me. We followed them to the armory."

She looked over at him sleeping against the door. "Finally," she muttered.

She continued, "Phone call to Dawson. He didn't know Terry was with me. He said there was someone in the system and it was a cyberattack of some sort."

She looked down at the speedometer. "Sixty-five. I need to slow down." She let off the gas and set the cruise at fifty.

"He told Terry to protect me and that I was in danger. We went back to the farm. Started packing. Then the deputies came in." It was all shorthand, but she knew what she meant, piece by piece, as she went through it.

"The glass was removed. Terry went to check it. I went in the garage with Jimmy. He had the jammer." Her eyes narrowed. "I had to hit him. Then Terry came in. He went back out and shot the other deputy. He came back and then Jimmy called me a terrorist."

She realized Old Fifty Road was coming up, interrupting her recap. Terry's estimate of how far north they were was short by about seven or eight miles. It was getting lighter now and she could see the stop sign. She knew the farm was still further east about ten miles so she could let Terry sleep a little more. He said he wanted to do some recon of the house and she knew the north edge of the property backed up to this road. The intersection of Old Fifty Road and P Road was the northwest corner of the property. The house sat in the southwest corner, almost a mile south. P Road was the one the driveway connected to. She assumed he would want to be away from the road as he approached the house, so she would have to either stop short or go beyond P Road. The property west of the house, on the opposite side of P Road, was completely pasture. There was no cover there of any kind. She decided to cross over P Road so he could come at the house from the northeast. She smiled to herself. She was thinking like an infantryman for once and not a strategist.

She made the left turn and started east. The predawn glow was getting brighter. Peggy knew the Higgenbottom property, north of theirs, didn't have much on it. She was trying to figure out where to park the Jeep out of sight. Nothing immediately came to mind. She needed Terry for this. She didn't want to shake him awake, but she didn't have much of a choice. She reached over and softly squeezed his arm, increasing pressure until he stirred. He looked over at her. He still looked tired.

"Hey," he said sitting up. "Where are we? How close?" He knew they were already heading east by the light shining in his eyes as he blinked them open.

"That's the north side of the property out your window," she replied. "I don't know where to park so we are out of sight." She could see he was still trying to clear the cobwebs. "There is an old barn on the Loeffler place to the east. It is half collapsed but we may be able to park behind it and then we can walk from there."

"*We*," he said dryly, "aren't walking anywhere." He realized he was still holding part of a PopTart in his hand and shoved it into his mouth. He spit pastry crumbs as he spoke, "Head to that barn and see if we can park there."

She drove silently. She had figured out the approach direction and the options for cover and concealment all on her own and now he was talking down to her. She was pissed for a second and then realized he wasn't part of that conversation inside her head. He didn't appreciate what she was so proud of just a few minutes before because he didn't know about it. She calmed herself.

"The property to the west is all pasture. There was no cover and concealment there," she went into briefing mode as if she was talking to a general about the Middle East. "And the road on the west edge of the property increased the chance of being spotted. I assumed you would want to approach from the northeast, through the property. The high prairie grass will allow you to get pretty close from that direction." He stopped chewing and looked at her.

"Anything else, S-2?" he asked her, impressed with her analysis. The designation of S-2 on a military staff was for the intelligence section and that title was worn by the officer who was in charge of the section.

"Yes," she said very matter-of-factly. "Coming from the east would actually be best because the sun would be behind you, making it more difficult for anyone looking that direction to see you." He drank from his Powerade bottle, trying to conceal his grin. "Unless you wanted to wait for darkness."

"Very good," he said. "I am very impressed." She smiled widely as she drove. "Was that the barn we just passed?"

"Shit," she said before she could think. She was distracted by his compliment and lost in her own head. She slowed the Jeep, downshifted, and turned it around in a quick three-point-turn. She goosed it and got back to the barn and off the road. The ground was hard packed after the dry summer and she pulled through what used to be an old feed lot that hadn't seen cattle in decades, nosing the Jeep behind the barn. He climbed out as soon as she stopped.

"I think we can probably get it inside," he said walking up to the barn. "I'll back it in." He walked back to the Jeep and whipped into the barn, ass end first. She stood inside, next to the Jeep, staring up at the roof of the old structure. She romanticized its history, thinking about all the horses and cattle that had moved through there in years past. The only thing living in there now were pigeons. She looked around at the ground level. The doors facing the road were off their sliding rails but were leaned against the frame. It was highly unlikely anyone could see them from out there.

He was in the back of the Jeep, pulling out gear. He grabbed one of the assault packs and pulled a camouflage uniform top from the main compartment. He put it on as he ducked back into the Jeep. He put a box of ammo for the Remington 700 into an assault pack, along with four bottles of water, the poncho liner, and the bag of trail mix he kept stashed in the Jeep. Next, he put the FNX with the suppressor in the bag. It wouldn't be quickly accessible, but if he needed to be quiet, he assumed he would have time to get to it before he needed it. Lastly, he added an old pair of Nikon binoculars. They had been his grandfather's and were handed down to him when he died. They were very good when they were new, almost sixty years ago, but they had seen better days. The lenses were clear though, and they were compact. Right now, they were the best he had and would hopefully be more than he needed.

"Stay out of sight," he said to her. "You should be safe here. Keep your daddy's pistol on you, just in case. The Model 12 is under the back seat and the AK is in the back." She was about to protest and demand to go with him, but she knew it was fruitless. He would move faster on his own and didn't need her slowing him down.

"What exactly are you looking for?" she asked. He hadn't really filled her in on anything. "This is literally returning to the scene of the crime. What are you trying to gain out of this?"

"A couple of things, really," he was throwing the assault pack over his shoulders. "If it is being treated as a crime scene, I'll be able to see it. Police tape and all that. If it isn't," he paused, "well, I'll be able to see that too. If there are any vehicles out there, it will provide some insight. Police cars versus FBI, or anyone else. All that stuff matters. And if it is nothing? No cars, no tape, nothing . . . that matters too." He was thinking in terms of who reacted and how, if at all.

"You're not planning on going inside the house," she said, making an assumption.

"No," he said, picking up his rifle. "Planning on keeping my distance. It's been long enough that anyone could have installed listening or monitoring devices if they wanted. I'm not planning on getting close." He moved in and kissed her.

"Maybe you should take this with," she said as she held the jammer in her hands. "If you run into anyone, they won't be able to call for help." He paused and looked at the Jeep. "You already said the Jeep was clear and I have my cell phone turned off so they can't track that either." She was right. He turned slightly, letting her put the small device into the pack on his back.

"Stay sharp. I'll be back in a few hours." He was reflexively giving her a contingency plan like he learned in Ranger School. "If I'm not back by midnight, you go straight to Brian and Emma's. Tell them everything. They will know what to do. If you hear shooting, same thing. Straight to their house." He turned and went to the corner of the barn and took a second to look out into the prairie grass before he jogged off to the southwest. He never turned back to look at her.

She stood there for a long minute and watched him. He disappeared quickly into the grass, crouching as he moved quickly. He had been wearing the same sweat stained baseball cap since they left. In fact, he rarely went anywhere without it. That cap was now blending into the tall grass, masking the top of his head.

There were a handful of things in his life that he was desperately attached to and that hat was one of them, the Benchmade knife was another. He never wore it in the house and never when they went anywhere nice, but since he spent most of his life in blue jeans, the hat was never out of place. He occasionally rinsed it out in the sink with liquid hand soap and then wore it until it was dry, keeping it from shrinking. He had torn the button off the top a long time ago so he could wear earmuffs over it without giving himself a headache

The cap itself was a color common to the military, and gun makers referred to as flat dark earth or FDE. It was tan or *dirt colored* as Peggy called it. On the front, the emblem of his unit had been embroidered in black. The black stitching had faded to almost match the color of the hat itself after all these years. Like the Benchmade, it had become a good luck charm of sorts, almost a part of who he was.

She could see it for about the next minute or so, peaking out of the grass here and there. After it disappeared completely, she took a long look around the outside of the barn. There was no one in sight and no noise coming from the road. She knew darkness was a long way off, but she decided to just settle in and wait, trying to ignore how nervous she was.

"Shit," she exhaled. "This accelerated quicker than I anticipated."

## CHAPTER 14

Terry Davis saw the roof of the house peeking through the grass and knew he needed to slow down. The day had started bright, with the sun behind him as he approached, but clouds moved in slowly. He could smell rain coming and hoped it wouldn't be more than a sprinkle. It had been a very dry summer so a little rain wouldn't hurt, but it also meant roads would become slick and creeks would flood quickly if there were more than a few inches of precipitation. He found a depression where he could stand upright and see the house through the waving grass. He estimated he was still about five hundred yards away and unless anyone was out looking for him, he was still a safe enough distance to take a drink and get the binoculars out of the pack.

He slugged down the whole twenty-ounce bottle and put it back into the pack and pulled out the old Nikons, looping the strap behind his neck. He unbuttoned the top button of the camouflage shirt, tucking the binoculars inside to keep them from bouncing and banging around, or dragging in the dirt, as he moved. He donned the pack and stood slowly, the rifle in both hands. He wanted to head farther south, so the horse barn masked his movement the last hundred or so yards to the back of the farmhouse. Terry moved slowly in a crouch for the next thirty minutes, occasionally standing a bit taller to keep the house in sight and on his right, then crouching down again and continuing forward.

He found another depression and dropped the pack. He had a pretty good sweat going and could feel it running down his back.

*This shit was a lot easier twenty years ago,* he thought. He sucked down another whole bottle of water. When he was a kid, his dad gave him books about Vietnam to read. He picked up a few tricks that he later learned were known as *field craft*. One of those tricks was to consume a whole canteen at once, that way there was no possible noise of sloshing water inside a half-drunk canteen. He didn't know if anyone could actually hear the sound of sloshing water, but he didn't risk it. Terry pulled the binoculars out of the front of the uniform top and stood slowly. He had drifted a little closer to the house than he intended. He was still about four hundred yards from the house and about three hundred fifty yards from the barn.

Looking through the binoculars, Terry didn't see any movement in or around the house. There was no yellow police tape to designate the place as a crime scene, at least from his vantage point. He watched intently for a minute and then ducked back down. Terry grabbed a handful of trail mix from the bag, carefully pushing any excess air out of the Ziploc bag before he sealed it and then wrapping the poncho liner around it to keep it from shifting inside the pack. He waited.

After five minutes passed on his watch, he stood slowly and looked at the house through his grandfather's binoculars. Still nothing. Nothing moving. No lights. No vehicles to be seen. He decided to move closer and look from a different angle. Grabbing his gear, he headed northwest. He wouldn't have the barn for cover, but he would be able to see more of the house and at a different angle. He moved much slower now, his steps more deliberate. Ten steps, stop, peek at the house, then another ten steps. He closed the distance a little more. When he was three hundred yards from the back door, he knelt in the grass.

Terry shouldered the sniper rifle, resting his left elbow on his left knee. He peered through the powerful scope at the house with his right eye. Still no signs of life or movement of any kind. He lost track of how long he had been peering through the narrow view of the sniper scope, focused on the house. As he opened his left eye and raised his head to look around, he saw movement by the barn. The horses were out in the small corral. He could see Peggy's woodpile and the horse tails swishing just beyond it. Movement to his left. *Closer.* He raised his head higher to find Larry approaching less than fifty yards away, with a lever action Winchester in his skinny hands. Terry gave a slight wave. Larry visibly relaxed and began to move at a brisk walk to Terry's location. Terry looked again at the house through the riflescope. Nothing. He waited for Larry to reach him.

"Mr. Davis," he said in a deep bass voice that didn't match his skinny frame. "You scared the devil out of me. Where is Ms. Baron?"

"Larry," Terry said still in a crouch. "Is there anyone at the house? Anyone at all?"

"No, sir. No one. I got the call yesterday from someone asking me to come take care of the horses," Larry must have been referring to George, "so I came out here to take care of them." Larry didn't know why, but he knelt down in the grass.

"Have you been in the house?" he asked.

"No," he responded plainly. "I drove up the side drive to the barn, checked on the horses. I knocked on the back door and no one answered so I went back out to the barn, then I saw someone out here and decided to take a look." He was referring to Terry. "What are you doing out here, Mr. Davis?"

Terry had asked Larry a hundred times not to call him *sir* or *Mr. Davis*, but it was just who he was, a polite man who had been taught manners at a young age. He called Peggy's parents *Mr. and Mrs. Baron* and Peggy was *Miss Peggy* all the way up until Peggy's mom died, then Peggy became *Ms. Baron*. Larry spoke to everyone that way, even at the protest of his son and two daughters who had gone off to college in Omaha and returned with a distaste for where they grew up. They implored their father to not bow down to White men and women and call them ma'am and sir. He never saw it as anything but being respectful, but his children didn't agree. After Larry's wife passed away, the children didn't come around much. Larry passed his time working with horses on farms all over the county, including this one.

"Larry," he looked the man dead in the face, "the less you know, the better off you are."

"Are y'all in trouble?" he asked with fear in his eyes. "I couldn't stand it if Ms. Baron was in trouble and I didn't help."

"You can help me," Terry said reluctantly. "I'm going to head for that house and head inside. You any good with that thing?" he nodded to the Winchester.

"Mr. Davis," he said with feigned insult in his voice, "I been shooting this rifle since before even *you* were born. What do you need me to do?"

"I don't want you coming inside because I don't know what I am going to find," he said. Larry's eyes got wide. "Peggy, um Ms. Baron, is safe. She ain't in there." Larry started breathing again. "I'm going inside. You stay outside and cover me. Anyone approaches, in a vehicle, on foot, on a fucking horse, anyone approaches, and you give me a whistle. That loud one you taught Ms. Baron."

"Yes, sir," Larry said with some confusion in his face. "Why did you ask if I was any good with this rifle?"

"Because, Larry," Terry responded plainly, "if someone starts shooting, I'm gonna need you to kill them."

"Yes, sir." There was steel in the old man's eyes, something Terry had never seen in him before. Larry had been to the farm a number of times and Terry always watched him around the horses and around Peggy. He was a gentle as he was old, but something in his face told Terry the old man had seen death before. It wasn't uncommon in the rural, hard-living folk that resided out here to see death. Animals died. People died. It was part and parcel of the lives they lived. The look Terry saw in the old man was different. He hadn't just seen death; he had likely caused it.

Terry picked himself up and the two moved quickly to the back of the barn where he dropped the pack and leaned the bolt-action rifle on the red painted wall. Terry could see the rear bumper of Larry's old truck now; it had been hidden by the barn as he approached. He was disappointed in himself. He was planning to use the barn to mask his approach toward the house but didn't think about what it was going to mask from *him*. It was almost like one of the legendary Murphy's Rules of Combat: *Tracers work both ways.* The military used tracer rounds for a number of reasons, but most commonly it was to make adjustments based on the flight and impact of the rounds you could observe. Tracers are what you saw in movies, the red flash that flew through the air looking like a laser beam. They helped a firer be more accurate when trying to kill the enemy, but they also helped the enemy find the man firing at them.

"You just stay here," Terry told him. "Stay with the horses and your truck. Keep your eyes and your ears open." Larry nodded and walked around the barn to the corral. Terry reached into the pack and grabbed the big pistol with the suppressor screwed onto the barrel. Terry knew he was taking a risk. He even told Peggy he wasn't going into the house because it could be bugged or could be monitored. The fact that he had shot a man and left another chained to a car inside the house less than two days ago wasn't lost on him, nor was it lost on him that it seemed the house was untouched since then.

He cracked open the back door wondering what he was going to find. Would the two deputies still be there—one dead and one handcuffed in the garage? Would anyone be in there waiting for him? Was it a trap? He pushed open the back door and lead with the pistol. He looked over his should before he went in and locked eyes with Larry. He nodded and Larry nodded back.

Terry was inside the kitchen and could see the holes in the wall where he shot the deputy. There was blood on the floor but no body, and much of the blood had been cleaned up. He checked quickly, curious if there was evidence of what happened to the deputy he shot. Nothing. Terry moved quietly toward the garage, cringing at every creak of the floor. *This fucking house,* he thought. The garage was added to the house in the late 1940s. Typical of farmers and farmhouses, the family cut a doorway into the exterior wall. It was crude work and was neither plumb nor true; there was always a gap between the door and the frame. He pushed the door open, finding Peggy's Audi still in the garage but Deputy Jimmy gone. In his place was blood—not a lot and it had been wiped up but enough there to notice. It looked like someone came in and killed him on the garage floor and then removed the body. It was a guess without much evidence, but it made sense.

Terry went back into the house and found Peggy's laptop in the living room, sitting on the coffee table. He grabbed it quickly, wrapping the power cord around it. Terry was going to head to the basement to get a few more essentials from his gun safe, namely his night vision goggles and possibly the two sets of body armor, when he heard the whistle from Larry out by the barn. Terry came out the back door with the pistol and the computer and locked eyes with Larry who nodded toward the front of the house. He needed to get to his rifle, but it was a long way away. The basement? Plenty of firepower down there, but not enough time. He heard the voices.

"Hey old man," it was coming from the front of the house. "What are you doing out here?" Larry put his hand to his ear as if he couldn't hear the man. Terry put down the computer and raised the pistol with both hands. "You see anyone else out here? White guy with a beard, maybe?" Terry could hear the voice clearly and could tell he was moving closer. He knew Larry could hear it as well but was trying to get them to move closer.

"No, sir," Larry finally answered, "just me and these here horses. Ain't seen no one else around." Terry decided to make a move. He circled around the house to get in behind whoever it was that Larry was talking to. As he came around the front, Terry spotted another black Chevy Suburban just like the one from the night before. *Assume at least three of them, maybe more.* Terry cleared the corners as he moved around the garage and then the front porch, spotting the driver's window was down and there was a man behind the wheel. Terry moved quickly and shot the man in the face, the suppressor making the pistol almost silent. Almost.

It didn't work like the movies. Guns with silencers, or suppressors, weren't actually silent. They didn't just make that *ffftt* sound when the trigger was pulled. In fact, if using supersonic rounds, even a suppressed gun can be quite loud—the bullet still makes a supersonic crack as it breaks the sound barrier. Terry's FNX-45 was chambered in .45 ACP and the rounds were subsonic, so no supersonic crack, but the mechanical sounds of the slide moving, the round ejecting, and the slide slamming forward on another round were audible. It was loud enough the two men in the driveway turned to look over their shoulders. They didn't see their compatriot with his brains splattered all over the passenger seat after Terry shot him in the left side of the head, but they did see Terry pointing the big pistol at them as he came around the corner of the house.

They were both dressed like the three guys last night—active or tactical clothing, sometimes referred to as *tacticool*. Terry shot the man on the left before he could react. The man on the right had his pistol out by the time Terry shot him with two rounds in the center of his chest. Terry was moving forward when he heard the shot. He thought he was dead, that there was a fourth man he hadn't seen, and he was just waiting for the lights to go out. He looked up to see Larry, Winchester on his shoulder, then back toward the Suburban to see a man lying on the ground with an AR-15 next to him. Larry had saved his ass.

"Thanks, brother," Terry said as the two met in the middle. He put out his hand. Terry reserved the term *brother* for those he had served in combat with and Larry had just joined that somewhat exclusive club. "You weren't lying about you and that Winchester. But right now, you need to get those horses and get the hell out of there. There may be more of these fuckers coming."

"Mr. Davis," he said. "What the heck is going on?"

"Like I said," Terry reiterated his point, "the less you know, the better. I'm going to load these guys up into that Suburban and dump it somewhere. You need to get out of here. They obviously know who I am and what I look like. They probably didn't let anyone know there was an old, Black guy out here. You need to scoot. They will be looking for me, not you."

"Yes, sir." Larry said back. "I'm going to hook up Ms. Baron's trailer and load these two horses in it and go."

"Good idea," Terry shook his hand again. "Thanks again, brother."

"You're most welcome," Larry stopped. "You take care of Ms. Baron. You hear me?" Terry nodded. "Stay safe now, Mr. Davis." Larry turned and walked to the barn as Terry went to work loading up the bodies. By the time he had them in the back and recovered his rifle, pack, and Peggy's laptop from the back of the house, Larry had the trailer hooked up and was loading the second of the two horses. Terry gave him a wave as he pulled out of the drive and headed north. He was going to circle around and link up with Peggy. She would follow him until they found somewhere to dump the Suburban.

He got to the partially collapsed barn in a matter of minutes, compared to the hours it took him to approach the house stealthily and on foot. As he pulled off the road, he realized Peggy may have taken off after hearing the shot from Larry's Winchester. If she followed the directions he gave her before he left, she should be long gone by now. *Shit,* he thought. He drove the big black Suburban off the road, through the old feedlot, and around the back of the barn. He rolled the windows down so Peggy, if she was even still there, could see him inside the vehicle. He wheeled the behemoth around only to be greeted by Peggy and the barrel of the .357 emerging from the barn. He jumped out of the vehicle.

"You should be gone by now," he said. "Didn't you hear the shot?"

"Happy to see you, too," she said dryly. This was no time for a tennis match, but her answer was a reflex. "Sorry. I didn't hear any shooting. Probably the wind and the distance. Too far from here, probably." She was walking over to the Suburban and he stopped her.

"Don't look in there," he grabbed her arm. "It isn't pretty. There are four more guys in there, probably from the same organization as the three from last night. We need to dump this thing. And I got your laptop." A surprised look came over her face. She had about fifty questions for him but realized quickly the Suburban was an urgent issue and her questions would have to wait.

"Um," she stuck her thumbnail in her mouth, "probably the quarry is best. Not really a quarry, but an old strip mine that is filled with water."

"Anyone out there?" he asked impatiently.

"No," she replied. "It's been closed since I was little. People don't even fish out there because the water is polluted. It's only about twenty feet deep though."

"That will have to work," he said as he moved back to the Suburban. "You lead, I'll follow." Peggy shuffled quickly to the Jeep as he put the Suburban in reverse and gave her room to pull out. He followed as she manhandled the Jeep down the blacktop, turning off onto a dirt road. He glanced in the rearview mirror at the pile of bodies in the back.

"Who the fuck are these guys?" he asked himself aloud.

## CHAPTER 15

The two of them stood at the edge of the water watching the bubbles from the Suburban as it sank to the bottom. Terry had quickly searched the four bodies before they put it in neutral and shoved it into the stagnant pool. All four of them had fake driver's licenses and all with the last name Smith. It was almost comical, but it also meant they were all connected and working for the same entity, be it a company or a person. When Terry was satisfied the bubbles were almost gone, he turned and walked back to the Jeep with Peggy trailing behind.

It was late afternoon and he had dispelled the idea of going to see Captain Anderson of the Nebraska Army National Guard. After a second run-in with the Smith boys, he knew there were people looking for them and they needed to get somewhere safe as quickly as they could. The Jeep was going to need gas to get to Brian and Emma's, especially since they were going to stay off the main roads, adding to the miles and time it was going to take to get there. Terry anticipated going through a full recap of the events at the farm with Peggy as they drove. She would probably be pissed that he went inside the house to get her computer and even more pissed that he had gotten Larry involved. Then they would brainstorm to see what else they could figure out. It was going to be a long trip.

They had driven this back-road route once before and Terry was going to try to do it by memory. Last time, they had Peggy's Audi and the navigation system in the dash. It took her fifteen minutes in the garage to figure out how to turn on and off all the right options to keep them on the country roads. She felt like driving that day, not necessarily being behind the wheel but taking the kind of drive she took with her parents on Sunday afternoons. Back then, they would drive aimlessly for hours. Her mother used to refer to them as *adventures* and they would eventually end up at some roadside stand or diner, eating ice cream. They drove for about a half hour in silence until they found a Casey's station. He filled the Jeep, keeping his head down and masking his face with the bill of his cap. As much as she wanted to grab some food from inside, it wasn't worth the risk, so he made her stay in the Jeep and put together peanut butter sandwiches courtesy of George and Juanita.

"So," she said quietly. "What happened back there?" They were back on the road and he had a mouth full of bread and peanut butter when she started in.

Swallowing down the clump of sandwich, he gave her the short version of his approach to the house. Her eyes got wide when he mentioned Larry. Terry told her what he saw and didn't see inside the house, specifically the deputies and the new blood on the garage floor. He told her about Larry giving him the warning and then everything that transpired outside the house, again sparing her some of the gory details. He was waiting for her to lash out when he told her about Larry killing the last man and saving his ass. He didn't expect her reaction.

"It doesn't surprise me," she said flatly. "When I was a teenager, Daddy told me a story about him. Larry was in high school and three White boys attacked him and were beating him pretty bad. Larry killed one of them with his bare hands and got arrested. It was nineteen sixty-six and the judge took pity on him because he knew those other boys were prejudiced against him because he was Black, so he gave him the option to join the Army or go to jail. Larry joined the Army and went to Vietnam. When he came home, one of those same boys tried to kill him . . . you know, for killing his friend." Terry was stunned. "Larry took another beating. He took it for as long as he could and then he fought back, and he killed that boy too." She looked at her hands. He could hear the sympathy in her voice. "There wasn't any trial this time. That boy just disappeared. Daddy said he was in the bottom of that strip mine, but he got what he deserved, and Daddy never held it against Larry."

"He told you all of this?" Terry asked. "Your dad did? How did he know about the second boy, the one that disappeared?"

"Daddy was Larry's lawyer," she said, "for the trial after he killed the first boy. He was the only lawyer in town and did it for free. When Larry killed the second boy, he came to Daddy for help. Daddy knew Larry wouldn't get off a second time. That's how I know about that strip mine. Daddy helped him." Terry put the pieces together pretty quickly. He could tell that was all she was going to say, so he sat quietly for a half second.

"Well, he helped me, probably to protect you," Terry said. She smiled. "I guess that was his way of paying your dad back."

"So, what about all these guys named Smith?" she changed the subject. "Obviously all connected. They got to the house pretty quickly and you said they described you."

"Yeah. They either had someone watching or they had cameras like I suspected. And they weren't far away. From the time I came out of the grass to the time they showed up was less than ten minutes. From the time I went through the door, less than seven minutes."

"But they didn't know where I was," she stepped in. "Otherwise they would have come and gotten me, probably first." He nodded. "So, they were only watching the house and they probably only had that one team of guys," she said.

"That's the second team," he said. "The first team was up at George's hideout. This was the second team. Like you said, they are clearly connected. Younger, fit, armed, dressed the same. Same vehicles. The fake IDs. They are like contractors in a bad action movie or something." He could see the lightbulb come on over her head.

"That's *exactly* what they are," she said. "We are in the middle of Nebraska. There are no private security companies out here. Not any good ones anyway. Those guys weren't professionals. They were probably the best available option. Probably the only available option."

"You're right," he said. "It seems like an eternity for us, but it has only been three days since this all started. And it's only been two days since it all went sideways with the deputies." His eyes narrowed. "This is because of me."

"What?" she didn't understand what conclusion he had come to. "I'm the one they called a terrorist. What do you mean this is about you?"

"Whatever this started as, it isn't anymore," he said. "This was about you, and only you. You're a lot of things Peg, but you're not a threat that requires security contractors. Once I was added into the equation, the threat to whatever this is changed. So, they found this bunch of fucking clowns and got them out here as quickly as possible." He chuckled. She looked at him like he was crazy. "Really, I should be fucking insulted. That's what I should be—insulted. They sent this bunch of morons out here to kill me. I mean, I'm not John Wick or anything, but I deserve a little more respect than sending these fucking guys."

"It was what they had available," she said with a slight tone of ego-stroking. "That's all. But, if these are second stringers, how did they find us at George's hideout? What assets do they have to find us in a place like that?"

"Good question," he said. The light was fading, and they were still a few hours from Brian and Emma's. "They aren't tracking us. We still have the jammer so that is weirdly keeping us covered. Is that thing still on?" It occurred to him that he had no idea how long the batteries lasted in something like that. She dug into the pack in the backseat. The light was still flashing. She nodded her head. "Okay. So only George knew where we were. I don't think he would give up his best hideout, let alone give us up in the process."

"I don't either," she agreed. "But, maybe that old man was full of shit." He snapped a look at her. She was sounding like him again. "He was a farmer. All farmers are at least a little bit full of shit. Maybe that spot wasn't as big a secret as he said."

"Well, that may be true," he chimed in, "but that doesn't mean anyone had any reason to look for us out there."

"Except that it's one of the few places to hide in the area," she countered. "If someone was looking for us, and they asked around, it's possible they may have been given a tip and with a little bit of work on Google Maps, they could have found the spot and come looking. They may have gotten lucky." It was a thin theory, but it was the only one that made sense. "You say it all the time 'LuckCounts.'"

"Well," he said with a wry smile, "you beat me. I can't argue with my own logic. So, these guys get hired and get fed some wild, bullshit story. They get paid plenty of money based on the rentals they are driving, the guns, and the number of people out here. They get sent out here to do what? Find us? Capture us? Kill us?"

"Kill *you*," she said. "Whatever it is they wanted from me, they probably still want it. They just need you out of the way. At that point, I'm helpless. That's probably why they picked me anyway. No parents. No kids or husband. No ties. Except to the Middle East." She was driving at something. "They were going to frame me. The deputy said it: 'She's a fucking terrorist.' That's what he got told by Captain Anderson. And who told Anderson?"

"General Dawson," he said. The words hurt. "Somehow, he is in the middle of this. Whether he is a willing participant or not, he is in the middle."

"Right," she said. "Dawson, the CENTCOM commander, a four-star, tells a National Guard captain that I'm a terrorist. He strokes his ego. It's a big secret and he is being trusted with it." The back and forth was picking up speed.

"So, Dawson tells Anderson," Terry said, making a left turn onto an eastbound blacktop. "Anderson boasts to his dipshit brother in-law, who tells us."

"But," she interrupted, "that brings us back to the jammer. Where did that come from?"

"Had to be Dawson," he stated plainly. "You said you can find them in the Middle East. That is CENTCOM AOR." AOR was military speak for area of responsibility. "CENTCOM owns all operations in the Middle East. They probably had more than a few jammers like this at their disposal. Anderson gets the package from CENTCOM the same day he gets the phone call from Dawson. Dawson just tells him to get it out to your place. Probably doesn't even tell him what it is or why. I can almost hear him now: 'It's a matter of national security, son. I'm trusting you.'" Terry was starting to get a sick feeling in the pit of his stomach.

"And when Dawson finds out you're involved," she added, "he has to get you out of the way. So, they hire the contractors. But, what happened to the deputies?" They were making some progress now. She was down in the weeds, which was unlike her, looking into the minute details. Normally, that was his role while she focused at the strategic level.

"No clue," he said. "But, I bet we find out and I bet it ain't good. The bigger question is what do they want from you? You said they were going to frame you. What did you mean?" He was trying to get her looking bigger again, engaging that brilliant mind of hers where it was most useful.

"Could be any number of things," she replied. Terry turned south again. "They could blame me for exposing my contacts." Terry was expecting her mood to sour at the thought, but she kept going. "They could label me as a sympathizer to any terror organization from the region—Al Qaeda, ISIS, whoever."

"But what does anyone gain from that?" he broke in. "There have been more than a few nutjobs that have gone over to Iraq and Syria to fight alongside ISIS. Or sent money. Or even done some low-level spying. If they pegged you for that, with your background working with DoD and all the other agencies, they would be the ones who looked stupid in the end. They gain nothing."

"Well, whatever it is, you sure fucked up their plans," she said in the growing darkness.

"Again," he said. "Again with the f-word."

She laughed. It seemed like the first time she had laughed in a lifetime. The last couple of days had been awful. Physically and emotionally exhausting. He could tell how tired she was, she looked like she could cry at the drop of a hat. Peggy Baron had lived a life, for sure. She had travelled the globe and been all over the Middle East, every country and every little corner, but she had never been in the middle of the action like this. She never knew why Terry had volunteered for all his deployments. He certainly didn't need to go on all of them, but he did. He wasn't what she would call a warmonger. He wasn't someone who thrived on the killing. She was finally relating to him and why he was what he was. *This.* This feeling of excitement, adrenaline, focus, and purpose.

"You didn't hear me, did you?" he asked her with a chuckle. "I really am rubbing off on you."

"Not even going to pretend," she said, stealing his line.

"I said, we are about an hour from Brian and Emma's." They were heading east again. Terry turned at an old windmill he noticed the last time they came through here. It was a straight shot on this road to their destination. "Why don't you get some sleep? You know once we get there, we will be up all-night filling them in."

"I know," she said. She looked forward to seeing them. The mention of sleep hit her hard. She was instantly tired, and her body was starting to shut down. She didn't know how Terry did it and had been doing it for so long. She admired his endurance and dozed off with a smile thinking about the next time she would be able to take advantage of it.

CHAPTER 16

Peggy awoke as they pulled into the drive. The headlights from the Jeep flashed across the front of the house. All the lights were still on, inside and out. Terry was opening the door of the Jeep when the biggest German Shepherd Peggy had ever seen bounded off the front steps and ran at them, a site that would scare the shit out of anyone who didn't know him. In truth, Jumper was just like his owner Brian—lots of barking and no bite at all. Terry began petting him and was getting his face licked when he heard the screen door bang shut.

"Boy," Brian said from the porch, "you ain't worth a fuck as a guard dog. Bite that sonofabitch." Brian was moving slowly down the steps. His accent was thick. He grew up in a house that was thirty feet from the Louisiana state line on the Texas side, but he claimed Texas and only Texas. He and Terry were as close as brothers. "Hey, baby," he said wrapping his arms around Terry. "What the fuck y'all doin' here? Not that I ain't glad to see you, but you coulda fuckin' called." Brian was moving around the Jeep to Peggy, talking over his shoulder. She met him halfway and hugged him. He kissed her cheek. "Hey darlin'," he said. "You still hangin' around with this shitbag?" Everything that came out of Brian's mouth was offensive, but it was all said with love.

A tiny redhead emerged from the house. Emma was down the steps in a flash and jumped into Terry's arms, wrapping her legs around him.

"Hey there, sexy," Terry said loud enough for Brian to hear. She kissed him on the lips. "Damn, girl, I don't think you're wearin' any panties!" It was a ritual the three had gone through a hundred times, every time getting a little more vulgar. Emma dropped to the ground and turned to Peggy. Terry slapped her on the ass.

"Wouldn't you like to know," she threw over her shoulder. "Hello, lady." She hugged Peggy. "Like he said, what the hell are you guys doing here?"

"We need your help," Peggy started.

"Whatever it is," Brian said turning to the stairs, "we can talk about it inside over some beer." Brian had been a paratrooper longer than even Terry had, and the price was steeper. He was moving on two new knees and a fused neck. He seemed slower every time Terry saw him. Brian was just a year older than Terry, but he wasn't aging well.

"Hey," Terry said, "can I put this thing in the pole barn?" Brian turned and looked at him, then Emma and Peggy, then back to Terry.

"Ah, shit," he said. "Yeah, go ahead. You can tell us all about it when you get inside. C'mon Jumper, git in the fuckin' house." He turned and went up the steps. Peggy and Emma followed him, arm in arm. Emma was younger than Brian by almost five years, which put her about fifteen years younger than Peggy. Peggy's five foot, nine inches towered over Emma who barely broke five feet. They were more like a cool aunt and a favorite niece than they would ever be like sisters.

At first Peggy was uncomfortable with the way the three greeted each other. It took her a bit to understand that it really was out of love and nothing more. Terry cursed often but it was mostly conversational and rarely really offensive. When he was around Brian, it was different. He said things he would never say if it was just the two of them. She didn't know if he was refraining out of respect for her or if he was putting on a show for Brian when they were together; the truth was likely somewhere in the middle. Neither Brian nor Terry refrained around Emma, mostly because she was as bad as they were. Peggy briefly thought the flirting between Terry and Emma was genuine and that there was a real attraction between the two of them, but she quickly realized it was their way of giving Brian a hard time, teaming up against him.

The three of them were around the island in the kitchen when Terry came through the front door. There were six open bottles of beer. Terry stopped, counted the people in the room, then the bottles, then the people again.

"Two for me," Brian said, "and two for you." Terry grabbed a bottle and downed half of it before taking a breath. "Now what the fuck is going on?"

"Good to see you too," Terry said taking another drink, "fucker." Terry and Brian had been captains and company commanders together twenty years prior. They had attended a number of schools together and had bumped into each other on deployments countless times. Brian was the closest thing Terry had to a brother in the Army. There was a true love between the two men, borne out of respect and lots of shitty days and nights spent in the worst places together. The two even retired on the same day.

Terry sat down on one of the stools at the kitchen island. Peggy started to lay out everything that had happened. Brian listened intently, chin resting in his hands and occasionally standing to drink from his bottle of beer. Emma came and sat on Terry's lap, listening to the story of the last seventy-two hours. Emma was a career Army officer as well, so there was no need to translate anything Peggy was saying into civilian speak. She was a Signal Corps officer and had spent the last few years working digital communications and networks. She and Brian met when both of their previous marriages had fallen apart. Emma was a tech geek in her own right and she knew how to build and repair computers and could set up a network with her eyes closed. Brian thought moving her to the country was going to be like fighting a pit bull, but she came willingly.

Emma slid off Terry's lap, one side of her little running shorts climbing up the crack of her ass as she did. Peggy kept telling the story as Emma walked away, casually fishing the shorts from between her cheeks as she went to the desk. *She really isn't wearing any panties,* Terry said to himself. Emma came back with a notepad and a pen. She started to slide back onto Terry's lap, and he couldn't help himself.

"I'm gonna have to ask you not to do that," he said. Everyone stopped and looked at him. "I've been thinking about Brian naked since you sat on my lap, trying not to get a hard on. I can't bare that thought any longer." Brian turned and spit his mouthful of beer into the sink, laughing. Peggy didn't think it was funny.

"Your loss," Emma said, walking back to the other side of the island. She gave Terry the finger. "Please continue Peggy." Emma started writing notes down. Brian was cleaning up his mess when Peggy got to the part about the first team of Smiths that had found them at George's hideout. He stopped and stared at Terry.

"Boy," he said standing stock still, "y'all really are in some trouble." He went to the refrigerator and came out with four more beers, handing one out to each of them. He resumed his position with his head resting on his hands. Peggy told the rest of the story. Emma had a page of notes. Brian stood up straight and looked at the ceiling. Peg sat there waiting for someone to speak. Brian opened his mouth and Emma beat him to it.

"Okay," she was reading from her page of notes, "I need your phones, your laptop, and that jammer thing. Terry, sweetie, can you go get those from your car for me?" She smiled at him. He scowled. "Oh, your Jeep. Excuse me. Please get them from your *Jeep* for me." He smiled and walked outside.

"Is he okay?" Brian asked her. "I know he is physically okay, I can see that. But how's his head? That's the toughest motherfucker I ever met, but I still worry about him."

"He is," Peggy said with a slight smile. "He's barely stopped since this all started. I actually worry more about him physically right now than I do mentally. You both know about his PTSD. And his sleep issues and the brain injuries. And everything else that the VA diagnosed him with. It is all so much and none of this is helping."

"We know, Peggy," Emma said, touching Peggy's arm.

Terry had been diagnosed with Complex PTSD. It was a different condition than was associated with the most common examples of PTSD. There were no singular or repeated traumatic events that impacted Terry, as had happened to many veterans of his generation and the ones that came before. He didn't have nightmares or flashbacks of any kind. Complex PTSD is a result of significant prolonged stress and Terry suffered from the results of that after multiple back-to-back, high-stress deployments.

"Listen," Brian said as he pointed toward the door with his half empty beer bottle. "That is the smartest, toughest, sonofabitch I ever met. If anyone can handle all this, he can."

Emma was still combing over her notes. Brian was drinking and thinking. He was waiting for Terry to come back in. Peggy looked at the two of them. She had almost forgotten that she knew the two of them before her and Terry had gotten together. The four of them were living proof how small the Army can be. Peggy sat on a panel that had been put together by Brian's unit before a deployment to Iraq. Brian stayed behind for an hour and picked Peggy's brain. They had stayed in touch from then on. When Brian started dating Emma, the two were stationed at Fort Leavenworth and Peggy was at Leavenworth for a few days to help a colleague with a doctoral dissertation. One night they all went out to dinner together. That was the night Brian had learned Peggy knew Terry.

Terry came through the door with the electronics Emma asked for. She disappeared into the basement and emerged with a blue plastic case with a series of small screwdrivers neatly lined up inside. She picked up the laptop first and flipped it over on the island, grabbing a screwdriver and started talking out loud.

"I'm going to take the case off this and look inside," she was working intently. "I want to see if anything, any hardware or devices, are inside that shouldn't be. That won't account for any software, but it's a start." Terry was watching when he felt Brian over his shoulder.

"You really think ol' Boo-Boo Dawson is in on this?" Brian said in a low tone. General Dawson was a college football player and had picked up the nickname *Boo-Boo* because he was always injured but kept playing. The whole Army knew about the nickname, but no one used it in public. In fact, only General Dawson's wife, Tammy, called him that.

"He almost has to be," Terry responded while keeping an eye on Emma. "If this is all going on and he is caught in the middle, without knowing? Well, then he isn't as smart as everyone thinks he is." Emma had the casing of the laptop pried open.

"Nothing," she said staring into the computer. "Everything here is normal. In fact, it's all still factory original." Peggy and Terry glanced at each other. That was both a relief and a bit of concern. There was no outward tampering, so if they wanted to put something in her computer, it had to be software or a file. "I'm going to check the other stuff first before we turn this thing on." She grabbed Terry's phone.

"Well," Brian said, opening a fourth beer, "he's about the smartest motherfucker I ever met. So, that ain't good." When Brian was a lieutenant, he was the aide de camp for the assistant division commander–support, Brigadier General William Zuteck. There are two assistant division commanders in every Army division, both one-star generals. At the time, Brian was in the historic 1st Infantry Division. The other one-star was none other than Boo-Boo Dawson. Brian didn't work for him, but he knew him well.

"Nice fucking phone," Emma piped up, referring to Terry's ancient piece of tech. It was a smart phone, but it was about six or seven years old. Terry never saw a need for a new one, so he never upgraded. "Vintage nineteen eighty-nine?" She was prying it out of the rubber case and taking the back off. Terry just shrugged and sipped his beer. "You're as bad as him." She pointed to Brian with a screwdriver in her hand. Brian mirrored Terry's shrug.

Brian wasn't a huge fan of being connected all the time. He was actually worse than Terry in that regard. His phone was a no-shit flip phone. He only made calls with it and never texted. The house had cable television only so Brian could watch football. There was no internet in the house, either wired or wireless, and cell reception was sketchy at best. Brian liked it this way. It was also why Emma was so eager to dig into anything technical. She moved out to the country with Brian and disconnected because she loved him, but after a career of dealing in high tech communications, it was worse than ripping off a Band-Aid. It was more like detox for a heroin addict. She would still go into town and sit at the Starbucks just to get connected on her laptop and phone at least once per day.

Terry knew coming here was as safe as they were going to get. Between the lack of connectivity, Emma's knowledge of computers and communications, and the dedication of these loving friends, this was the perfect place to stay for a bit. Emma had the phone apart and back together. She pushed it off to the side, grabbing Peggy's phone. At that very moment, Peggy remembered something that had escaped both of them.

"We gave our phones to Captain Anderson," she blurted out. Terry looked up. He remembered. Before they went into the armory, Anderson had asked for their phones. Terry didn't think anything of it at the time because it was normal security protocol—cell phones are not allowed inside a secure facility.

"You're right," Terry said. "Dawson wanted to talk to us on a TS line, but the armory didn't have one, they only had a Secret line. He made them clear the building. Anderson asked for our phones before we went in to make the call." Emma slid Peggy's phone out of the case. Under the phone, attached to the case was a small circle. It looked like a sticker, but denser, thicker.

"I assume this isn't yours?" Emma asked. She could see the answer on Peggy's face. "My guess is that little thing is actually what is blocking reception to your phone and not the black box."

"Well," Brian jumped in, "Git rid of that fuckin' thing." Emma looked at him, exasperation on her face.

"No, dear," she stopped him, "not yet. We need to figure out what this is first." She held up what Terry and Peggy had thought was a jammer. She laid it on the table and grabbed her screwdriver again. They all leaned in as she opened the casing. Inside wasn't much, but she recognized the structure. When she was in Iraq, they started issuing PLBs or personal locator beacons to key individuals. If you got separated, captured, or in a really bad spot, you could activate the beacon and the whole world would know where you were. It was a bad Army habit, but everything that was digital, related to communications, or remotely electrical ended up being given to the commo section to maintain. Emma learned about PLBs very quickly, both inside and out. What she saw in front of her looked a lot like what was inside those beacons.

"What the hell is that?" Brian asked. He was on beer number five now. Emma's brain was turning. Brian had recognized years ago that he was smart, but in this room, everyone was smarter than him. Peggy was a PhD and a world renowned expert on the Middle East. Emma was a tech genius. Terry was Brian's best friend in his whole Army career, and they were peers in almost every way, but Brian knew Terry was smarter than he was. He wasn't afraid to be the one to ask the obvious questions.

"Well," Emma started as she got up from her stool, "I think you guys came to all the right conclusions, you just had your devices mixed up." She grabbed her pack of Marlboro menthols off the counter. "Anyone mind?" She lit a cigarette. They were all standing there waiting for her explanation. Terry's mind was spinning.

"The jammer was in the phone," he started as Emma inhaled. "That's not a jammer, is it? It's something else. A locator?" Emma blew a smoke ring.

"Fifty points for the sexy man," she said pointing at Terry with the cigarette. Brian handed him another beer, but Terry held his hand up. He was tired and already had three beers in him. Any more than that, and he'd pass out in the kitchen. Terry pulled his can of

Copenhagen out of his back pocket and tapped it on the counter. Before he could open the lid, Brian snatched it from him and took a pinch for himself. Emma continued, "This is what was blocking your cell phone reception." She held up Peggy's cell phone case and pointed to the white sticker.

"Which was probably put in by Captain Anderson when we were inside talking to General Dawson," Peggy added.

"Probably," Emma said. "This," she held up the black box, "is a beacon of some sort. I am guessing that when it is close to the phone, the signal is blocked. Honestly, these two being in close proximity is probably why you two are still alive."

"Peg," Terry butted in, "when we were at George's little hideout, we left the beacon in the Jeep, right?" Peggy nodded. "We didn't know if the Jeep was being tracked, so we didn't want to separate them, hoping what we thought was a jammer would block any signal. Where was your phone?"

"My phone?" Peggy asked. "It was turned off."

"That's not what I asked," Terry said bluntly. "Where was it? Was it in the Jeep?"

"No," she said. She felt a wave of guilt, as if she had done something wrong or been careless. "It was off, and I had it in my pocket. Force of habit, I guess."

"That's how they fucking found us," Terry said looking down. Emma and Brian could see the look in Peggy's eyes and the tears welling up.

"And at the farm," he said. "You put it in my pack, separating it from the phone. That's how they knew I was there. The time it took me to get there on foot is about how long it took them to pick up the signal and move to the house."

"Baby," Brian broke in. He was talking to Peg. "You didn't do a goddamn thing wrong." Terry looked up to see Peggy's lip quivering. Emma moved to Peggy and wrapped her arms around her. Terry felt like there was an apology in order, but it wouldn't come out.

"I could've gotten us killed," Peggy said fighting back tears. "I could have gotten *you* killed."

"Fuck that," Brian said spitting into one of the empty beer bottles. "I know this sonofabitch," he pointed at Terry with the bottle, "and it would take a lot more than three cherries to kill him. And he damn sure wouldn't let them kill you." Peggy looked up at Brian and smiled. She loved his Southern charm, as vulgar as it could be sometimes.

"Listen," Emma said putting her hands onto Peggy's cheeks, "you two are exhausted. I am going to dig into this computer to see what I can find. Asshole is going to sit up with me and keep me company," she was lovingly referring to her husband. "You two take the guest room in the basement and get some rest." Peggy nodded and stood up, hugging little Emma.

Terry got off his stool and turned into a brotherly hug from Brian. Everyone switched partners, Brian hugging Peggy and Emma hugging Terry. He whispered in her ear. "Thanks, sweetie." He kissed her on the cheek and squeezed her ass. Terry led the way downstairs to the guest bedroom with Peggy in tow. She looked briefly over her shoulder to see Emma already back at the laptop, putting the case back on and Brian cleaning up empty bottles. They were good friends.

# CHAPTER 17

Peggy awoke to Terry's hand on her thigh. The two had showered
quickly and crawled into bed, falling asleep almost instantly. She
didn't know if he was awake or if he was touching her in his sleep.
She was lying on her stomach, her face turned away from him. It
was dark and she had no idea what time it was. His hand moved up
to her ass cheek and squeezed. He was definitely awake. He rolled
closer to her.

"I'm sorry," he whispered in her ear. She smiled to herself,
reaching back to pull him closer.

"For hitting on Emma?" she whispered back.

"You know what I mean," he said quietly. He was close now.
They didn't have anything to sleep in, so they were both naked. He
kissed her shoulder and she moaned soft approval. She grabbed his
hand from her ass and moved it to her breast, pulling him in even
closer. She could feel him getting hard, pressed up against her. They
needed this. She needed this.

Still with one hand squeezing her breast, he grabbed her hair
with the other and kissed her neck. She moaned softly again and
rolled beneath him onto her back. His hand fell between her thighs.
She was ready and he climbed between her legs, she wrapped them
around him. It was fierce and short and a little rough, but they were
both satisfied and fell back to sleep after.

She awoke to an empty bed and sunlight peeking through
the curtains. There was a pair of sweatpants and a T-shirt lying
on a chair in the corner. Definitely not her style, but she needed

something to wear and Emma had likely put forth the effort. She threw on the clothes and went upstairs, the scent of coffee and bacon getting stronger as she climbed the steps. Brian was cooking, as he always did. It was one of those things that bound Brian and Emma together; he loved to cook and she was known to burn meals as simple as macaroni and cheese. Terry was drinking coffee at the island in the kitchen. The two had likely been up for a while. Emma was nowhere to be found. Peggy didn't even know what time it was.

"Nice outfit," Brian said moving strips of bacon from the frying pan onto a plate with paper towel on it. "You look damn good naked." Peggy's eyes got wide.

"Asshole," Terry said to him. "He didn't come down there, Emma set those clothes in there this morning." Peggy sighed relief and Brian laughed out loud. "She was up all night digging into your laptop." Peggy grabbed an empty coffee cup and decided to play along with Brian a little.

"I do look good naked," she said to him. He turned and looked at her. "Probably more than you could handle, though." She poured coffee and Brian laughed out loud again. Terry had a surprised look on his face. Peggy talked like that to him, but not anyone else. She sipped her coffee. "Close your mouth, dear. Now I know why you and Emma flirt so much. This is fun." Brian laughed again.

"Except Brian doesn't really know how to flirt," Emma was emerging from the hallway leading back to their bedroom. Her red hair was still damp, and she was wearing a T-shirt that hung down low enough to cover the shorts she had underneath. "He is like the little boy that pulls a girl's hair because he likes her."

"Hey," Brian said with a piece of bacon in his hand, "you never complained about me pulling your hair before."

"That kind of hair pulling is different," she leaned in and kissed him, standing on her tiptoes.

"Nothing wrong with a little hair pulling," Peggy said. Everyone stopped and looked at her. "What?"

"Damn," Terry said with a smile. "Something got into you this morning."

"You did," she said with a wink and a smile. Brian almost fell on the floor laughing. "Okay, okay, enough with the dirty talk," she turned and looked at Emma. "Tell me you found something in my computer."

"I did," Emma said grabbing the laptop. "It's a good thing we live in the fucking stone age out here," she gave Brian a side-eye look. "When I started digging around, I found a new file that was put on your hard drive about the time you said you got the email from Whiteman."

"A file?" Peggy asked. "I didn't download anything or start any new work. What is it?"

"Well, it looks like a manifesto," she said. Brian, Terry, and Peggy all came around the computer. "It's a document about a hundred and twenty pages long and it talks about all the things the United States has done wrong in the Middle East. I haven't read the whole thing, but it is signed by you."

"Signed by me?" Peggy was shocked. "I never wrote anything like that."

"I thought not," Emma said. "So, I dug a little bit. Every piece of evidence associated with that document points to you. Every digital fingerprint says it was done on this computer and nowhere else."

"Go to the last couple of pages," Brian said. "Manifestos are normally associated with an act. An action." He was serious and the bite of his accent was diminished. The change in his tone was something Terry recognized long ago. When the accent disappeared, things weren't good. Emma was scrolling. "There. Stop."

The four of them started to scan quickly. Terry focused on a few key words *I am doing this in retribution* . . . Brian saw them at the same time. They looked at each other.

"Retribution?" Peggy said. "For what? What am I supposed to be doing in retribution?" They were all thinking. Emma broke in.

"So, that gets us to the second thing I found," she said. She minimized the document and opened a separate window. "This shows all your activity. It's a log basically. This computer was never plugged into a classified network, right? Not even by mistake?"

"No, never," Peggy said. Her thumbnail was in her teeth again.

"According to this, it was," Emma pointed to the screen. She was the only one who really understood what they were looking at. "Your log says you plugged this in at Leavenworth, at Whiteman, and at the Pentagon. All three times you plugged it in to a classified network and you downloaded a bunch of files. Classified files."

"What?" Terry said. "How is that possible?"

"My guess?" Emma said, lighting her first cigarette of the day. "When you got that email from inside Whiteman, this stuff was all piggy backed on top of it. Digitally inserted. You didn't even know it happened."

"So . . ." Terry was trying to put pieces together. It always bothered him in movies that no one ever figured out the bad guy's plan until right at the end. He knew it was part of movie storytelling, but it drove him nuts. "It looks like Peggy has been stealing classified info, wrote a manifesto that vilifies the US in the Middle East, and is taking responsibility for some act. But, what act?"

"I dunno," Brian said with a little of his accent coming back, "but they are framing the shit out of her for whatever it is. I need a dip. Gimme your box of snuff." Terry tossed the tin and cardboard can of Copenhagen to him.

"I'm the perfect person for whatever this is," Peggy was being analytical now. "Expert on the Middle East. I've literally spent years of my life there. My late husband was even from there. Painting me as a sympathizer is pretty easy. The US has done so much damage over there in the last thirty years, it wouldn't be a leap for someone with my background and exposure to become radicalized."

"Here," Brian said. "Eat some fuckin' bacon. You damn sure ain't a sympathizer if you're eatin' pork."

"Not funny," Emma said with a glare. "But, you're not wrong, Peg. With your background and this computer, they could certainly make you look like you've been radicalized."

"For what?" Terry spoke up. "Radicalized for what? To do what? Retribution how? What exactly were they going to frame you for? And what do they gain?" Everyone froze. Those were the big questions. They were diagnosing the how, but not the why. Terry was looking at the big picture and getting ahead of Peggy again.

"It would be something big," she said. "A lot of effort is being put into this. It wouldn't be small. This would be national news-type stuff."

"Yep," Brian said. "Like 9-11 big."

"Exactly," Terry said. "And what happened after 9-11?"

"Patriotism," Emma chimed in. "National unity. We bonded together."

"A war," Brian said. He looked at Terry. "Actually, two fucking wars. We fought in both of 'em."

"Right," Terry said, "and what's happening to those wars now?"

"They are ending." Peggy said quietly.

"Yes," Terry agreed. "They are ending. And all this money that DoD, CIA, State Department, and everyone else has been getting fed for the last twenty years is drying up."

"I'll do you one better," Brian said spitting into the trash can next to the kitchen cabinets. "You know what else is ending? All these fucking deployments and all these promotions for all the fuckin' generals."

"They are doing this to keep the war going?" Peggy was incredulous.

"No," Brian said. "These fuckers are sinking the Maine again. This is about starting a new war. Well, maybe it is more about fighting the same war, the war on terror, but somewhere else and against someone else."

"We need to slow down a bit," Terry said. "These are some

awfully big conclusions we are jumping to. I'm not saying we are wrong—"

"But we damn sure better be right," Brian broke in.

"But how do we know we are right?" Emma asked. "How can we prove any of this?"

The four of them stood silently in the kitchen, staring at each other. Emma had just asked the million-dollar question.

"Listen," Terry said. "We've already put you two at enough risk. You don't need to get involved any more than you already are."

"Yes," Peggy chimed in. "You don't need to be in the middle of this."

"Fuck you," Brian said, "and fuck you." He pointed to each of them. "Me and you been through so much shit together and you think I'm walking away from this? Fuck that. And you, young lady," he was talking to Peggy now. "Whether you know it or not, all that shit you taught me kept me and a bunch of other dudes alive in Iraq. I figure I owe you. No, no fuckin' way. I'm in this shit."

"Me too," Emma had sidled up next to Brian. "I'm in it too. Whatever we can do to help, we are in."

Peggy was getting emotional. It was making Terry uncomfortable. "Well, if it is an open offer," he said, "I'm gonna need Emma for about a half hour . . . in private."

"What are you going to do with the other twenty-four minutes?" Peggy asked.

"Damn," Brian said. "That's two minutes longer than me. She does this thing—" Emma slapped him in the chest, and they all laughed. There was still a cloud hanging over the room. Everyone took a breath.

"So, what do we do next?" Peggy asked.

"Keep moving. Keep shooting," Terry said. Brian had heard that phrase from his closest friend dozens of times and every time it meant a fight was coming. He shook his head.

## CHAPTER 18

Emma decided that since the sticker on Peggy's phone case had been blocking the beacon for so long, it was a safe bet that no one knew where they were. She turned off both Terry and Peggy's phones and disconnected the WiFi receiver on Peggy's laptop. Emma wanted to ensure there was no internet connection by any of those devices. No need for them to pop up on the grid by accident. Terry decided it was important for Brian and Emma to maintain their routines. If anyone even suspected Terry and Peggy were at the house, any deviation from the norm by Emma or Brian would cause them to investigate. Emma decided to go into town like she would most days. She also decided, against Brian's protests, she would go alone, like she normally would.

One of the beauties of living in Kansas was permitless carry. Any Kansas resident with a Kansas driver's license who isn't a felon, can carry a concealed weapon. Brian wasn't a gun guy like Terry was but he was a country boy and both he and Emma had spent their adult lives in the Army. There were guns in the house and Emma was more than comfortable using them. Brian didn't have any pistols small enough for Emma to conceal, so Terry gave her a quick class on his Glock 19, and she was heading out the door.

"Listen," Brian told her, "git your coffee, git whatever news updates you can, and git your ass back here." She got on her tiptoes and kissed him.

"I know," she said. "I'll be fine. Even Terry thinks I'll be fine. And he's more paranoid than you are."

"Yeah," he said. "If he thinks you're gonna be fine, why did he hand you a pistol to take with?" She hadn't thought of that. She kissed him again and headed out the door.

Peggy was doing some laundry and getting their stuff cleaned up in general, her mind always thinking about what was going on, but keeping herself busy just the same. Brian sat down and turned on the television, scanning the news channels for anything that might be related to Terry or Peggy. Terry busied himself out in the pole barn. He pulled everything out of the Jeep, floormats, carpet, everything. He wanted to straighten up the inside. It had been a mess since they left, even with the few occasions they had to straighten things up. He wanted it ready to move, and to fight from, if needed. Maybe he was paranoid, but his paranoia had kept him alive through all his time in combat so there was no sense bucking it now.

"Goddam, man," Brian said, coming up behind him. "You got a whole fuckin' arms room in there. You sure you need all that shit?"

"Nope," Terry told him as he put the Model 12 under the back seat. "Better to have and not need and all that shit." Brian picked up the AK-47 George had given them. He removed the magazine and pulled the bolt back, ejecting the round in the chamber.

"Ain't seen one of these in a while," Brian picked up the round that came out of the chamber and was putting it back into the magazine. "Last one of these I saw, somebody was tryin' to kill me with it."

Brian knew what Terry was doing and there wasn't much he could do to help, except to keep him company. As they worked, they told stories about when they were much younger men, Brian handing Terry things as he asked for them. Terry had just put the last of their gear in the Jeep and was closing all the hatches when they heard Emma's Volkswagen pull into the drive. The two men walked out of the pole barn and met her in the driveway. She was excited and had information to share. The trio climbed the steps into the house and Terry called for Peggy to join them.

"Well, on the surface there is some good news," Emma started. The four of them were huddled around the island kitchen. Emma downloaded a number of articles onto her computer and was pulling them up, one by one. "Evidently, there was a joint operation between the National Guard and the sheriff's department that led to some fatalities." Terry and Peggy looked at each other. "According to a local paper, the Guard and the deputies were doing some local drug interdiction operation where they were looking for marijuana and meth labs in farmer's fields when a trailer with a meth lab inside exploded. Ten dead. Two from the sheriff's department and eight from the Guard. By the way, no mention of this in the national news anywhere."

"That accounts for the two deputies from your house," Brian said from inside the refrigerator. He came out with beers. "I bet them other dudes that came after you were the Nasty Girls in the article." He was using a not-so-flattering term for National Guard that was popular in the 1990s.

"That math doesn't add up," Peggy said. "There were only seven of them. Three up north and four at the farm."

"Does it give any names or details?" Terry asked. "Anything more than what you told us?"

"It only says that names are being withheld until family members are notified," Emma replied, scanning the article again. "And that one of the fatalities was a National Guard officer."

"Anderson," Terry said. "He is number eight."

"Told you they were a bunch of cherries," Brian said after swallowing from the bottle. "This shit sounds like a bad movie. They may as well have said it was a goddamn training accident."

"They are cleaning up the mess," Peggy said flatly.

"That's what I thought, too," Emma said. "Then I found this," she was referring to another article she saved to the drive. "It's a BOLO that is in a couple of local papers up there." BOLO was a term that became common for all of them while they were deployed. BOLO stood for *be on the look out* and was commonly used when there was a description of a vehicle associated with a terrorist. "It has a partial still photo of you, Terry. No name. And a description of you possibly driving a dark SUV or Off-Road vehicle."

"You guys kept a low profile, right?" Brian asked. "Took the backroads an' shit to git here?"

"Yeah," Terry replied. "Didn't see a single vehicle between there and here."

"The picture is grainy as hell," Emma said. "Looks like you're clearing a building or something." Peggy moved to look at the picture.

"That's inside my house!" Peggy exclaimed. "They put a camera inside my fucking house!" Terry and Brian both moved to look at the picture. She was right, they both were. The camera was mounted inside the back door, probably on top of the cabinets in the kitchen. You could see Terry with his suppressed pistol. The picture was grainy for sure and you could only see part of his face because of his baseball cap.

"I didn't even realize it was you until I looked at it a few times," Emma said. "And then I recognized that nasty ball cap of yours." Terry looked at the underside of the bill as the cap was perched on his head. "They only have you identified as 'a person of interest' and if anyone sees you, they should contact the police."

"But," Terry said, "it's not tied to the other article? The one about the explosion and the Guard guys?"

"No," Emma said. "There is no connection. In fact, the paper that talks about the explosion isn't even carrying the BOLO. It's the only one in the area that isn't. If someone wasn't looking to connect the two, they never would."

"I guess you're shaving that fuckin' beard of yours," Brian said with a smile. Other than putting on a little weight, Brian looked exactly the same as when Terry had met him more than twenty years ago. Still clean shaven every day and still wearing a high and tight haircut. He had given Terry a hard time about his longer hair and beard since he started growing them. "Fuckin' hippie."

"What about me?" Peggy asked. "Is there anything out there about me? Missing person report? Anything?"

"No," Emma responded. She brought up another article. "I thought that was weird, too, so I widened my search. I opened up the aperture a little and this is what I found." She pointed to the screen. It was an Op-Ed from a scholar at Kansas State University. "This is running in the paper out in Manhattan, in Lawrence, here in Leavenworth, Topeka, and Kansas City."

"That's Jim Scarab," Peggy said. Dr. Jim Scarab, PhD., had sat on a number of panels over the years with Peggy, enough that Terry recognized the name. He was always the one offering an opposing view to hers when it came to the Middle East. He was anti-Muslim and Peggy wasn't afraid to tell him the only reason he stayed in Kansas was because that was the only place his blatantly bigoted views would allow him to keep his job. Peggy was scanning the article.

"The article is about radical Muslims," Emma said as Peggy read, "right here in the middle of America. He goes on to talk about how no one is safe from Islam, even here, and that the Muslim faith is a danger to our entire existence."

"How very 2001," Terry said. "Why in the world would so many papers carry that shit?"

"Because, dumbass," Brian said flatly, "they got fuckin' told to." They all stared at him. "You really think with that BOLO and them other articles about the dead National Guard dudes, that this is a fuckin' coincidence?"

"This isn't about me, though," Peggy said. "I'm not in here anywhere. Why do you think this is linked to me?"

"You're being set up," Terry said.

"We already established they are setting me up," Peggy snapped.

Terry knew he needed to remain calm. Him getting worked up too wasn't going to help.

"Yes," he said calmly, "they are setting you up, but the article is part of that. They are using it as a setup. The article itself. The article is about people *like you* or what they are going to portray you as, after whatever they have planned. They are validating whatever event is supposed to happen, even before it happens."

"It's a big damn *I told you so*," Brian broke in. "Once they have you do whatever it is, they can point to this and say, 'I fuckin' told you so.'"

"Who is this guy, anyway?" Emma asked. "Scarab. What's his deal?"

"Jim Scarab and I go back a long way," Peggy started. "And all the way back to the beginning, we have looked at the Middle East through opposite lenses. He despises Islam and has criminalized everything about the people and the culture since he started his PhD. He is a bigot, and a racist, and an Islamophobe." She was leaving out a detail that Terry thought was important, but he was reluctant to mention it because of her mood. *Fuck it.*

"He also lost his brother in the Embassy bombing in Beirut," Terry added.

Peggy snapped a look at him. "And that is supposed to justify the filth that comes from that man?" she said.

"Not justify," Terry said calmly. "Just give some background." Terry turned to Brian. "His brother was a Marine and was in the embassy in eighty-three." Brian gave a subtle nod.

"So, they get this guy," Emma was reeling everyone back in, "who knows you, who disagrees with you, to write this article. It gets published and everyone sees it. Then, you get blamed for whatever it is they frame you for, and not only can they say *I told you so*, but he can specifically say *I knew her and I told you so*. It adds a level of credence and credibility."

"So," Brian stepped in, "We got the National Guard, the Sheriff's Department, Boo-Boo fuckin' Dawson, the media, and some asshole doc all in on this together. Gimme your box of snuff." Terry handed his tin of Copenhagen blindly over his shoulder. It was a pause that was common if you spent any time around Brian. He had more to say but needed to get some Copenhagen in his lip first. It wasn't a pause for dramatic effect, it was just his priorities—Cope first, talk second. Everyone waited for him to continue. "Okay, maybe not the *whole* National Guard, but still. Now, what the fuck did they have planned for Peggy?"

They still didn't know. They really had no idea. Terry realized that if General Dawson was involved and the press was being manipulated, this was far-reaching, possibly to the highest levels of government.

"Something big," Peggy said. "Nothing says *radical Islam* like an attack on American soil. Is that all you found, Emma dear?"

"Yeah," Emma responded. Brian putting a dip in prompted Emma to light a cigarette. Other than an occasional cigar, Peggy didn't use tobacco of any kind. Her father smoked a pipe when she was little, but eventually gave it up. She loved the smell of good tobacco, but never took up the habit like the other three in the room. She had a feeling of being left out at this particular moment. "That's all I could find. Or at least that was everything that popped up. I didn't want to search too deep. I didn't search either of your names because I knew that would alert someone, somewhere."

"You know," Terry said, "they could have exposed us both. By name. And they didn't."

"I know that tone," Brian said. "Alright genius, why didn't they?" Brian had fallen into this trap more than once through the years. Terry would ask a question to the room, already knowing the answer and knowing that no one else in the room did.

"Because they aren't done with us yet," Terry said flatly. "They are cleaning up the mess as they go and keeping us out of the headlines because they are keeping Peggy in play. And since I am in the middle of this, when she goes down, they are going to put me down with her."

"Well," Brian said. "Ain't that some shit. Motherfucker spends his whole life serving, putting his fucking ass on the line for God and country, and they are going to shit on all that to start a fuckin' war."

"Yep," Terry agreed.

"Fuck that," Brian said. "I think we need to git ol' Boo-Boo on the phone."

## CHAPTER 19

"Are you insane?" Emma asked. "Sweetie, I love you, but that's the dumbest shit you've ever come up with."

"What?" Brian was feigning being insulted. "I've come up with much dumber shit than this. Hell, I married you." He smiled. She gave him the finger. "Listen, we got about all the intel we can git. We got Peggy's computer, so they don't have that. They don't know where y'all are and they are scramblin' to clean up dead bodies all over Nebraska thanks to this motherfucker." He flashed a thumb at Terry. "We need to create some reaction from them without showing our hand. Recon by fire, just like the old days."

"Except," Emma said, "if we call him, he will know exactly where they are. And he isn't going to tell us anything anyway."

"Dawson is never going to reveal anything over an open line. Emma is right about that," Peggy spoke up. Emma smiled a snotty smile at Brian. "But he is on to something. Recon by fire." Brian returned the same snotty smile to Emma. The tactic of sending out a small unit hoping the enemy would attack them to reveal their strength and position was something that had been around for centuries. "If we can get them to move, to act, to do anything that gives us some insight into what their plan is, it is worth the risk."

"It's either that," Terry said, "or we spend the rest of our lives hiding in your basement."

"I love y'all and everything," Brian responded, "but fuck that." He laughed then turned to Emma. "Alright, my young, sexy, techno-geek of a wife. How do we call him and not let him know exactly where they are?"

"An old landline is the best bet, actually," she said. "One with a blocked number. And don't call his office, call him at home. Do you know his home number?" Terry was thoughtful and then nodded. "Eventually, they will be able to track it down, but it will take some time. A public place with a blocked number and call his house."

"Shit," Brian said with a smile. "That's easy. Go shave your beard, hippie. We are going to the VFW."

"The VFW?" Peggy asked.

"Yeah," Brian said, "them crusty ol' bastards still have a landline in the back room and the number is blocked. They do it so they can call their wives and they won't know where to find them." Emma gave a shocked look like Brian had done exactly that to her in the past. "Yes, dear, you now know my secret hideout."

"Okay, let's not rush into this," Terry said. "Once we make that call, we are leaving. I don't want us anywhere near you guys when they come looking." Emma looked heartbroken. "We will get everything packed and ready to go. You and I will go make the call, then I'll get Peggy and we will take off."

"Where will you go?" Emma asked quietly. "And how? I am sure the police have your vehicle and license plate by now. That BOLO was for the public, but I am sure law enforcement is looking for you guys at this point. With details."

"They can take Big Blue," Brian said. It was Terry's turn to be shocked. Big Blue was a Chevy truck Brian bought used as a teenager and was currently sitting in the pole barn with Terry's Jeep. Terry had ridden in the truck more times than he could count. It was completely original and still ran like a top. Brian wasn't a mechanic, but he always paid good money to keep that truck running. It wasn't much to look at; there were some rust spots in the body and the paint was faded, but it would certainly drive as far and as long as they needed it to. "We will just have to put all their shit in it before we go to the VFW."

"Thanks, brother." Brian offering Big Blue was like a parent offering up one of their children. The gesture wasn't lost on Terry. He stood up and hugged his friend.

"That just leaves the question of where," Emma persisted.

"S-2," Terry looked at Peggy. "You're now a certified expert on terrain analysis. Where to?"

"This isn't that," she said. "This is a tactical move and that's your department." Terry opened his mouth to speak and she cut him off. "But I think we either go to them or force them to come to us." Terry's jaw snapped shut. She had taken the words right out of his mouth.

"Well done," Terry said. There was genuine approval in his voice. She really was brilliant. "Let's see how the phone call goes with Dawson, but you're right. Start packing up our stuff. Brother, if you can start moving all our gear from the Jeep to Big Blue that would be great."

"And what the hell are you gonna do?" Brian asked him.

"I'm going to shave my beard, as ordered," Terry said as he turned and headed downstairs.

Terry got to the guest bedroom in the basement and grabbed his shaving kit. He'd had the kit for his entire career. The bag was dark green nylon with a black zipper and had stains on the outside from a tube of toothpaste that exploded upon landing during a particularly rough night jump when he and Brian were captains. He stood there looking at the old stains and thinking about various points in his Army career. Brian's earlier statement rang in his subconscious. Ain't that some shit. Motherfucker spends his whole life serving, putting his fucking ass on the line for God and country, and they are going to shit on all that to start a fuckin' war.

Terry hadn't cried since his dad died, but he could feel it coming now. The realization hit him that everything he had done, his whole career, was being thrown away. Not by him, but by Dawson and whoever he was working with. He looked at himself in the mirror. His eyes were red and watering. He felt abandoned by the very institution and the very people he had dedicated his adult life to serving. Worse than abandoned—sacrificed. He turned on the hot water and dug through the kit for his razor. Once the water was hot, Terry soaked his beard and started rubbing in the blue gel that transformed into shaving cream. He looked at himself again. Not just his face, but his body. He stood there shirtless and took account of the physical shape he was in.

At a glance, he was in much better shape than his old friends from high school. He had never gotten the *dad-bod* that overcame so many men his age. He was still muscular through the chest and arms. He was a little soft around the middle, not the lean warfighter he used to be. Upon closer inspection, the impact of his career was visible. His left shoulder fell a little lower than the right, the result of multiple dislocations. One of the ribs on the right side poked out a little after being broken during a fall from a snowy cliff in Afghanistan and never healing properly. He could see a faint scar at the base of his neck where a hot casing from an M240 machine gun got stuck between skin and body armor, leaving a permanent mark. That was from Baghdad. His hands were beat up and scarred, fingers jutted in slightly different directions from being broken.

He grabbed the razor and noticed Peggy in the mirror, standing behind him, leaning against the doorframe.

"I'm sorry," she said. He turned off the water. "I'm sorry for all of this. You just wanted to retire and live a quiet life."

"Peggy," he said, "I couldn't find quiet if I tried. You don't end up on five deployments if you are looking for quiet." He turned and looked at her.

"Yeah," she was whispering now, "but this is because of me. You came to the farm because of me. And you're in this mess because of me."

"*We* are in this mess because of someone else," he said as he touched her shoulder. "You didn't do this. They did."

"But . . ." she was starting to cry. She wiped the tears from the tip of her nose with her fingers.

"Stop it," he said. It was a comforting tone, not harsh. "We are going to get out of this. I promise."

"How?" she said. There was dread in her voice. It was a tone of impending doom. "How are we going to get out of this?"

"Keep moving. Keep shooting," he said. "Eventually, we are going to outmaneuver them."

"And then what?" she asked. "What do we do then?"

"Then, then I am going to kill every person responsible for this," he said as he turned back to the sink. He was focused now. His resolve had returned in an instant. She turned and walked out of the bathroom to pack their stuff.

# CHAPTER 20

He hadn't seen his face without a beard in over a year. It was strange, younger maybe, as he looked at himself in the mirror. He wiped the remaining shaving cream from his neck and earlobes and pulled a clean T-shirt over his head. Terry dug into the shave kit and pulled out his dog tags. Somehow, he had kept the same set his entire career and wore them exactly as they were issued—long chain, short chain, two tags. No black rubber silencer around the tags themselves. No gutted parachute cord over the chain. The only addition was a Saint Michael's medal his mother had given him before he went off to Airborne School to learn to jump out of planes. Saint Michael was the patron saint of paratroopers and his mother was Irish and Italian Catholic. The medal had been with him on every jump and every combat operation of his career. He wasn't superstitious, but he wasn't dumb enough to tempt fate either. If things were going to get violent, having an archangel on your side was never a bad thing.

Peggy had cleaned out the room, leaving him only with his shaving kit. Everything else was packed and moved upstairs. Brian was waiting for him in the kitchen, the two women were nowhere in sight. Terry grabbed his ballcap out of habit then put it back down, realizing it was one of the few distinguishable things in the grainy newspaper photo. Brian picked up his keys and the two men headed out the door. Terry veered off to the pole barn to put his shaving kit into Big Blue and found the two women there, packing up the truck. He tossed the shave kit inside and gave Peggy a quick kiss.

"We will be back soon," he said. "And then we are leaving."

"I know," she said. He patted her on the ass.

"Nothing for me?" Emma said with some sass. He smacked her on the ass, probably hard enough to leave a handprint. "Woo!" she said.

"Where's the Glock?" he asked Emma about the pistol he leant her.

"Do you think you'll need it?" she said with a furrowed brow. "It's under the front seat."

"I sure as hell hope not," he said as he fished the pistol out of the cab. "But, hope isn't a course of action." He turned and headed to the door. "Back soon," he said over his shoulder. Brian already had his brand-new Chevy Silverado running in the driveway. Terry climbed in the passenger door. "Damn. This is nice. Sure as shit ain't Big Blue. Maybe you should let me take this instead," he said with a chuckle.

"Shut the fuck up," Brian laughed in response. He put the big truck into drive, and they headed out toward the VFW. The two friends laughed and made jokes for most of the ride, telling old stories and talking about the good old days. When they were a few minutes out, Brian changed the subject. "You sure you want to do this?"

"What?" Terry said with an incredulous tone. "This was your fucking idea!"

"Yeah, that's what I'm worried about," Brian replied. "Listen, man. You're the smart one. I got promoted because I'm a good motherfucker and people like me. You got promoted because you're good at this shit."

"What's your point?" Terry asked.

"If this is such a good goddamn idea," Brian replied, "how come you didn't think of it?"

"This is the right play," Terry said as he stared out the windshield. He could see General Dawson in his mind, sitting at that table in eastern Afghanistan with his bottle of peach tea. "Dawson will make a move. He never could stand it when someone poked him. So, I'm going to poke him."

"You know what you're going to say?" Brian asked, one hand casually on the steering wheel of the big Chevy.

"More or less," Terry responded. "And look, you're not stupid. No one who knows you thinks you're stupid." He paused. "You just *sound* stupid, that's all." He grinned.

"Asshole!" Brian said laughing. "Alright, let's go poke ol' Boo-Boo Dawson and see if he flinches." He wheeled the truck into the gravel lot outside the VFW building. It looked like every VFW in every small town in America. There was an old anti-aircraft gun that needed a paintjob at the edge of the parking lot and a 75mm towed howitzer at the base of the flagpole. The building itself was low and long and made of cinderblocks with a pitched roof. There were two windows covered by curtains along with a door on the front side of the building. Terry followed Brian inside.

It took Terry's eyes a second to adjust to the darkness and smoke inside. It was five o'clock and there were already ten people at the bar and the hightop tables. State law said there was no smoking allowed inside any public buildings. Clearly this crowd of veterans didn't give a shit. Terry laughed to himself.

"Hey, look what the cat dragged in!" The voice came from the man behind the bar. He was the stereotype of a Vietnam vet if Terry had ever seen one. He was wearing an olive drab green fatigue top with the cuffs rolled up and patches sewn all over it. His face had a gray goatee and there was a long ponytail of the same color sticking out of the back of his red USMC baseball cap. "Lemme guess—you want a beer."

"Hell, yeah," Brian said, "as long as you're buyin'. I never turn down free beer." It was like Norm walking into the bar on *Cheers*. Everyone inside knew Brian. He got close to the bar and leaned in. "And we need to use the phone in the back." The Marine gave a sideways look at Terry.

"Is this something I even want to ask about?" the bartender asked.

"Not really," Brian said. "Classified. Do me a favor and make sure we have some privacy." The bartender handed him a bottle of beer.

"Well, you know where it is," the bartender threw his thumb toward the back. "Leave a quarter when you're done." Brian grabbed his beer and headed to the back with Terry close on his heels. Terry glanced over his shoulder at the bartender. His mind drifted to Larry the ranch hand and how different the old Black man was from the man behind the bar. Two men, same war, very different outcomes. Terry followed Brian into a small office cluttered with cheap memorabilia from the different services. A USMC flag hung on the wall and a Dixie Cup sailor cap sat atop the file cabinet. Brian pushed a deeply stained Air Force coffee mug out of the way to grab the black desktop telephone and drag it to the front of the desk. There was a glass jar with a *US Army Retired* sticker on it, full of quarters. *I guess the bartender was serious about leaving a quarter.*

Terry grabbed the handset for the phone and dialed General Dawson's home number from memory. On the third ring a female voice answered.

"Hello, Dawson residence."

"Tammy, it's Terry Davis," Terry said.

"Terry!" the woman said. It was Tammy Dawson, the general's wife. "So good to hear from you. How are you doing? How's retirement?" Tammy had been like a second mother to Terry when he was Dawson's aide. Terry had assumed duties as the aide in Afghanistan and didn't meet Tammy until months later when Dawson was called back to the States for a series of meetings at the Pentagon, but from the minute he took over she treated him like her son. Whenever the general received a care package from home, there was one for Terry as well. She sent him Christmas gifts and even sent him emails just to ask how he was, never mentioning her husband. Terry later learned that her reputation across the Army was very different. Many saw her as more of a careerist than her husband and felt she would do anything to help him advance. Terry hadn't seen that side of her while he was in Afghanistan. To him she was just a sweet woman.

"I'm doing well, ma'am," Terry winced as he said it. That was her golden rule; she was not *ma'am*, she was Tammy.

"Terry," she chastised, "that's your one freebie. You know better."

"I do," he said.

Brian rolled his eyes.

"It won't happen again," Terry continued. "I'm doing well, but I need to ask your husband something. Is he around?" It struck Terry that he didn't even know what day it was and if the general would even be home. He got lucky.

"He just walked in the door," she said. "I'll get him." She was about to yell for her husband when Terry cut in.

"Don't tell him it's me. Please?" he playfully begged. "I want to surprise him."

"Deal," she said. "It was good talking to you. Come visit us soon. Hang on." She pulled the phone away from her face and yelled "Boo-Boo! There is someone on the phone for you . . . yes, someone from work . . . how the hell should I know?" Terry could hear the handset being handed off.

"General Dawson speaking," Terry inhaled. Brian leaned forward in the chair to listen more closely.

"Hey, sir," Terry began. "It's Terry Davis. It's been a few days."

"Terry?" he said, with a mix of surprise and confusion in his voice. "Yes. It has been a while. Um, what can I do for you?"

"I was just wondering if you can fill me in on a few things," Terry replied. Brian sat motionless. "You got a minute?" Terry could almost see the gears turning in Dawson's head.

"Yeah," Dawson said. Terry could sense some anger in his voice. He assumed Tammy had left the room. "What do you need to know? Everything going okay?"

"I was just wondering, sir . . ." Terry hesitated. This was the point of no return. *Keep moving, keep shooting.* "Are you planning on framing both of us? Or just her?" Brian's eyes got wide.

"F-framing?" Dawson was stumbling. "Terry, I don't know what you're talking about. What do you mean?"

"You know exactly what the fuck I mean, General." Terry flashed back to Peggy calling Anderson *Captain* and how it had made Terry cringe. He knew it would piss Dawson off for the same reason. "I've got you figured out. I know what you're up to and why. I just didn't know if you were going to frame her and let me die in the process."

"You little shit," the general snapped back. "You always were too smart for your own good. Terry, this is so much bigger than me. It's bigger than all of us. And if you *really* knew what was going on, you'd already know that, which you clearly don't. You got yourself into this and now you get to pay the consequences."

"Consequences?" Terry was angry. "Let me tell you what the consequences of this are, motherfucker. If anything happens to her, I'm going to kill you. I'm going to drag you out onto that very well-groomed parade field across the street from your house and I'm going to beat you to death. Those are the fucking consequences." Terry hung up the phone. Brian stared at him.

"Well," Brian finally said, "we ought to get some movement now." He stood up. "Put a fuckin' quarter in the jar." Brian finished his beer as they walked through the bar to the front door, setting the empty bottle on the bar.

"Just one?" the bartender yelled. "You never have just one beer."

"Eat shit and die Marine," Brian said as he opened the door into the sunlight. "I'll see y'all next week." Outside, the two climbed into the truck. Brian looked at his good friend Terry and laughed while he shook his head.

"You liked that shit," Terry said. "Didn't you?"

"Brother," Brian said as he started the truck. "I ain't never, *never* heard a lieutenant colonel call a four-star a motherfucker. You got some balls."

"Well," Terry said, "we wanted some movement. I think that was enough to cause some movement."

"Yeah," Brian said laughing and putting the truck into gear, "no shit." They weren't far down the road when Brian asked "So, you goin' south or goin' north?"

"That's a damn good question," Terry replied. "You think they are sending someone to find us?"

"After that shit back there?" Brian laughed again. "You can bet your sweet ass he is sendin' someone after you."

"Then north it is," Terry said staring out the windshield. "I'd rather fight on ground I know. If I have to go to Tampa after that, then I will."

"Dude," Brian said, "whatever you need, you let me know. Emma and I are in, all the way. Just like me and Cindy Peters on prom night."

"Thanks brother," Terry replied. "Except I might be asking for more than just the two inches you gave to Cindy Peters." Brian laughed so hard, he almost put the truck into the ditch.

## CHAPTER 21

The ladies were in the kitchen when Terry and Brian got back to the house. Terry stood there and recounted the phone conversation to Emma and Peggy while Brian shook his head and chuckled. Emma was wide-eyed and Peggy held her head in her hands. He couldn't see her face, but he imagined it was a cross between regret and disgust. There was a moment of silence after Terry finished. Peggy raised her head out of her hands.

"So, you're going to the farm," Emma said.

"Yes," Terry replied. "To the farm." Emma popped her cute little self from her stool with a smile.

"Good," she said. "Then we are going with you." Brian picked his head up to speak and she looked at him and pointed. "I don't want to hear a fucking word out of you. He is your best friend and we are going with them." She turned back to Terry. "We decided while you were gone. We're already packed. When are we leaving?"

"You're not going," Terry said. "Emma, I love you. Really. I can't ask you to come with. You two have each other and this house and that worthless dog. You guys can't risk this."

"Well," Emma said, "you don't get to tell me what to do."

"Emma, stop," Brian said. "Dammit, woman, you didn't listen to what he said. And he hasn't said it out loud yet, not even to me, but none of us are going to the farm." He paused and looked at Terry. "You're going up there alone, you sonofabitch."

"I am," Terry said flatly.

Peggy snapped a look at him. "Not without me, you're not," she said. "That is *my* house. My family's house. If you're going up there, I am too."

"No, Peggy," Terry said calmly. "You're not. There are people coming after us. After you and me. And it's going to get ugly. People are going to die. I cannot put you at risk."

"And you move faster on your own," Peggy said.

"I do," Terry said. "But I do need the three of you to do something else. Peggy, go back and look at that op-ed by Scarab and then reread the manifesto on your computer."

"You think he wrote it?" she asked.

"That's my guess," he said. "See if you can find a connection of any kind. Something that puts his fingerprints on that document."

"Why do I get the sneakin' suspicion," Brian broke in, "that we are taking a road trip to Manhattan, Kansas to talk to that asshole?"

Emma turned and looked at Terry.

"Because you are," Terry replied. "Except *she's* going to be the one to talk to him. Peggy has been back and forth with this guy for years. She knows him well enough to rattle his cage."

"And what if that doesn't work?" Emma asked.

"Well," Terry said adjusting his ball cap, "he's a skinny little shit, so Brian can just scare the hell out of him."

"And what if *that* doesn't work?" Brian added.

"Then Emma gives him a lap dance," Terry said. "Maybe that will work." Emma gave a shocked look.

"That'll *damn sure* work," Brian said with a laugh. "What do you want to know from this guy?"

"Peggy is going to see if she can find a connection between the documents," Terry said. Emma and Peggy were getting Emma's computer up and running to read the op-ed. "That's a lead, but not proof. If she can find anything that makes her believe he wrote that fucking manifesto, I need you to go there and get him to admit it. Or at least get him to admit he is involved in all of this."

"Roger," Brian said. He was back in military mode. "You know they aren't sending any more cherries after you, right?" Emma and Peggy looked up from the computer. "This is no-bullshit. It's gonna be a bunch of Delta dudes, or a fuckin' SEAL team, CIA ground guys, or some shit. They're gonna tag this as a training exercise to get the assets, but them boys aren't gonna be fuckin' around. It's gonna be real bullets and guys who know what the fuck they are doin'."

"I know," Terry said. "But listen, you guys can't stay here either, for the same reason. Once they figure out where the call to Dawson came from, they are going to figure out we are here. No one can be here when they figure that out, because it is gonna be some Delta dudes or a SEAL team that are gonna knock on your door. So, you guys need to get this shit done and head to K-State and find Scarab."

"And then what?" It was Peggy. "You go up there and kill all the bad guys and we go talk to Jim Scarab. Say all that works out. What do we do next?"

"We can't go to the media," Terry said. "And going to the cops is probably hit or miss. So, I guess we go to Tampa."

"That's the link-up plan?" Brian said incredulously. "The fuckin' link-up plan is *Tampa*?"

"I'm fucking working on it!" Terry yelled back at him. Throughout this whole ordeal, he had kept his cool, until now. His tone lowered. "Look, I'm making this shit up as I go. I don't have all the answers, so Tampa is the best I can do."

Emma came and stood between the two men. "We will go to Manhattan. Then we will go to Tampa. We will meet you there," she told them. "You've been there before, right?" Terry nodded. "There's a McDonald's right up from the main gate. We will meet there at eighteen hundred. Every day go there until we meet up. It may take us a few days, or it may take you a few days. But, go to that McDonald's every day at eighteen hundred until we link up."

"Shit," Brian said, impressed again with his wife. "That works for me. That work for you?" Terry nodded again. "Damn, you're smart *and* sexy. I love you girl." Brian kissed her on her forehead.

"I'm going to head out then," Terry said. Peggy stood up from her stool. "Brother, I'm going to leave you that AK and the old 1911 from George. If you need to dump them, then dump them. No serial numbers on either of them, so get rid of them if you need to," Terry said to Brian.

Peggy was standing next to him now. "Why are you going up there?" she asked. "It doesn't make sense. If you know they are going to find you there, why are you going? It's a diversion, isn't it?"

"Yes. First, I need to get them to focus somewhere besides Manhattan while you guys talk to Scarab," he was starting to feel antsy, like he needed to be moving, but he knew she needed this explanation. "Second, my guess is they can probably only get two teams to act on this without raising suspicion. Brian is right, it's probably a team from Bragg and a team of SEALs. One of them will come here. So, the other team is probably on a string to go after us as soon as they find us, which I am going to let them do." She was still waiting for an explanation that made sense to her. She folded her arms. "Lastly, there is still something about your car that doesn't make sense. The jammer or tracker or whatever it is. They wanted you out of that house and they wanted you in your car and they wanted to know where you were. I want to go back there and take another look."

"I still don't get it," she said, unfolding her arms and wrapping them around his neck. "But I know you have your reasons, or at least your instincts. And they've kept you alive this long, so trust them." She kissed him.

"Yes, ma'am," he said. He looked at Brian over her shoulder. "Help me get that shit out of Big Blue." Brian stepped out from behind the kitchen island.

"Roger," he grabbed the very worn keys for the old Chevy from the key rack on the wall and headed out the door. Terry gave Peggy a long look in the eyes and a short kiss on the lips then broke her embrace and followed Brian outside. She stood there and watched his back disappear out the door.

"He knows what he's doing," Emma said from behind her. "Brian always says he is the best officer he's ever seen."

"I know he does," she said. "But, like he always says, *luck counts*. And we haven't had the best luck lately." Brian came in with Peggy's laptop and handed it to her.

"Y'all are gonna need that," he said. "I think." Peggy took it from him, turned to Emma, and put it on the countertop. She opened it up and pulled up the manifesto from the file directory, just like she watched Emma do.

"What exactly are we looking for?" Emma asked her, peering at the screen on her own computer.

"Um," Peggy stopped and thought. "Key words and phrases, I guess. Start with complex, multisyllabic words. Even educators don't use them that often, so if we can see a pattern with those, that might help." The two searched for a few minutes, picking out bits and pieces and comparing. They hadn't found anything that stuck out. Peggy saw some similarities in word use, but nothing that would be out of place for anyone who studied the Middle East in detail.

"Is this guy American?" Emma asked. "Or British?"

"What do you mean?" Peggy turned and looked at her. "He's an American but studied at Oxford. He either got his masters or his doctorate there. I can't remember which."

"He certainly spells things like a Brit," Emma said. Peggy moved to the island and looked over Emma's tiny frame. "Lots of o-u-r endings where normal people just use o-r." She pointed. "See, behaviour, ending in o-u-r instead of o-r. And here, honour, ending in o-u-r. Americans don't spell like that, Brits do."

Peggy went back to her computer and quickly scanned the manifesto. "I found it!" she exclaimed. Emma jumped up and came over. "Really, *you* found it. Look there. Colour ending with o-u-r. Honour . . . o-u-r." There was excitement in her voice. She turned and hugged Emma. "Thank you, Emma."

"Do you think that's enough?" Emma asked. "Is that enough to prove he wrote this shit?"

"It's enough," Peggy said turning back to the computer, "to prove I didn't. And enough of a link to make Doctor Jim Scarab believe we are on to him." Terry came through the door. "Terry, come look at this. We found something. Really, Emma found it."

"*We* found it," Emma cut her off. "I noticed that he spells like a Brit. Peggy put the pieces together." Peggy pointed out the examples of o-u-r in the manifesto and then lead him to Emma's computer with the op-ed pulled up and pointed them out there as well.

"Pretentious little shit," Terry said, raising his eyebrows. "That's great. Really. Now take this to him and call him out."

"You think this is enough?" Peggy asked.

"For him? Yes." Terry responded. "It wouldn't hold up in court or anything. Purely circumstantial. But you said that guy is a pussy. Watch him melt when you show him this. That will tell you everything." Brian came through the door. Emma gave him the short version of what they found.

"Ain't that some shit," Brian said. "That's enough for me. Let's go talk to this fucker."

"And I need to head north, too," Terry said. The four of them stood there in the kitchen for a moment. It was dark out now and they all needed to get moving. It had been a busy twenty-four hours. Terry was amazed at the two of them and what they were willing to do in the name of friendship. "Thank you two. For all of this."

"Shut the fuck up," Brian said. It was already too mushy for him. "You'd do the same shit if it was me. Probably more." Emma walked over and hugged Terry. She pulled back and kissed him on the lips. Brian pushed her out of the way. "Alright, alright. That's enough of that shit." He came in and hugged Terry. "Love you, baby."

"Love you, brother," Terry said as he patted him on the back.

"If I didn't know better, I'd swear you two were sleeping together," Peggy stated. Everyone in the room laughed.

"Alright," Terry said. "I'm heading out." He turned toward the door.

Peggy intercepted him. "That's it?" she said. There was an undertone of frustration in her voice. "She gets a kiss. He gets a hug. I get *see ya later*?" He was a little speechless. He knew what to say but couldn't bring himself to say it. He did the only thing he could do—he kissed her.

"I'll see you in a couple of days," Terry said quietly. "Please be careful." He was a hard man, inside and out. He didn't need to say things out loud and she wasn't a schoolgirl who needed to hear them.

"You be careful, too," she said. "And don't destroy my house, please."

"Yes, ma'am," Terry said. He turned and walked out the front door, heading for the pole barn. He opened the door and took a last look at his beloved Jeep before he got into the big truck. The engine fired up and he pulled out, heading back to the farm. He put the FNX on the seat next to him, tucked behind one of the assault packs so it wasn't out in plain sight. Terry turned on the radio, finding a classic rock station. The Nazareth song "Hair of the Dog" came through the speakers. *How appropriate*, he thought. He sang to himself.

"Now you're messing with a—a son of a bitch." He smiled. "Yep, that's what they're gonna get, a son of a bitch."

# CHAPTER 22

It was almost midnight when they got on the ramp to Interstate 70 heading west. Brian and Emma talked about it. It was highly unlikely that Dawson and his people had tracked the call, put the puzzle pieces together, and linked Terry or Peggy to the two of them already. No one was looking for them or this truck. The highway was the safest and quickest way to get out to Manhattan, Kansas. Brian knew that if he drove like he normally did, it would take them less than two hours to get to the "Little Apple," as Manhattan was known. He set the cruise control at two miles over the speed limit and got in the right lane. He was listening to sports talk radio because he always listened to sports talk radio. Emma was trying hard to stay awake in the passenger seat. Peggy was already asleep with Jumper's head in her lap in the back seat of the crew cab truck.

Brian didn't know exactly what they were going to do when they got to Manhattan, except find Dr. Scarab. He didn't think parading into his office was a good idea, but he didn't know where he lived. It would be almost 0230 by the time they got into town. It was a college town, so people moving around at that hour wouldn't necessarily be out of place. He wasn't worried about drawing attention necessarily, but he was trying to figure out the timing of their next move. He looked around the cab again. Emma was asleep now, too.

"I guess I gotta figure this shit out on my own," he said quietly. About forty-five minutes later, they hit the east edge of Topeka and passed through the toll booth. The lights woke Peggy in the backseat.

"You doing okay?" she asked him. "You've got to be tired."

"You know," he said, "your boyfriend ain't the only old soldier around. We lived like this for a long time. I may not be able to move like him anymore, but I can damn sure stay awake and pull security." Brian was a good man and she knew how much he meant to Terry.

When they were majors and Terry was the aide for General Dawson, Brian and Emma were deployed together in eastern Afghanistan. On Christmas Eve and Christmas day, Dawson wanted to travel around and visit a bunch of the outposts to spend the holiday with soldiers. Terry planned the trip weeks in advance and made sure Brian and Emma's unit was on the list of places to visit. Seeing his friend on Christmas Eve was the only thing he could think of to make the two-day trip bearable. The two Blackhawk helicopters carrying Dawson, Terry, and the rest of their party landed at the rock helipad to be greeted by Brian and his boss. There were salutes all around and a hug between Terry and his close friend.

Terry, Brian, and Emma were all sitting in Brian's plywood office about fifteen minutes later when the rockets came in. The Afghan insurgents launched them from the mountainside that overlooked the camp. It was a barrage of seventeen rockets, all the big 122mm ones. Terry heard the alarm right before the whirring sound of the first rocket as it passed over the camp, not landing inside the walls. The rest of the impacts were scattered all over the small camp, inside the felt and wire baskets full of dirt that made up the perimeter wall of the tiny camp. Terry knew Dawson was on the other side of the plywood wall with Brian's boss. He leapt out the office door to grab him and move him to one of the concrete bunkers outside. It was his job. Out in the cold night air, Terry had General Dawson by the uniform top, dragging him to the nearest bunker when a rocket hit nearby, knocking the pair to the ground.

When Terry regained his senses, he was being dragged into the bunker by his body armor. Brian had grabbed the drag handle behind his head and was pulling him on his back to the protection of the concrete. Dawson was inside with Emma. It turned out the rocket that knocked them down was the final rocket in the barrage, but Brian had no way of knowing that when he ventured out to grab his friend. They sat there quietly for ten minutes waiting for the *all clear* signal. Terry wasn't wounded and Brian hadn't done anything heroic by Army standards. There were no medals awarded for what happened during that rocket attack, but the two men never forgot.

"So," Peggy said from the backseat, "what do we do when we get there?"

"I was just tryin' to figure that out," he said, rubbing his chin. "You got any idea where this fucker lives? Where his house is?"

"I do, actually," she said. Emma was awake and sitting up now, listening as the other two spoke. "He lives right off campus. Big house. I had dinner there once, a little over a year ago."

"Is he married?" Emma asked. "Anyone else in the house?" Brian looked at her. Her hair was a mess. He knew what she was thinking and didn't like it, but it was probably their only option.

"Not that I know of," Peggy said. "He isn't married. I'm actually pretty confident he doesn't like women."

"That don't mean he's alone," Brian said. Peggy knew he was right, but she decided in the Midwest, even in a somewhat liberal college town, if Dr. Scarab was actually a homosexual, he wasn't going to flaunt it.

"Agreed," she said. "I think the risk is low, though. And we don't have many other options." Brian was turning off Interstate 70 and taking the state highway, K-177, north into Manhattan. They were less than fifteen minutes away from the campus. He looked at the clock—0209 hours.

"I guess we just go knock on his door, then," Brian said. "Or are we gonna add breaking and entering to our rap sheet?"

"Actually," Emma said, "I think knocking is our best bet. When he answers the door, we just push him inside. Less chance of him calling 911."

Peggy gave directions to Brian as he drove through town toward the campus. They drove past the house as a precaution. It was a big house, old. Probably built not long after the campus was established in the 1860s. The exterior was a mixture of stone and wood. There were no lights on. Brian made two passes and finally parked on the street about a block away and around the corner. The three climbed out of the truck and Brian looked at Jumper in the backseat. He cracked both rear windows to make sure the pooch didn't overheat. It was late summer and hovering around eighty degrees that night. The dog barely moved, putting his head on the warm seat that Peggy had just vacated.

"Useless fuckin' dog," Brian said with a chuckle. They closed the doors quietly and walked casually toward the old house. Brian had George's 1911 tucked into the back of his waistband. *I sure as fuck hope I don't need this thing,* he thought as he pulled his shirt over it. The three of them stood on the front step of the house, Peggy knocked. They waited. Peggy knocked again. Finally, Brian saw a lamp turn on through the curtains on the first floor.

Doctor James Scarab, PhD opened the oak door, still tying his robe and trying to adjust his glasses, all at the same time. Emma was the first one through the door and moved like she was the number one man in a four-man stack, clearing rooms. She put her hand on his chest and pushed him back inside the house. Peggy followed behind her with Brian taking up the rear and closing the door.

"What the—" was the only thing Scarab could manage before the door shut. "What is going on? Who are you people?" He recognized Peggy. "Margaret? What are you doing here? What is this?"

"Shut the fuck up," Brian said. "Just sit your ass down and shut the fuck up."

"I'm calling the police," Scarab said. He began to turn.

"No, you're not Jim," Peggy said. He stopped and looked at her. "You're not calling the police. We know. And we know what and who you're involved with."

"Me? What I did?" he said with a cluck. "The people I'm involved with are the same people—" Peggy slapped him, knocking him down.

"Dr. Scarab," Emma broke in. "If you try to call the police, three things are going to happen." They all looked at Emma.

*What the fuck is she doing?* Brian thought.

"First, you'll find that you can't use your cell phone. It's being jammed. So, trying to call the police is useless. Second, if you do find a way to call the police, we are going to give them every piece of evidence we have that proves you are trying to frame Peggy as a radicalized Muslim. Pretty sure that won't get you arrested, but it will get you fired. Lastly, if those two don't deter you from picking up that phone, I am pretty sure getting shot in the leg will."

Brian followed her lead and pulled the pistol from the small of his back. *We just added aggravated assault to the charges.*

"I don't know what you are talking about," Scarab said as he got to his feet. He plopped his small frame into a highbacked chair in the living room and crossed his legs. "I've done no such thing to Margaret, or anyone else for that matter."

"You're lying, Jim," Peggy said standing over him. "I know you're lying because you won't look me in the eye. Who put you up to this?"

"You're being very dramatic, Margaret," he said. "Though, you were always dramatic. No one is making you out to be a radical. You do that without any help, at all."

"Stop the double-talkin' bullshit," Brian said. "We know you wrote the document. We just want to know why you wrote it and who you wrote it for."

"I wrote no such document," Scarab said. "And if I did, I wouldn't have the faintest idea how to put it on Margaret's computer."

"No one ever said it was on my computer, Jim," Peggy said. "But thanks for confirming what we already knew. You wrote it and someone else did the digital dirty work." Scarab's face went gray. "If you won't tell us who you are working with, you are of no use to us.

Shoot him." Peggy turned and started to move away from him. She took a page from Terry's book and hoped Brian could sell it like she did. "Let me get out of the way first."

Brian cocked the hammer on the old pistol and pointed it at Scarab.

"Wait, wait," he was scared. "Please don't shoot me." They all noticed the wet spot on the front of his robe. He was pissing himself. He began to cry. "I was promised. They promised me a job at the CIA in the Operations Directorate. And a book deal. And to get out of this godforsaken town. She—" he was pointing at Peggy.

"What did you have to do?" Peggy asked bluntly, cutting him off.

"Just wr-write a document," he stammered. "Write it as if I were you. As if I were you and you had been radicalized. You're a fucking disgrace anyway. You legitimize what they do, those—those filthy animals. You legitimize what they do, and —and you give them resolve." He looked up at Peggy, his composure returning. "*You're* the security risk."

Peggy punched him in the face. His nose bled. Her hand hurt.

"So, you wrote the document," Emma said. Scarab was trying not to wail and to keep the blood from spattering on his carpet at the same time. "Who did you write it *for*? Who told you to write it?"

"There were three of them," he said through the dripping blood. Peggy grabbed the bottom of his robe, avoiding the piss stain on the front, and held it up to his nose to catch the blood. She stared at him intently as he continued. "They came to me after a speech I gave in the Beltway. It was an Army general, another man, and someone from the State Department."

"Who was this other man?" Peggy asked.

"I don't know. He might have been Army too. Longer hair and a beard, but he acted like the general, like a soldier."

"What about the guy from DoS?" Brian asked. "Was he a suit? Someone higher up, or just a worker bee? Is he the one that promised you the CIA gig?"

"I don't know who he was!" the Doctor was regaining his composure once again and now he was outright angry. "This is absurd! You people need to leave. I'm not saying another thing. Get out of my house!" He stood up. This time Emma punched him, again in the face. If Peggy hadn't broken his nose when she hit him, it was certainly broken now. He fell back into the chair.

"We aren't done yet," Peggy said. "Who was the general? What was his name?"

"I—I don't know," Scarab said.

"Bullshit, Jim," Peggy said. "You're a self-absorbed, narcissistic son of a bitch. If any general spent five minutes talking to you about anything, you'd have his name and his email address so you could brag to all your friends about it. Who was it?" Brian leveled the pistol at Scarab's head.

"Dawson," he said. "It was General Dawson, from CENTCOM."

"Thought so," Peggy said. Brian manually lowered the hammer on the pistol. Emma and Peggy helped Scarab stand up. "Now go clean up, Jim. And go to bed."

"Dr. Scarab," Emma said, "If you call anyone, if you tell anyone, if anyone knows about this visit, we will know about it. And we will come back. And there won't be any friendly discussion. You'll end up dead on the side of the road or out in a farm field somewhere. Do you understand me?"

"I—I understand," Scarab said as he wiped blood from his nose.

"Not a word, Jim," Peggy said, staring again. He nodded in agreement. The three of them turned and walked out of the house, closing the door behind them.

"Remind me not to piss you two off," Brian said as they got back to the truck. Peggy and Emma glanced at each other and smiled.

## CHAPTER 23

It was just before midnight when Terry pulled up to the small ranch house. There was a lone light in the picture window and a single light attracting bugs on the side of the barn. When he got out of the truck, Terry could hear the dog inside begin to bark. He knew not to approach the house at this time of night, he just stood in plain view by the tailgate. He could barely see the backend of Peggy's horse trailer behind the barn when he heard the screen door open. Larry was standing there, holding his Winchester rifle. He didn't immediately recognize Terry without his beard. Terry put his hands up.

"Larry," he said, "it's me, Terry Davis."

"Mr. Davis?" the elderly man said. "I didn't recognize you. Hell, I didn't think I was ever gonna see you again." Larry approached him and stuck his hand out. Terry took it and gave it a shake. "Is Ms. Baron with you?"

"No, Larry," he said, "she isn't." He could see concern between the wrinkles on the old man's face. "She's okay, she just isn't here. Larry, I need another favor."

"Anything," the old man replied. "We already spilt blood together. Ain't nothing more you can ask of a man after that. Nice truck." He was eyeing Big Blue with a curious look. "C'mon inside and we can talk." The two men went through the front door and Larry shooed away an Australian Cattle Dog that was wagging his tail just inside the door. The house was spartan but lived in. Terry guessed it hadn't changed much since Larry's wife passed away. The place was clean; there wasn't any dust on anything, which was a miracle out here in rural Nebraska. Terry followed the old man into the kitchen.

"What can I help you with, Mr. Davis?" The old man went into one of the kitchen cabinets and pulled out two glasses.

"I need to keep that truck here for a little bit," Terry started. Larry went into the small cabinets above the refrigerator and emerged with a bottle of Old Charter. It was terrible bourbon as bourbon goes, not that Terry was much of a connoisseur. Terry had never heard of it until he started living at the farm with Peggy, but it was a local favorite and could be found at every small-town bar in the area. Larry splashed a little into each glass. "And I need you to drop me off near the farm so I can walk back in there."

"That's easy, Mr. Davis," Larry said.

"And then I'm going to need you to cover my ass again," Terry said reluctantly. The old man looked at him.

"Mr. Davis," Larry looked into the glass of whiskey as he spoke. "I've done a lot of things in my life. Some good, some not so good." Terry just let the man speak. "I was a soldier, like you, a long time ago. I went to Nam and came back, but I came back different. Not in a bad way, just different. I got married and raised a family. All that is gone now. The only family I got left is Ms. Baron and that dog over there." He sipped from the glass. Terry took a sip, too. It burned like hell going down. "I got no problem killin', Mr. Davis. Never have. And if that's what you need me to do, and that's gonna keep Ms. Baron safe, then that's what I'll do."

"You're a good man, Larry," Terry finished his whiskey in one shot. It was awful, but he damn sure wasn't going to leave a drop given to him by a man like this. "I really hope it doesn't come down to you having to kill anyone, but it might."

"What do I need to know?" The old man finished his whiskey. "Don't tell me more than that—just what I need to know."

"They got cameras inside the house," Terry began. "I know they do because they got a picture of me from when I was in there the other day. The day you helped me out. I don't know how many and I don't know where they have them, except maybe one. But, I need to get into the garage to look at Peggy's car and I need to get into the basement. I got some stuff down there I need to get to." Larry got up and went over to a cabinet next to the landline telephone on the wall. He opened it and reached inside.

"The car is easy," he said turning to face Terry. He held out his hand. "This here is the garage door opener for the Baron place. Had it for years. Ain't never used it but once. Mr. Baron had an old truck and when he died, it wouldn't run. Ms. Baron and Mrs. Baron couldn't get it out of the garage, and they didn't want to watch it being hauled away. So, when they was at the funeral, I rode my tractor over there and hauled it out so the tow truck could hook it up. They never asked for it back and it's been sittin' in this here cabinet ever since." Terry did some quick math. It had been over ten years since her dad died. They probably needed some new batteries. "Gettin' you into the basement ain't all that difficult either. If them storm doors are unlocked, that is."

Terry knew exactly the doors the old man was talking about. A month or so after Terry started living at the farm, he was wandering around outside and found a set of metal doors set into a cement doorway about halfway between the house and the barn. They were Bilco doors, similar to the ones George had hiding his still northwest of there. Terry asked Peggy what they were for and where they went. She pulled open the doors and led him down into an unlit stone cellar. It was fairly large inside and the walls were lined with empty shelves. Generations of the family had used the cellar to store food through the winter and it even saved the family from a nearby tornado before Peggy was born. One of those Midwest tales of a tornado passing through, missing both the house and the barn, but tearing everything else to pieces.

Terry remembered watching Peggy disappear into a corner of the cellar. She vanished in the darkness. He thought his eyes were playing tricks on him until a light suddenly appeared. There was a narrow passageway that led all the way into the basement of the house, barely wide enough for a grown man to move through. Once she turned the light on, he could clearly see the passageway and followed it to emerge underneath the house. He could only hope no one put any cameras in the basement.

"I forgot about those," Terry said. "Let's just hope no one locked them. My guess is that once I walk into that garage, we've got about somewhere between two and four hours until someone shows up."

"Mr. Davis," Larry interrupted, "if you got that much time, why not just do what you got to do and leave? Why hang around and wait for them people to get there?"

"Larry," he responded, "I'm buying some time. There are some other things happening right now, in other places." The old man nodded. "If I can keep all the attention here, at the farm, that will help keep Peggy safe."

"I got it, Mr. Davis," the old man sat back in his chair and folded his arms across his skinny frame. "When are we leaving?"

"As soon as you're ready to go," Terry said. "And I get some stuff out of that truck out there."

"Well, you get whatever it is out of your truck and gimme ten minutes," Larry said.

"I'll be outside waiting," Terry said. He stood up and walked outside. He dug through the truck quickly. He knew what he needed and where it was. He needed the gear in the basement before company arrived. Terry stood in the drive with his uniform shirt on, a packed assault pack, and the AR-15 slung across his chest, waiting patiently for Larry to emerge.

The old man emerged from the house in a set of jungle fatigues that had probably been in his closet since they day he got home from Vietnam. Terry couldn't help but smile. The uniform still fit the old man and the creases were still sharp. It wasn't until he got close that Terry could see the Special Forces patch on the left sleeve and the white embroidered parachutist badge sewn above the left pocket. He was holding the Winchester.

"I'll be damned," Terry said.

"I figured if I needed to do some killin'," Larry said, "I oughta be dressed for it. You got one of them for me?" He gestured to the AR-15.

"Not yet, but once I get to my gear in the basement I will," Terry said with a smile. "Thank you, Larry." The two men got into Larry's big pickup and headed toward the farm. Larry stopped about a quarter mile short. Terry hopped out. "Come pick me up at the house in an hour. One hour." The old man looked at his watch and nodded. "Once I open that garage door, they are going to know I'm there. Won't be any need for hiding at that point. Not until they show up." He closed the door and banged the window frame. Larry wheeled the pickup around and disappeared back down the road. Terry started a slow shuffle toward the barn. He knew he could get past the barn and to the Bilco doors fairly easily, even in the dark. He assumed they didn't have anyone watching the house and were relying on the cameras.

The house was dark as he approached. He stopped short of the barn, listened, and watched. No sound and no movement from the house. He moved to the backside of the barn, stopping again. He had already burned ten minutes of his hour. Terry made a dash to the Bilco doors and pulled, hoping to God they weren't locked. The right door swung open with a creaking sound that Terry thought would raise the dead out of the family cemetery a few hundred yards away. He paused. Still no movement or sound. He was confident there was no one in or around the house.

Once inside the cellar, Terry dropped his assault pack and rifle, pulling out the FNX-45 with flashlight mounted underneath the barrel. He moved quickly through the passageway and into the basement. The room where he stored all his guns had no exterior windows, which was one of the reasons he liked the room as much as he did. Knowing he didn't have to worry about light showing outside the house, he pulled the chain on the light over the workbench. He checked his watch—forty minutes left. Terry grabbed a set of body armor from the corner and his bump helmet. He dragged them both to the cellar and returned to his gun room. Two more trips and he had everything he needed—body armor, helmet, night vision, more ammo, his short-barreled AR-15, and his war belt complete with Ek knife and an experimental holster for the FNX-45. He also grabbed a suppressor for the short-barreled AR-15 and another for the Remington 700.

Terry put on the body armor, war belt, and helmet. He tipped the night vision up, so they were out of the way. Once he put the FNX into its holster, there was plenty of room for the extra magazines of ammo he picked up. It had taken him two months of work and three holsters to finally get one set up that would carry the big pistol securely with the suppressor mounted. It ended up being a holster that rode below his belt and high on his thigh, which he wasn't a fan of, but it was the best solution he could come up with. It wasn't designed to draw the pistol in a hurry. Davis hoped he wouldn't end up in that situation in the coming hours.

Terry put the suppressor on the short-barreled AR and strapped it to the outside of the assault pack. He took a deep breath and looked at his watch. Twenty minutes before Larry showed up. Terry climbed up the cellar steps and realized how much weight he had just added to himself. There would be no running with all this gear on. *Getting old is a bitch,* he thought as he closed the Bilco door. Terry moved to the front of the house and took a deep breath. He hit the garage door opener. The lights on the chain drive opener came on and before the door was completely open, Terry could see the Audi was gone. He stood there for a second dumbfounded.

"I guess that confirms my theory," he said out loud as he pushed the remote for the garage door again, lowering the big steel door. Now he just had to wait for Larry and hope the response time by whatever special operations team he was expecting wasn't less than an hour. He flipped down the AN/PVS-14 over his left eye and turned it on. Through the green glow, he scanned the horizon. Nothing moving. He saw the glow of the headlights behind him and flipped the goggles back out of his field of view. Larry was pulling up, five minutes early. Terry dropped the pack into the bed of the truck and took off his helmet as he climbed into the cab of truck.

"Did you get what you needed?" Larry asked as they pulled away.

"I did," Terry said. "Let's go stash this thing and then move back this direction."

"Did you get me a rifle?" Larry asked.

"I did," Terry told him. "You can use this one," he shook the rifle on his chest, "I'll use the one in the back." Larry drove the truck back toward his house and pulled off the road about three quarters of a mile from Peggy's. There were some sections of concrete sewer pipe and road construction equipment about twenty yards off the road. Larry tucked his big truck into the construction site. The two men climbed out of the truck. Terry flipped the sling of his AR over his head and handed it to Larry. The old man dropped the magazine and cleared the chamber, then reloaded the rifle. Terry stood there and watched him.

"Blessed be the Lord, my Rock, who trains my hands for war, my fingers for battle," Larry said out loud. Terry handed him three additional magazines for the AR. "If I need more than this, we got us some serious problems. How many are we expecting?"

Terry had thought through this twenty times on his drive up. "I am assuming it will be eight to twelve men. If they arrive by freefall parachute, which I am guessing they will, they will land west of the house and assault from that direction. If they come by vehicle, it will be blacked out and they will be wearing night vision. Those are the two most likely courses of action." Terry knew that if there was a team sent to the farm, it was going to be from JSOC, the Joint Special Operations Command. It would either be a SEAL platoon or a team from Delta Force at Fort Bragg. Like the raid that killed

Osama bin Laden, the special operators would be on loan to the CIA and not working for the military. This whole thing would be filed as a training exercise to get the vehicles or aircraft and to allow them to operate on American soil. In reality, they were violating the Constitution, but based on everything that had happened in the last couple of days, Terry decided no one gave a shit about the Constitution anymore.

"Mr. Davis," Larry said, "how do we want to do this? Where do you want me and what do you want me to do?"

"I want you to follow this road and set up in the ditch across from the house. Find yourself some cover. If they come by parachute, you'll see them as they come across the road. If they come by vehicle, you'll see them much sooner than that. Regardless how they show up, you don't fire until I do. When I do, you start killing the closest guys to you and don't stop shooting until they do or you're out of ammo. If they start maneuvering on you, haul ass."

"I can do that," Larry nodded. "If you got that silencer on your rifle, how am I gonna hear you shoot?"

"You probably won't," Terry said, shouldering the assault pack. "But, when you see the first motherfucker's head come apart, you'll know." Terry reached out his hand. The old man shook it. "Thanks again, Larry."

The old man turned and headed off down the ditch. He disappeared quickly into the night. Terry flipped down his night vision and headed off toward the farm.

## CHAPTER 24

It was faint when he heard it, but he knew what it was instantly. The drone of the C-130 cargo plane was familiar to Terry after all the years he had spent jumping out of them. It was under ten thousand feet, for sure, so he knew the JSOC team would be jumping without oxygen masks and be out of their parachute harnesses quickly once they hit the ground. He looked up through the night vision monocular and could clearly see the flashing lights of the big cargo plane. They were flying in civilian airspace, so they had to keep them on. If they were jumping in a combat zone, they would have been completely blacked out.

It was an assumption, and Terry knew the dangers in assuming, but his guess was this was more likely a SEAL platoon and not a team of Delta. Actually, it was probably half a SEAL platoon—only eight men instead of the full sixteen. He had worked with SEALs on a number of occasions during his deployments. Every experience he had with them landed him at the same conclusions: they were fit as fuck, strong, and fast, but they were also overly brash and arrogant as a result. They wanted to start every operation with a high altitude, low opening or HALO jump because it was sexy, and not necessarily because the mission called for it.

In his gut he felt this was exactly that—underestimating their foe, overestimating their ability, and doing things because they were cool and not because they were tactically sound. This wouldn't be a cakewalk, but he felt more confident he and Larry could pull this off against eight SEALs than if a dozen operators from Delta had shown up in armored SUVs. He watched the sky intently, looking for any sign of movement. He saw the first parachute and then counted five more. He knew there were more out there that he couldn't see. He kept watching. Number seven. Number eight. He looked for more but didn't see anything. They landed in the pasture across the street like he had assumed and were approaching from open terrain. He hoped Larry would be able to see them coming.

The silhouettes came slowly. Eight men spread out in a line, coming across the field. He couldn't tell much more. Nothing distinguishable about them from this distance. Terry was north of the house, not far from the cemetery, and the house was their focus. They were moving quickly, carelessly. Either they were being cocky, or they assumed he had already left the area, and this was a wasted effort. Either way, they weren't on their game. The SEALs crossed the road in twos, Terry counted them easily through his night vision. Definitely eight men. One man came to the corner of the structure nearest Terry; it was actually the garage and not the house itself. He could see the man wasn't wearing a helmet as he crouched next to the house. The downspout creaked as the man leaned on it. A second man joined him, standing above him, both peering into the darkness. Terry was lying in the grass just at the edge of the yard. It was about a twenty-five-yard shot. Terry took aim at the standing man when the two began to move slowly from their corner.

The outlines of the two men were clear against the white siding that covered the structure. The lead man came out of his crouch and moved toward the rear of the garage, focusing forward. The second man was two steps behind him, weapon oriented out toward the high grass. Terry didn't have the PEQ-15 infrared aiming device on his short-barreled rifle; it was on the one he gave to Larry. At twenty-five yards in the daytime, this would have been a cakewalk, but the darkness and no aiming device made this a challenge. Terry could see now that both men were wearing body armor and communications headsets, probably like his Peltors. Thankfully, both men were presenting him a side view where he knew the ceramic plates in their vests offered the least amount of protection. Terry had a very simple Aimpoint red dot sight mounted on the rifle. His left eye was seeing green through the night vision monocular, his right eye seeing a black silhouette against the white background. He put the red dot on the shoulder of the second man and pulled the trigger.

As soon as he saw the blood from the man splatter onto the garage siding, Terry transitioned to the lead man. He was turning toward Terry to return fire, but Terry got there first, this time firing two rounds. The first round struck the man in the neck, the second in his forehead. Although Terry had a suppressor on the rifle, these were not subsonic rounds and each of the three rounds he fired had made an audible 'crack' as they broke the sound barrier. He didn't think either of the men had time to radio the rest of their team through their headsets before they died, but Terry knew it was only a matter of time before more men would arrive.

Terry was moving in a crouch when he heard the shot from the other side of the house. Then another. Then another. It was Larry, banging away with Terry's rifle. He must have heard the three shots from Terry and decided to start engaging targets. He smiled briefly. Just as Terry reached the corner of the garage previously occupied by the two men, he was bowled over. One of the attackers was moving to a covered position, out of Larry's line of fire and had chosen the same corner as Terry, arriving at the same time. The two men hit chest to chest and ended up in a heap on the ground. His AR was pinned underneath his body, so Terry reflexively reached for the FNX strapped to his leg.

His experimental holster was designed for movement and not for rapid draw. With one pull, Terry knew the pistol wasn't coming out of the holster in time. He could see the man was wearing the desert camouflage pattern the SEALs had essentially stolen from the Marines. It was the first time he could see it clearly, confirming his theory. The man seemed stunned, almost like he assumed he had run into another SEAL and not Terry. Terry took the opportunity and jumped on him, leading with his elbow. The elbow smashing into the man's face made him quickly realize this wasn't one of his teammates. He swung back, hitting Terry in the side of the head with a closed fist. Terry knew he had to keep the man as close as possible, limiting his ability to draw his pistol or bring his rifle to bear. He grabbed the man's body armor and pulled him in.

The SEALs had come in light. This man, like the other two, wasn't wearing a helmet and wore a plate carrier instead of a heavier set of armor. Terry didn't know if it was because of the HALO insertion or because this was how they operated normally, but the only protection was from the ceramic plates themselves. The vest was nothing more than nylon webbing and material that kept the plates in place to cover vital organs front and back. There were no side plates under his arms and he only had minimal gear attached to the vest itself. He was a big man, though, and if Terry didn't kill him quickly, he knew the man would eventually overpower him.

Terry reached down to his war belt and immediately found what he was looking for—the handle of his Ek fighting knife. With a jerk, the Ek came free from the Kydex sheath and Terry plunged it into the man's ribs, under his arm. The lung punctured and the man fought to breathe. Terry swung the knife a second time into the man's neck. The big SEAL grabbed for the wound, trying desperately to cover it and stop the bleeding. Terry rolled off him, sheathed the knife and grabbed his AR.

The first 9mm round hit him and knocked him off balance. He could feel the impact in the center of his back. The second round spun him, and he tripped over the SEAL bleeding at his feet. Terry didn't have the ceramic plates the SEALs were wearing; his plates were coated steel and rated to stop military grade 5.56mm rifle rounds like the ones in his AR. Terry had trauma pads between his body and the steel plates, meant to take some of the sting out of the impact. That didn't mean the shit didn't hurt. *Fuck.* He was on his back again and could see the man approaching with his pistol drawn. The SEAL was still in front of the house but closing rapidly when Terry heard the shot. The big man collapsed in front of him, a gaping hole in the side of his head. Larry had covered his ass once again.

Terry was getting back to his feet and trying to do some quick math: *two next to the garage, the guy I killed with the Ek, this dude that shot me. That's four. Three shots from Larry. Maybe seven. That leaves at least one more, possibly two.* Terry came around the garage corner with the AR-15 at the ready. He couldn't see any of the SEALs in his immediate view, so he began moving forward. He could feel the ache in his back where the two pistol rounds hit him. *That's going to hurt like a motherfucker when the adrenaline wears off.* He kept moving forward. *Keep moving, keep shooting.* The front door was still closed when he reached it. They hadn't gotten into the house yet. He moved to the far corner of the house and peered into the darkness. Nothing. Now it was a game of cat and mouse. Grown men with guns playing hide-and-seek in the dark.

Terry peeked over his shoulder to make sure no one had maneuvered in behind him, then moved around the corner of the house. He could see in the green of his night vision the Blico doors to the cellar were still closed. Just as he shifted his view to the barn, he heard a series of shots from across the road. It was Larry, but they were coming from a different location than before. Terry moved quickly, covering the open ground next to the house and across the road. He jumped into the high grass that filled the ditch next to the road and could see three different paths of beaten grass leading west. The SEALs were moving on Larry and based on what he could tell, Larry had left his position, like he should.

Terry moved cautiously down the ditch, using one of the paths already broken through the grass. The house was over Terry's right shoulder as he moved further away from the farm. He moved quickly, stopping to listen and look every few steps. Terry couldn't

see or hear anything and was beginning to worry the SEALs were
going to find the old man before he could get to him, if they hadn't
already. He heard the sounds of vehicles approaching at a high rate
of speed. He stood only tall enough to peek over the top of the high
grass. There were four SUVs pulling up in front of the house, driving
with no lights on. More men piled out. Terry watched and counted
the men. He felt a hand on his shoulder. He turned.

"Mr. Davis," Larry said in a whisper. Terry jumped and then let
out a huge sigh. He hugged the old man.

"Jesus, Larry," Terry said in a low tone. "You scared the shit out
of me. You okay?"

"I'm good," the old man replied. "I got a little scratch, but I'm
good. Two of them guys tried to come after me and I moved, just
like you said. But I circled back on them just like we used to do in
the jungle. I got them before they got me."

"Good work. Thanks for covering my ass—again," Terry said.

"Who's that?" the old man pointed to the vehicles in front of
the farmhouse. Terry could see them inspecting the bodies of their
comrades through his night vision. He realized Larry couldn't see
what he saw and probably only saw the shadows of the vehicles.

"That's their exfil," Terry responded. Terry made a rookie
mistake when he thought through the assault. Most young
commanders plan training all the way through clearing an objective
and then stop. Experienced commanders force their subordinates
to go through the steps of redistributing ammunition, treating
casualties, and calling in radio reports. The best commanders plan
training exercises all the way through leaving the objective, or the
exfiltration. Terry hadn't thought through how the SEALs were
going to leave the farm after arriving by parachute. Seeing the SUVs
now, he knew the rest of the SEAL platoon had staged not far away
with the four vehicles and that was how they planned on leaving
after they killed him. He cursed himself for missing it.

"We going to kill them, too?" Larry asked. There was no reluctance in his voice. It wasn't eager either. It was a question from a soldier who just wanted to know what the mission was.

"Let's watch them for a little bit," Terry said. "I am sure one of these guys made a radio call. The guys in the vehicles knew they were in contact. Right now, they are just trying to figure out what the hell happened." The two men sat quietly and watched. Terry was trying to figure out why they pulled right up to the house when they knew there was shooting going on. He knew there were drivers sitting in each of the vehicles; they had never gotten out. There were five men on the ground moving around. No one was pulling security of any kind. "They are putting the bodies in the back of the vehicles," Terry was narrating because he knew Larry couldn't see. "They have no security out at all. Eventually, they are going to come looking for the two guys that came after you. They aren't going to just leave them for the coyotes."

"Then they are going to find us," Larry whispered. "Them boys are only about fifty yards up the ditch, behind us." On cue, the five men on the ground turned and began to fan out like they were looking for something. They had the six bodies loaded in the rear of the SUVs and now they were on the hunt for their last two comrades.

"You any good with a pistol?" Terry asked.

"No, sir," the old man replied. "Never was. The only thing I ever did with a pistol was put down old horses."

"Okay," Terry said. "Once these guys come across the road and get into this high grass, we are going to cross back over into that pasture," Terry pointed to the open ground where the SEALs landed under parachute canopy. "You can have this rifle. We are going to go take care of those guys in the vehicles first."

"Then what?" Larry was looking for the rest of the plan. Terry didn't have one.

"One step at a time, Larry," he said. He saw the men moving across the road. "Let's go. Follow me." He got up and moved quickly across the road, hoping the drivers didn't see them and the team moving through the grass didn't either. The pair got to the barb wire fence at the edge of the pasture. There was no cover here, so Terry wanted to move quickly. He handed Larry his suppressed rifle and got the suppressed FNX out of the failed experiment of a combat holster. Larry leaned the other AR on the fence post.

"So, we know where to find it later," he whispered.

"I'll move in close and come around from the garage," Terry told him. "The passenger doors are still open. I don't know if those vehicles are armored, but I assume they are. Once I shoot the first driver, the rest will start getting out. You get as close as you can, and once they get out, shoot 'em. You work from the last vehicle forward and I'll work from the first vehicle back. Got it?"

"Yeah, Mr. Davis," he nodded. "I got it."

"And watch for those fuckers across the road. Once you start shooting, they are coming for you," Terry said. He got up and moved at an angle, gaining some space so he could cross the road and into the yard, where he was positioned when he killed the first two men. The whole maneuver was ludicrous to him, but he could only work with what the SEALs were giving him. They had repeatedly divided themselves up, making it easier for him and Larry to kill them piecemeal. He knew he didn't want to face five men ready for a fight in high grass when he had four sitting ducks. Terry was almost a hundred yards from the house when he crossed the road.

Terry used the house for cover as he closed the distance to the SUVs. He couldn't see Larry across the road, even through his night vision. He had to go on faith that the old man had made it to a position where he could fire on the vehicles. Terry had the pistol in his hands when he came around the corner of the house. He made it to the open passenger door of the first vehicle and shot the man inside. He moved quickly to the second vehicle and was met with gunfire. The driver had seen Terry shoot the man in the first vehicle and had drawn his pistol, firing as Terry approached. It was a smart move. He didn't try to clamber out of the vehicle or use the rifle next to his leg. He used his close quarters weapon in the manner it was intended. Luckily for Terry, the man made one mistake—he forgot the glass was bulletproof.

The first round hit the window frame and buried itself in the vehicle's armor plating. The second round hit the glass of the open door and ricocheted into the night. Terry cleared the door and fired three rounds of .45 ACP into the man. Driver number three was out of his vehicle and had his rifle between the open door and the A-Pillar of his vehicle, using the armor for cover. He fired across the hood as Terry got to the right rear corner of the second vehicle. The SEAL was using a suppressed rifle and subsonic rounds. Terry heard the impacts instead of the report from the weapon. *Where are you, Larry?* Terry poked the suppressor of his big pistol around the back corner of the SUV and fired four rounds at the man, forcing him to duck into the cabin.

Terry heard the supersonic crack of the incoming 5.56mm round from Larry's position, somewhere across the road. Driver number four fell into Terry's view, dead from Larry's shot. He had gotten out of his vehicle and was using vehicle number three as cover, trying to maneuver on Terry. *One more.* Terry heard the impacts of more rounds coming from driver number three. He was pinned. Another shot from Larry and Terry heard the rifle rattle to the ground. *That's four.*

Terry knew the other five men were coming and he wanted more than the FNX in his hands when they did. He came around the SUV and grabbed the rifle from the dead driver along with the three thirty-round magazines mounted on the front of his vest. This rifle was more than the standard M-4 issued to every soldier in the Army. This was a tuned instrument, set up for the suppressor and subsonic rounds. Terry was confident the ammunition he had on his vest and his war belt would function in the Navy issued carbine, but he didn't want to take the chance. He moved quickly to the right rear corner of vehicle number four, loaded a fresh magazine into the newly acquired rifle and tucked the FNX back into the holster on his hip. He watched the road for the men he knew were coming.

When Terry heard the scream from across the road, he knew immediately it was the old man. He moved back up the passenger side of the vehicle and looked over the hood and could see men moving across the pasture through his night vision. The SEAL carbine was equipped with the same PEQ-15 aiming device as his AR currently leaning against a fencepost in the darkness. He squeezed the pressure switch attached to the front pistol grip of the AR and could see the infrared beam clearly. He aimed at the lead man and pulled the trigger three times, watching the man jerk at the impact of each of the rounds. One of the men moving with him turned and returned fire wildly, not knowing where Terry was. Terry plastered him with the laser and fired again, five rounds this time. He went down in a heap.

Terry scanned the field in front of him. He could still hear Larry moaning from somewhere in the darkness. There were no enemies to engage but he knew he needed to get to Larry quickly. Terry raised into a crouch and began moving to the front of the lead vehicle, putting distance between himself and where he expected the SEALs to come from. As he passed the open passenger door of vehicle number two, he felt a hot flash under his right bicep. *Shit.* He didn't know where the shot had come from, but he never heard it, so it came from one of the other SEALs. He dove between the first and second vehicles.

Terry darted across the road toward the pasture. He could see a single infrared laser beam through night vision to his front left. Someone was searching for Larry. He knelt at the fencepost and fired at the man, squeezing the pressure switch, just as he pulled the trigger. The laser disappeared and the man went down. Terry got as low as he could and began to crawl toward the sound of Larry's moaning. On knees and elbows he crawled through the pasture, stopping only briefly to ensure no one was around him. There were still two men out there.

Terry knew he was bleeding from under his arm. It was wet and sticky, but not life threatening. He would deal with that later, right now he was focused on Larry. He found the old man in a small depression. He was still conscious but just barely. Terry looked the man over and found that his lower left leg had been mangled by a bullet and was bleeding through his pant leg. Terry fished the tourniquet out of the first aid kit on his war belt. Manufactured tourniquets had become mandatory during Terry's later deployments and he had acquired a number of them. He had one in the Jeep, one in Peggy's now missing Audi, and the rest spread across his range bags and wherever he thought he made need one. Thankfully, he had this one on him. He was in the middle of tightening the black webbing around Larry's leg when the shot came in. *Bang.*

Terry assumed it was from a pistol because it wasn't suppressed, and it was close. He grabbed his rifle and fired at the two men approaching from the house. The man on the left, holding the pistol, died when the second round went through the bridge of his nose. The man on the right took three rounds to the front of his body armor and went down. Terry moved quickly to the second man, believing he hadn't killed him, and he was right. The SEAL was unconscious, knocked out from the impact of the rounds or his head hitting the ground when he fell. Terry pulled a set of zip-tie cuffs from the webbing on the man's plate carrier and secured his hands behind him. He returned to Larry to find him awake and aware, but still in obvious pain.

"Hey brother," Terry said. "Glad to see your eyes are open. I gotta stop this bleeding, so I'm going to put this tourniquet on you. It's gonna hurt." Terry pulled the tourniquet band tight and turned the spindle, locking it into the metal triangle to keep it in place. Larry moaned. "Stay here, I'm going to get one of those vehicles."

"I ain't going nowhere," Larry said with a half-hearted laugh.

"Couldn't if I wanted to."

Terry ran back to the last SUV, jumped in and started the engine. He looked in the back and could see at least two dead SEALs back there as he put the beast in reverse. Terry bounded the vehicle across the road, breaking the barbwire fence and approaching Larry with the headlights on. When he got to him, he dragged the dead SEALs out of the back, leaving them in the pasture. Terry got Larry into an upright position and helped him hop to the vehicle, lying down in the backseat.

"I'll be right back," Terry said as he closed the door on the old man. Terry moved to the zip-tied SEAL and kicked him awake. "You're going for a ride, motherfucker." He got the big man to his feet and walked him over to the back of the SUV. "Get in," he told the sailor. The man stood silently. "Have it your way." Terry hit the man in the back of the head with the butt of the carbine, knocking him out once again. He lifted the big man into the back of the vehicle and closed the rear door. Terry grabbed Larry's rifle from the ground and tossed it in the passenger seat.

Terry wheeled the big vehicle around and headed toward the road. He stopped briefly at the fence post where Larry had leaned the other rifle. *So we know where to find it later.*

## CHAPTER 25

Terry stood over the old man as he sat on the couch in his living room. Once he had gotten Larry inside and cleaned up, he saw that the wound was better than it had looked in the dark. The bullet had passed through the calf, breaking the fibula and tumbling on its way out. There was some muscle damage and the broken bone and a decent amount of blood loss, but the old man was tough. Between Terry's first aid kit and the stuff Larry had lying around for dealing with injured animals, they got him patched up. Larry knew he couldn't show up at the local clinic with a gunshot wound to his leg without drawing attention. He would wait until later in the day and see how he felt before heading to an emergency room. He wanted to give Terry time to get out of the area before people started asking questions.

Terry had driven the SUV to the construction site and then transloaded his wounded partner into the cab of Larry's stashed truck. The unconscious SEAL got to ride in the bed back to Larry's house. Terry decided the mess out at Peggy's farm was too much to cover up and since the bad guys had done such a bang-up job cleaning up the mess with the deputies and the seven dead National Guardsmen, he would let them handle this one too.

"I wish we had some anesthetic for you," Terry said. "Something besides that whiskey." The old man tipped his glass in appreciation. "I can't thank you enough for this, again."

"Mr. Davis," he said, "I ain't seen this much action in over forty years. If this didn't hurt so bad, I'd be thanking *you*. What are you going to do with that guy outside?"

"I'm going to have a little talk with him, find out who put them up to this," Terry said, "and why. If he is smart, he'll cooperate, and I'll dump him on the side of the road somewhere. If not, we will see how long that SEAL can swim in a quarry with his hands and feet tied together." Larry gave him a sideways look but decided not to ask. "I'll be back in a few minutes." Terry turned and walked out the door. The sun was coming up and he wanted to get moving. He knew it was only a matter of time before someone came to clean up the mess at the farm and he wanted to be long gone by then.

Terry walked into the barn where he had stashed Larry's truck. The big SEAL was still asleep, but Terry had wrapped his hands, feet, and mouth with tape before he took care of his wounded comrade. He grabbed the man by the feet and dragged him out of the truck bed and onto the barn floor. The man slowly regained consciousness. He rolled over and looked up at Terry squatting over him. Terry ripped the tape off his mouth.

"I know you," Terry said. "You were the aide to the SOF commander in Afghanistan."

"And I know you," the SEAL said.

"You're a sorry motherfucker," Terry replied, "coming here and trying to kill me, a fellow officer."

"You're the sorry one," he said. "Harboring and aiding a domestic terrorist. Fucking traitor."

"Is that what they told you?" Terry laughed. "You fucking SEALs just do whatever you're told and never ask questions. You never thought any of this was a little sketchy? A combat operation inside the US, probably briefed as a kill-capture mission, right? That didn't seem like something you needed to question?"

"Not when it comes to the security of the nation, I don't," he spat back.

"You guys done this kind of shit before?" Terry asked him. "Inside CONUS?" The military was not authorized to operate inside the Continental United States; it was against the Constitution.

"This is the first of many," the SEAL responded. Terry knew this man's ego. He had met him more than a few times when they were both aides de camp, standing outside meetings their bosses were attending. He was an arrogant prick who believed all the press about how badass Navy SEALs were. Terry knew this guy couldn't help himself but to talk.

"The first of many," Terry quoted the man back. "That's the plan, then, huh? Frame an innocent woman as a domestic terrorist to convince the politicians and the public that the military needs to be able to operate inside the borders. That's some real Patriot Act shit right there."

"She's a fucking terrorist," he said bluntly. "And so are you."

"Yeah," Terry laughed. "And they sent you assholes to kill us. How's that working out?" He laughed again. "You guys on loan to CIA, like the bin Laden raid? Working domestic terrorism outside the bounds of the military, right? Department of Defense would never buy off on this shit." *Or would they?* Terry thought. The man said nothing. "Hey, I'm fucking talking to you. You've been real accommodating so far. Let's not make this ugly." Terry pulled the Ek knife from his war belt. There was still blood on the blade from the night before. *Gotta remember to clean that.*

"You're a fucking coward," the man said, "and a traitor. I'm not telling you shit."

"That's fine," Terry said. "Don't tell me anything. Since I took an oath to defend this country against all enemies, foreign *and domestic*," Terry poked the man lightly with the tip of the blade in emphasis, "I am well within my rights to kill you." Terry stood up and raised his arms out to his sides. "Right here in this barn."

"You won't kill me," the man said from the ground.

"Oh, no?" Terry said with a smile. "I killed those other, what, sixteen motherfuckers last night. Why wouldn't I kill you, too?" The man's face went gray. "That's right. If they are going to try me for murder, or even treason, what's the difference between sixteen and seventeen counts? Don't make a damn bit of difference to me."

"Go ahead," the SEAL said. "Kill me. I'll be a fucking hero and you'll still be a traitor."

"Yeah," Terry said. "But, you'll be a dead hero." Terry's eyes narrowed as he leaned down over the man. "So, let's start this again. Are you guys working for CIA? Who's in charge of this shitshow?" The man came to a quick realization that Terry was no longer negotiating. He hesitated as he tried to figure out what to say. "Listen, I gotta hit the road pretty soon. Someone is probably on their way to pick up all your teammates and I don't want to be around for that. So, you better start talking soon, or I'm just going to end this conversation and head on out." He poked him again with the knife.

"It's everything and everyone," the SEAL said. His arrogance was bubbling up again. He was in on the big secret and he couldn't wait to tell someone. "DoD, CIA, Military Industrial Complex, Armed Services Committees, everyone." Terry's eyes widened. Dawson wasn't kidding, this was bigger than him or anyone else. "Your girlfriend and you are the catalyst. You two are the keys to the kingdom. A retired soldier and an American PhD, radicalized and staging an attack inside the US."

"Except," Terry said, "it's all bullshit. She isn't a radical and neither am I. You and your boys got set up. Everything they told you about us is a lie. Every fucking word. We are being framed and you believed all of it, just like the public would have. And for what?" It hit Terry like a ton of bricks. "This isn't about starting another war in the fucking Middle East. This is about starting a war right here at home. Something that can be controlled and can go on for as long as you assholes need it to." The expression on the SEALs face changed. He just realized he had been lied to and his men had died because of it. Terry knew all he needed to know. He put the tape back on the man's mouth and walked out of the barn.

"You got a cellar," Terry said as he walked into the house, "like the one under Peggy's house? I need a place to ditch all this gear."

"No," the old man said, still sitting on the couch with his leg elevated. "No cellar, but there is an old, dry well back in them trees. Ain't been water in it since forever. You could put it there. No one will ever find it."

"Okay, back in the trees," Terry said. "I'll be right back." He turned to leave.

"Mr. Davis," Larry said. "What did you do with that man out there?"

"He's still out there, and he is still breathing," Terry said. "I'm going to dump him off with the rest of his guys when I leave. He can deal with that fucking mess. Write home to all those families." He walked out.

The well was tucked back in the trees behind the house. Only half the stone wall around the hole was still standing. Terry pulled the two spare magazines for the FNX and the Ek off his war belt and dropped it into the hole. He peeled off his body armor for the first time in hours and dropped it next. He could immediately feel where the two pistol rounds hit him in the back. After a few trips to the truck, everything was in the well with the exception of the FNX, the Ek, and his Model 12. He didn't want to drop the old gun in the well and he figured anyone driving a redneck truck like Big Blue with a shotgun behind the seat wouldn't be very out of place.

He pulled Big Blue up to the barn and walked inside. The SEAL was lying on the floor sweating from trying to break his binds. Terry put a piece of tape over his eyes and dragged him to the door of the barn. Hoisting the big man in a fireman's carry, Terry again felt the ache where the two 9mm rounds hit his back and he could feel the bandage under his right arm come loose. He dropped the big sailor into the pickup bed and looked at his watch—0721. He definitely needed to get moving. He stowed the pistol and knife in the cab of the truck, catching a glimpse of himself in the rearview mirror. He looked like hell. Tired and dirty. He would stop and clean up at a rest area or a truck stop on his way to Tampa.

Terry walked back inside the house to find the old man dead, holding a framed picture of his family. His reaction was to start CPR, but he knew better. Larry had died peacefully. The dog had run off when they pulled up in the middle of the night, so Terry knew the old man would be safe until someone found him. He touched him on the hand.

"Thanks, brother," Terry said softly. "Tell Saint Michael I said hey." He turned and walked out.

## CHAPTER 26

It had been a long two days of driving for Terry by himself. After dumping the SEAL at the farm, he had headed southeast. He was confident that no one was looking for Big Blue, but he wasn't taking any chances. Sticking to the backroads until he got into Missouri, he finally jumped on the interstate. He made it to the north side of Atlanta before he needed to sleep. It had been thirty-six hours of running on adrenaline, Copenhagen, Mountain Dew, and vending machine snacks with no real food or real sleep. He pulled off the highway and found a wooded spot in Red Top Mountain State Park to get some rest. He awoke almost twelve hours later. The sun was up, and his watch said 0906.

"Holy shit," he said to himself, rubbing his face. Terry started the truck and headed south again. His map estimate put him in Tampa at around 1600. He figured even with rush-hour traffic and trying to find the McDonald's, that gave him plenty of time. He pulled the truck back onto the highway and headed south.

The drive south was mostly uneventful. Terry had taken for granted how nice it was to have search and scan features on a radio, let alone his beloved Sirius/XM satellite radio. He spent most of his time fiddling with the plastic nobs on the old radio, trying to find something to listen to. He picked up a road atlas at a gas station in Missouri and had been using it to navigate. He thought of his dad, pouring over maps as they planned their summer vacations, teaching his son how to read the most intricate details embedded in them.

He was about thirty minutes into Florida when the news headlines came across the radio about a team of US Navy SEALs dying in a deep-water training accident, seventeen sailors in all. None of the bodies had been recovered and names were being withheld pending next of kin notification.

"Jesus," he said out loud. "Training accident. You guys need to get some new material." He realized the number was seventeen and not sixteen. That meant the SEAL Team commander from the barn ended up dead anyway. *Poor bastard.* The next headline caught his attention as well.

*"It was reported today that Middle East expert and college professor, Doctor James Scarab committed suicide at his residence in Manhattan, Kansas,"* the voice announced over the airwaves. *"Doctor Scarab was found by his partner who reported the suicide to police. No foul play is suspected."*

"Nice little bow on top," Terry said. "Wrapping everything up, nice and clean." It suddenly struck Terry that Scarab's death could have meant more than just Dawson and his people cleaning up a mess. I could mean that Peggy and Brian and Emma were dead too. Or if they were alive, they were the ones that killed him. "Fuck." His mind was racing. His gut said he needed to get into Tampa as quick as he could to make sure the three of them were okay, but he knew he couldn't afford to get pulled over.

Terry spent the next two and half hours thinking. He constantly changed the radio station, even occasionally switching over to AM, looking for any other news and bit of detail that could add to what intel he already had. He was following the signs to MacDill Air Force Base as he drove through Tampa. MacDill was the home of CENTCOM and where Dawson lived and worked every day. Terry knew this was all coming to a close in the very near future. He just needed to ensure Peggy was safe.

The McDonald's flashed by and Terry almost missed it. He could see the signs for the main gate of MacDill and was thinking about how to get onto the big base with everyone looking for him instead of watching for the fast-food restaurant. He looked down at his watch, 1704. Plenty of time. He pulled into the drive-through with the intent to order some food to eat in the parking lot while he waited for one of the three to show up. He stopped the truck in line and was looking at the menu when Emma jumped in the passenger seat.

"Jesus Christ, woman!" he shouted. Emma hugged him. "You scared the living shit out of me. Why are you here so early? We aren't supposed to meet for another hour."

"East Coast time, dumbass," she said. "We are in the eastern time zone. It's after eighteen hundred." Terry had completely forgotten about the time change. "Pull out of line."

"Emma," he said, "I'm fucking starving. I haven't eaten in forever."

"We have food at the motel," she said. "Let's go. C'mon, c'mon, c'mon."

"Alright," he said. "Don't get your panties in a bunch." He pulled the truck out of line and through the parking lot.

"You know I don't wear panties," she smiled a naughty smile. Emma gave him directions back to the motel. She didn't say anything, so he assumed everyone was safe.

"Scarab is dead," Terry said.

"We know," she replied as she pointed at the parking lot of a shitty looking motel. "We saw it on the news." He saw Brian's truck in the lot and parked across from it. The two climbed out and he followed her to Room 17. The motel was a dump. It was a single-story building and offered rates by the hour. All the doors were painted a teal-blue color and all the windows were painted with pink trim. It looked like a set from the TV show *Miami Vice*.

"You guys seen Crockett and Tubbs around here busting drug dealers?" he asked as they approached the door.

"Oh my God," she said. "You two are exactly fucking alike. Asshole said the same thing when we checked in here." The two walked through the door.

Peggy paused when she saw him, then leapt from the double bed farthest away from the door and ran to him, wrapping her arms around his neck. He kissed her cheek.

"Thank God you're okay," she said. She could see the bandage under his arm had soaked through with blood. "What happened?"

"Them Navy SEALs that died in a training accident," Brian used air quotes when he said training accident, "was that you?"

"Yeah," Terry said. "That was me." Brian gave his friend a hug. "I'll fill you guys in, but I need a shower and some fucking food." He looked around the room. "Wow, this place is lovely." The sarcasm was thick. The room was lined with cheap, dark wood paneling. The two double beds were both covered in stained bedspreads. He could see cigarette burns in the nightstand between the beds and on the dresser where the TV sat. "I'm gonna need a tetanus shot after this."

"Yeah, well," Emma said, "the Four Seasons was full." Peggy was still staring at his face. "We got you some clothes too."

"All the way down to a pair of britches," Brian said plopping down onto the nearest bed, next to Jumper. "Peggy didn't want to tell us you wear extra small, but she gave you up." He smiled.

"Yeah," Terry smiled back, "Emma never complained." Things were instantly normal now that they were together, even though the four of them had been through hell in the last week. "I'm heading to shower." He walked to the bathroom, Peggy behind him. They closed the door.

"Are we conserving water," he asked as he took his shirt off, "or are you here to keep me company?" She stared at him. He smelled bad and his skin was salty from sweat, but she didn't hesitate. She undid his belt and opened his pants, reaching her hand down into his crotch. She kissed him and stroked him until he was hard and then leaned back against the sink and began to pull her pants down. She wrapped her bare legs around him and let him slip inside her. "I missed you too," he whispered in her ear.

It didn't take long and neither one of them cared. Once they were done, he turned on the water and finished undressing. She cleaned herself up and then sat leaning against the sink while he showered. Peggy handed him what the hotel considered a clean towel when he shut the water off. The bathroom was filled with steam. He dried himself off and climbed out of the tub. When he turned around, she could see the two bruises on his back from the pistol rounds absorbed by his vest. She had thrown away the bandage on his arm while he was in the shower and she could see the gash as he dried himself. It was starting to bleed again.

"What's that from?" she pointed to his arm.

"That, my dear," he said, "is from a five-five-six round. Luckily it just caught my arm."

"What about those bruises on your back?" she inquired. "What are those from? Clearly, they aren't from bullets, or you'd be dead."

"Actually," he replied, "they are from bullets. My vest stopped the rounds." He could see the concern in her eyes. "I'm fine, really." He slipped the boxer-briefs on and then the black T-shirt and jeans they had bought him. He opened the door and waved her through. He finished dressing while Emma and Brian got the food out. Belt, socks, boots. He was missing his hat. It was out in the truck with the one assault pack he hadn't dumped in the well at Larry's. *Shit, I have to tell her about Larry.*

"So, tell us what happened," Emma said as she heated up some Little Caesar's pizza in the tiny microwave. It was sacrilege for anyone from Chicago to eat chain pizza like this, but he was starving and didn't care. Brian handed him a cold beer from the mini fridge. Terry recounted the events from two nights ago, including Larry's heroics. When he told Peggy the old man died, she cried. There was no wailing and no sobbing, but she cried because he was the closest thing to family she had left. Even Brian kept his mouth shut long enough for her to regain her composure.

"Who was the SEAL dude you left alive?" Brian asked. Terry

didn't even have a chance to answer before Emma put a printed copy of a black and white photo in front of him.

"Was that him?" It was. In the photo, he was in civilian clothes, sitting next to Dawson in some kind of auditorium. On the other side of Dawson was a man in a suit.

"Yeah, that's him," Terry said. "How did you know? And where is that picture from?" Peggy started into the story about their visit with Jim Scarab and how he told them that he was approached by Dawson and two other men after giving a speech in Washington DC. With some work on Google, Emma found all the photos from that speech and pulled the one she showed to Terry. "I guess you guys didn't kill Scarab."

"Fuck no," Brian said. "These two beat the shit out of him though. Hell, they scared the shit out of me, too."

"Then his suicide was another clean up job," Terry said.

"Yes," Peggy stepped in. "Just like the others. These are some powerful people to clean all of this up."

"They are," Terry agreed. "And I don't think Dawson is leading the charge on this. He's just a cog in the wheel."

"You know that motherfucker is retiring, right?" Brian said.

"What?" Terry was shocked. Emma handed him the free newspaper from MacDill. The front-page story was all about Dawson and his career and announced his retirement. The ceremony was coming in two weeks. "You gotta be fucking kidding me."

"No," Peggy said, "he is. The article says he is being considered for a number of boards inside the defense industry and as a candidate to be the Director of the CIA. Isn't there some sort of waiting period after retiring before you can take positions like that?"

"Supposed to be," Brian said, "but there is a waiver for everything. Ask Emma, she had to get one to come in the Army 'cause she's so short." Emma gave him the finger.

"What about Peggy's car?" Emma asked. "You said it was gone. What happened to it?"

"I think that is where all this is or was heading," Terry responded. "I have been thinking through this and I think they pulled it and are making a VBIED out of it." Terry was referring to what a car bomb had been labeled during the Iraq war—vehicle borne improvised explosive device. "Before we fucked up their plans, I think they were going to rig it up and then let you drive it to somewhere important, maybe a military base or even something in the beltway and then remote detonate it, probably with you in it. That's why I think they had the tracker and the jammer. They needed to know where you were." Everyone's eyes got wide. Peggy had her thumbnail in her teeth again. "Now, I think they will probably stage it somewhere and once they kill you, they will stuff your body in it and then detonate it. Either way, they have the manifesto. The guy who wrote it is dead. They have your car. They have an email trail between you and all your contacts in the Middle East. They have you as the widow of a Muslim."

"And they have the media in their pocket," Emma said, "to make the story whatever they want it to be."

"And you said the SEAL dude told you," Brian shook his head interrupting himself. "This sounds like some school-kid-telephone-game. The SEAL dude told you they are doing this so JSOC or whoever can start killing motherfuckers stateside?"

"Yes," Terry said. "It's the perfect war. It's domestic. They can generate whatever threats they need to and keep it going forever. It keeps the military funded and it keeps the defense industry rolling in money."

"And it changes the rules," Emma said. "It will allow CIA to operate inside the US, along with the military. And it will allow the government to specifically target US citizens *inside* the US as terrorists. Not law enforcement, but the military and the CIA."

"Shit," Brian said. "This is like sinking the Maine, Gulf of Tonkin, killing Kennedy, and WMDs all rolled into one."

"Worse," Peggy said. "This paves the way for total government control, short term and long term."

"So," Emma said quietly, "how do we stop it? We can't go to the press. We can't go to the Army. We can't go to the government. What do we do?" The three of them all looked at Terry, expecting an answer. He gave the only one he could come up with.

"We need to kill Dawson," he said.

## CHAPTER 27

"Terry," Emma said, "we can't."

"Have you lost your goddamn mind?" Brian said. "Look, them sonsabitches that you killed up north, that's one thing. They were tryin' to kill you. Like tryin' hard to kill you. This is something else. He's a fuckin' four-star, man!"

Terry sat quietly. He knew this would be the reaction.

"He may be right," Peggy said. That took Terry by surprise. "I don't think it solves the bigger problem, but it solves the immediate problem."

"What the fuck does that mean?" Brian said.

"How long do you think they've been planning something like this?" Terry asked. "How long do you think they have been cultivating Dawson and dropping ideas in his head? How long do you think they have been looking to find the right guy, the right four-star who they can bullshit into believing all this *and* be capable of moving from the military to CIA?"

"Years," Emma said quietly. "They've been planning this for years." It was a realization Terry had come to in the cab of Big Blue during the hours of driving to get to Tampa.

"This is a chess game," Terry said. It seemed Brian was the only one in the room that still needed convincing. They were all talking to him as he laid on the bed petting Jumper.

"Brian," Peggy said, "I have dozens of contacts all over the Middle East. It has taken me decades of travel and repeated contact to get those people to trust me, to build those relationships. Decades."

"Baby," Emma said, "this isn't something they threw together. This isn't haphazard. Someone has been putting this plan together for a long time. They have been moving puzzle pieces around. It's chess, like Terry said."

"I know this sounds like some conspiracy theory shit," Terry said, looking his best friend in the eye, "but I'm right on this one."

"Oh my God," Peggy said suddenly, "I'm part of this too. They have been manipulating me too, just like they did Jim Scarab. Do you know how many times both of us were invited to sit on panels together by DoD or State Department?"

"Probably," Terry said. He hadn't extrapolated the situation out that far, but she was probably right. "That rivalry between you two, the public nature of your opposing viewpoints, they either took advantage of something that was already there or maybe even built it themselves."

"Jesus," Brian said. "So, you're tellin' me that through generations of the military and generations of the CIA, they have been planning this shit?"

"Maybe not them, specifically," Terry said, "but someone has been. Administrations change, policies change, but there are some people inside and outside the government who maintain influence. Some congressmen stay for a lifetime. Presidents of weapons and tech companies stay for decades. Whoever is orchestrating this had a framework in place and have probably been waiting for the right people and the right time."

"I am wondering if," Peggy said, "the big pieces of this have been in the works since after 9-11. You said it yourself, 'WMDs.' In 2003, they convinced the country we needed to go to war based on intelligence that was basically bullshit. This could be the same thing."

"Go back, Peggy," Brian said. "You said short-term and long-term solutions. What did you mean?" His accent was fading again. He was thinking and this wasn't for show.

"I said bigger problem and immediate problem," Peggy corrected him. He was about to throw out a profanity laced protest, but Peggy kept talking. Brian closed his mouth. "The immediate problem is having someone they can move from DoD to CIA who is on board with all this. Without Dawson, they don't have that, and they have to start that process over. Find someone else. A new general."

"It delays it," Emma said, "but it doesn't stop it."

"Exactly," Peggy confirmed. "The plan still exists and the endstate remains the same for whoever is planning this. It just changes their timeline."

"And the bigger problem," Terry said. "I'm not trying to overuse this chess metaphor, but if we get rid of Dawson, that takes a big piece off the board. It doesn't end the game, but it makes it more challenging."

"Well," Brian said, "I never played any goddamn chess, but I get what you're saying. He's still a fuckin' general and you're talkin' about murdering him. That's what this is."

"I don't see it that way," Terry said. "He's a fucking insurgent against our own government. That's what this is."

"You may be right on that one," Brian replied. "Can't we just get him to quit? Or catch him admitting all this shit on tape or something? That always works in the movies."

"I don't think we have an option on this one, brother," Terry responded.

"Unfortunately," Emma said, "I agree with Terry. We are all missing a much bigger problem, though."

"What is it, dear?" Peggy asked.

"How does this end for all of us?" Emma replied. "If these people are this powerful and they can bring in a damn SEAL team after us and they can manipulate a general and they can kill a college professor, then what happens to us? Even if we kill Dawson, that doesn't mean it ends for us." She was right. Terry stood up. Peggy stood as well.

"Fuck," Terry said. Peggy was staring at him with her thumbnail in her mouth.

"Hell," Brian said. He was smiling. "That's shit's easy. There's three motherfuckers that are in on this, for sure." He got off the bed. Jumper sat up for a minute but laid back down in the now vacant warm spot. Brian picked up the black and white photo. "We know this fucker is dead," he pointed to the Navy SEAL. "And we are planning on killing this one," he pointed to Dawson. "We just need to git rid of this dude," he pointed to the unnamed third man they all assumed was CIA.

"I would definitely not define that as *easy*," Terry said. "We don't know who that is, not even a name, or where to find him."

"The retirement," Peggy said. Terry thought she was talking about the ceremony.

"That guy is *not* coming to the retirement ceremony," he told her.

"No," Peggy said. She shook her head like she was trying to clear cobwebs. Terry realized how frazzled she looked. Peggy had never been much for make up or doing her hair, but she was tired, and he could see it in her face. She wasn't built for this sustained pace and she wasn't groomed into it over decades like Brian, Emma, and Terry had been. It was all catching up to her. "Not the ceremony, but his retirement. Dawson's retirement. The ceremony isn't for a couple of weeks, right?" The three all nodded. "And they want him to move straight in to be the director of the CIA."

"The paper said he was being considered," Emma said. "That or some defense industry boards."

"No," Terry said. "She's right, they want him at Langley. As soon as possible, I bet. That other stuff is just bullshit cover. They can't say he is going to be the director of the CIA until he gets confirmed."

"Yes," Peggy said. "And if they want him up there right away, and they want to get him confirmed quickly, he is going to get prepped for his confirmation hearing. Didn't you do that for him once?" she asked Terry.

"Sort of," Terry elaborated. "We did a murder board for him before he got his fourth star." All four-star officers must be confirmed through the Senate. It can be a grueling experience, so officers will spend weeks preparing in many cases. Their staff will prepare a mock hearing or *murder board* and the officer will go through it a number of times, rehearsing responses to questions they know or assume will be asked in the confirmation hearing.

"We can assume he is going to go through the same prep before his confirmation for CIA," Peggy said.

"And if that other bastard is CIA," Brian broke in, "then I guaran-goddamn-tee he will be part of it."

"So, what are we going to do," Emma asked, "bust into CIA headquarters and kill him too?"

"Baby," Brian said, "they won't prep him at Langley. They can't even bring him into Langley. If they prep him, it will be outside somewhere. Maybe in DC someplace."

"It would have to be a secure facility," Peggy said. "They are going to talk about classified information, and they won't do that in some hotel room."

"The Pentagon?" Brian said.

"No," Terry spoke up. "They will do it here." They all looked at him. "His house is a top secret SCIF." Terry was using shorthand for any facility that is cleared to keep, store, or discuss classified information. The National Guard armory was a SCIF rated secret, but not rated for top secret, that's why they had cleared the building for the call from Dawson in the first place. "The house for the CENTCOM commander is rated as a TS SCIF. Or at least the basement is."

"Seriously?" Emma said.

"Yes," Terry said. "Most four-star houses are. That way, if they need to get on a secure call in the middle of the night, they don't need to come all the way into the office to do it. And CENTCOM runs ops twenty-four hours a day."

"That's a lot of late-night trips to the office," Emma said.

"Exactly," Terry said. He came to another realization. "I bet that's where he was when we talked to him. His house, not the office. That's why he answered his own phone and not anyone else."

Peggy's eyes narrowed. Terry was right.

"Back the fuck up," Brian said. "So, you think that CIA dude is going to prep him at his *house?*"

"I do," Terry said.

"Okay," Brian replied, "even if he is, we can't get onto MacDill. The whole fuckin' world is lookin' for us. We try to go through that gate, and we get arrested or fuckin' shot on sight."

"I will figure that piece out," Terry said. "But first, we need to make sure that CIA guy is the one, or maybe one of many, who are preparing Dawson for his confirmation."

"And how do we do that?" Peggy asked.

# CHAPTER 28

Terry and Brian sat in the cab of the Silverado in the McDonald's parking lot. They had been there for about an hour, watching traffic coming in and out of the main gate of MacDill, looking for a very specific car.

"What does she drive again?" Brian asked.

"We've been here for a fuckin' hour and you're asking me that now?" Terry was poking fun.

"Fuck you," Brian responded. "What is it, again?"

"Tammy drives a black Porsche convertible," Terry told him. "Little two-seater. She will probably have the top down and be in a baseball cap with her blond hair sticking out."

"That's pretty fuckin' specific," Brian said.

"Tammy is pretty specific," Terry said. After Terry and the general had come back from Afghanistan, he had learned about the other side of Tammy Dawson. She was a well-manicured personality as much as she was anything else. Her image as the wife of a general was something she and her husband paid close attention to. It was important for her to look and act the part, contributing to his ascension and not taking away from it. She was in her late fifties, but you wouldn't know it. She kept her hair long and blond, her body tan, and her nails and makeup always perfect. She was fit, working out daily but also blessed with the body of a Division I college swimmer. She was at the University of North Carolina when she met Dawson. He was a lieutenant at Fort Bragg, serving in Brian and Terry's beloved 82nd Airborne Division and they met when he was partying with a bunch of other lieutenants in Raleigh one night. She didn't have a plan after college and attached herself to Boo-Boo when she heard the other lieutenants say he was probably going to be a general someday.

Terry figured she still stuck to her Saturday morning routine and would be exiting the base soon to get her nails done. The couple never had any children; she wasn't going to ruin her body for the sake of having a child. That freedom allowed her to do what she wanted whenever she wanted. It also allowed them the financial freedom to buy things like the Porsche convertible she loved so much. Terry was hoping he would catch Tammy coming off MacDill and follow her to wherever she got her nails done. His gamble worked.

"There she is," Terry said. He pointed to a black Porsche turning left in front of them. Brian put the truck in gear, and they followed her. Terry's description was accurate from where Brian sat. The Tampa morning was comfortable, so she had the top down and was wearing a white baseball cap like golfers and long-distance runners wear. Brian stayed close and followed her into a strip-mall parking lot. She parked the Porsche right in front of the nail salon located at the other end. Brian pulled up behind her and Terry jumped out.

"Damn," Brian said quietly as he watched the woman climb out of the convertible. Tammy was in yoga pants and a sports bra. Her figure was stunning for a twenty-two-year-old, let alone a fifty-nine-year-old. Terry called out to her.

"Tammy!" she turned to look for whoever was calling out her name. She smiled big, exposing her bleached teeth and wrapped her arms around him in a hug.

"Terry!" she said, kissing him on the cheek. It was all for show. Terry had seen her greet every one of Dawson's former aides in the same way. "I didn't know you were in town. Does Boo-Boo know? He never said anything."

"No," Terry said. "I didn't call." She feigned a stern look at him and then smiled again. "We were just at the McDonald's and I thought that was you that drove by. I just had to come say hi."

"Are you hear for the ceremony?" she asked, looking at her watch. "It isn't for a few weeks, you know."

"Sort of," Terry said. He was trying to draw out the conversation, knowing she had a nail appointment. "I figured I would come down and surprise him, shake his hand. How are you?"

"Terry," she said, fidgeting a little, "we are great. I have a nail appointment and I need to go inside. Can we catch up at the ceremony? Or after?"

"Yeah," Terry said, "of course. Hey, can I borrow your phone? I'll call him from your phone and surprise him." She was rushing to get inside, and he was holding her up. "I'll call him and then just walk the phone back inside."

"Sure," she said digging it out of the waistband of her yoga pants. "Sure. He'd like that. It will be funny." She unlocked the phone and handed it to him. "I'll be right inside. Just bring it in when you're done. Talk to ya later." She smiled and gave him a kiss on the cheek again. "Good seeing you!" She turned and ducked into the nail salon. Terry turned and looked at Brian in the truck. He opened her contacts and touched *Boo-Boo*. The phone started ringing.

"Don't tell me you got pulled over again," Dawson's voice came through the phone.

"No, sir," Terry responded.

"Davis?" Dawson's voice was immediately cold. "Is that you? Where is Tammy?"

"She's inside," Terry said calmly. "Getting her nails done, just like every other Saturday morning. She looks great."

"You're in Tampa," Dawson responded.

"Yes, sir. Came for your big retirement ceremony," Terry said. "Tammy said I could have stayed at the house with you guys, but with all the people coming and going—the movers, the people from the CIA prepping you for confirmation—there's a lot going on."

"She . . ." Dawson was at a loss. That woman never could keep her mouth shut. She loved to talk about his career and everything he had going on. It never occurred to him that Davis was lying. "Listen to me, Terry. You don't know what you've gotten yourself into. Or the people you are dealing with."

"Sure I do," Terry said with more anger in his voice than he intended. "You, the Navy SEAL guy, that dark haired guy from Langley. Hey, how's the SEAL? I heard he died in a training accident." Davis wanted him to know things were unraveling.

"Yeah, damn shame about that," Dawson's tone changed. "You're responsible, Terry. For all of it. Everything that happened and everything that *will happen.* Remember, you caused all this to turn out this way."

"What do you mean?" Terry asked. "*You* did this. Not me. I didn't start this, but I'm damn sure going to end it."

"No," Dawson was cold now. "No, Terry. You're not going to end it. *They* are going to end it. They are going to end you. And her. And your friends. And they will get what they want in the end, no matter what you do." Terry went cold. He was drenched in a feeling of dread.

"Motherfucker," Terry said. "I made you a promise. If anything happens to her, I'm going to fucking kill you."

"Terry," Dawson said, "you should get back to that shitty little motel." Terry hung up the phone and tossed it into the open top of the Porsche as he ran to the truck.

"Go back to the girls, now!" Terry yelled. Brian reacted, putting the truck in gear and squealing out of the parking lot.

"What the fuck did he say?" Brian asked as they sped through traffic.

"He knows where we are staying," Terry said. "He said to go back to the shitty little motel."

"Fuck," Brian was swerving through traffic in the big truck. Terry's heart was racing. He didn't know what they were going to find when they got to the motel. He reached into the glove compartment and found the sterile pistol George gave him. It was the only weapon they had with them. As they passed the McDonald's Brian saw Big Blue in the drive through lane. He dove into the parking lot and pulled up next to his old truck. Only Emma and Jumper were in the cab.

"Where's Peggy?" Terry yelled to her through the open windows.

"At the motel," she could see something was wrong. The two men sped away, Emma pulling out of line to follow them. They were about two hundred yards from the motel when the explosion rocked the truck.

## CHAPTER 29

Oh *my God*. Brian slammed on the breaks to avoid rear-ending the silver Nissan in front of them. Terry jumped out and began running down the sidewalk toward the motel. Brian called after him, but Terry kept going. He came to the edge of the parking lot and stopped dead in his tracks. The front of their room was gone and so were the doors and windows for the rooms on either side. Still on fire and sitting in front of the building was the carcass of what used to be Peggy's Audi. Terry ran toward the gaping hole where their room used to be. The building sprinkler system was only spitting little bits of water after the damage from the explosion knocked it mostly out of commission. Terry vaulted over a pile of debris into the room.

"Peggy!!" he called. He could hear sirens outside. "Peggy!!" he called again. The room was in shambles. Both mattresses and bedframes were blown against the bathroom wall. The mini-fridge, TV, and dresser were in a broken pile in the back corner of the room. Terry pushed the mattresses out of the way, hoping to find her underneath and fearing it at the same time. He was frantic. "Peggy!" he kept shouting over and over. There was nothing under the pile. He threw chunks of dresser and TV out of the way to get to the bathroom door, kicking it open. She was lying unconscious and bleeding over the edge of the tub. He could see her bare back, only a white bra strap cutting across the center. He pulled her off the tub, blood coming from her ears and her mouth. She was breathing, but barely. He could hear the sirens right outside when Brian came through the bathroom door.

"Help me," Terry said, sitting on what was left of the toilet, Peggy leaning on him. Brian grabbed her legs and the two men carried her out of the bathroom. Firemen were inside the room now urging them to get out. They carried her through the debris and into the sunlight. Firemen were hosing down the remnants of the Audi. Terry and Brian were met by two emergency medical technicians as they opened the back of their ambulance.

"Put her here," the EMT told them, pointing to the gurney rolling out of the doors of the white vehicle. Brian and Terry lifted her up and laid her on red padding.

"She was in the bathroom," Terry told the second EMT, a young Hispanic female with glasses and a neck tattoo.

"She is breathing. Pulse is weak." The young woman said as she put her stethoscope in her ears and listened to Peggy's heart. "Come on, we have to get her to the ER," she yelled at the other EMT. Police were on the scene now and the area was getting crowded. Terry looked at Brian.

"You need to get Emma and get out of here," he told his friend. "Go."

"What are you going to do?" Brian asked.

"I'm going to keep my promise," Terry said. "Just go. Go back to Texas. It doesn't matter. Just get away from here as fast as you can." Brian hugged Terry.

"Love you, baby," he said.

"Love you too, brother," Terry responded. The men broke their embrace and Brian walked off. "Hey!" Brian turned around. "Leave Big Blue at the McDonald's." Brian gave a thumbs up and headed off. Terry stood there for a second, watching the ambulance doors close on Peggy.

"Sir," said the female EMT. "Do you want to ride with her?"

"No," Terry said, "which hospital are you taking her to? I'll just meet you there."

"Kindred," she said. "It's right up the road."

"Okay," Terry said. "I'll meet you there." Terry had no intention of meeting them. He knew Peggy didn't have any identification on her and if he wasn't there, she would be admitted as a Jane Doe. He hoped that would buy both her and him enough time to figure out what to do next. The hospital would provide care for her and keep her alive and that was all Terry cared about.

He looked back at the Audi. The firemen had doused the flames at this point. It was a smoldering heap but not actively burning anymore. More police were showing up. Terry knew he needed to get the fuck out of Dodge. The cops may not know enough to arrest him, but he wasn't taking any chances. *How the fuck did they know where we were?* Terry thought to himself as he turned and ran out of the parking lot toward the McDonald's. Peggy's ambulance passed him about fifty yards up the sidewalk. He couldn't do anything but watch as the big machine sped forward with traffic dutifully getting out of its way.

Terry got to the McDonald's parking lot within a few minutes of jogging on the sidewalk along the busy street. Big Blue was there, with Brian and Emma nowhere in sight. *Good.* He pulled open the driver's door and climbed in. The keys were tucked under the visor and fell into his lap when he flipped it down. He pulled the keys from between his legs and started the old truck. The assault pack was still on the passenger seat, he reached behind and felt his FNX still tucked away. Reaching under the seat, he could feel the cold steel of the old Model 12 still hidden. Terry backed the truck out of the parking space and drove away, not yet knowing where he was headed, but knowing he couldn't stay in the immediate area.

He needed to regroup and think. His body was aching, but so was his heart. Seeing Peggy like that was worse than a gut punch. He felt nothing but failure in his bones. He didn't protect her. She was in a hospital bed and he felt responsible. She may even die, and it was his fault. Terry had lost soldiers in combat, men he considered friends and brothers. It seemed weird, even to him, but he took some solace knowing those men knew the risks and they volunteered anyway. They died doing their duty, serving their country. Peggy didn't ask for that. She didn't volunteer. She got blown up because of someone's agenda. The pity was leaving his psyche and slowly being replaced by anger bordering on rage.

Terry knew he had enough Army buddies spread across the country that he could disappear long enough for things to die down, but that wasn't really an option. He knew they would find Peggy, probably in a matter of a few hours and if she wasn't already dead, they would kill her. He didn't have much time and he needed to move. But where? General Dawson was on MacDill and he wasn't likely to leave the base anytime soon, knowing Terry was in Tampa and looking for him. Terry needed to get onto the base to get to Dawson. With any luck, the CIA guy would be there too, and he could end this all at once.

*How did they find us?* he kept thinking. He didn't know everything the trio had done before Emma jumped into Big Blue and scared the shit out of him. *But that was only yesterday. Jesus.* It felt like a lifetime ago. He couldn't even count backward to figure out how many days it had been since the morning he found Peggy chopping wood. He had to assume that not only were they looking for him, but for Big Blue as well. He needed a new vehicle and a way onto MacDill. He knew his name on any form of identification would be a red flag going through the gate. Even his blue retired military ID card wouldn't work.

"I need a new ID card," he said to himself. "And a new vehicle. Where can I get a new ID and a new vehicle?" Terry knew the answer lay somewhere in that thought, but he couldn't think straight. He needed to pull over and stop somewhere. He saw a blue sign on the side of the road with an arrow for Kindred Hospital. He headed that way. Terry knew Peggy was there and he could find something, somewhere near there to take a breather. Terry found the hospital, hoping for a covered parking garage that he could hide out in, but no such luck. He wanted to stay within walking distance but keep Big Blue out of sight as best he could. The muscle memory of old training resurfaced.

Terry unconsciously made a large cloverleaf around the hospital. It was a reconnaissance technique he learned as a Ranger School student so many years ago. Approach the objective from one direction, observe and take notes. Back away far enough to be out of sight of the bad guys, move right, then approach again to get a different perspective. Observe and take notes. You continue the process until you are confident you've seen everything, from every angle. If you drew the process on a piece of paper, it made what looked like a clover with four leaves. In this case, Terry wasn't trying to look at the hospital from every angle, he was looking for something around the hospital, somewhere he could safely park Big Blue, somewhere he could possibly rest and think, and somewhere within walking distance to the hospital.

Terry drove the big truck up a block, over a block, then back toward the hospital. After a few of these 'clover leaf' moves, he found something he thought would give him the respite he needed—a Catholic church. Terry wasn't a religious man, not in the sense his Irish-Italian Catholic mother would have liked. He hadn't been to mass in years. Terry told a number of people throughout his career that he had a good relationship with God but didn't feel the need to sit in church to prove it to anyone. That response generally fended off those trying to encourage him to attend church, most just shrugged and walked away.

Two dumpsters sat at the back of the parking lot in a corner farthest away from the church itself, and out from under the trees that lined the asphalt lot so the big trucks could lift them up and dump their contents without hitting the branches. Terry backed Big Blue into a space next to the dumpsters but under the leafy branches, giving him some shade and maybe even a little cover. He checked his position before he turned off the truck. He couldn't see the street in front of the church, so no one could see his truck unless they pulled into the lot. The dumpsters and trees created some blind spots that he couldn't see around, even after adjusting all the mirrors. It wasn't optimal, but it was good enough for now.

Terry spotted himself in the rearview mirror, his face was covered in ash from the hotel room and his stubble was starting to grow back already. How long had it been since he shaved at Brian and Emma's? Three days? Four? Terry looked down at his clothes, they matched his face. He was filthy. Terry climbed out of the truck and locked it behind him, making for the rear doors of the church. He knew they would have a bathroom inside where he could clean up and maybe a clothing donation box. If he was lucky, he might be able to walk out of the church with a clean face, and even new clothes. Terry climbed the seven steps to the back doors and found them locked after a few good tugs on the worn brass handles.

Assuming the front doors facing the street were open, he decided to walk around the big stone building. Terry turned and began walking down the stone steps only to hear the door open behind him. An elderly man with glasses stuck his head out the door. Terry could see the telltale black shirt and white collar of a priest.

"Can I help you, son?" the priest said.

"I'm sorry, Father," Terry replied. He suddenly felt like an eleven-year-old, late for altar boy duty. "I was just coming in to, um, pray a little bit," he lied.

"Young man," the priest had frustration in his voice, "if you're homeless, I can call the shelter. I can even give you something to eat, but you can't stay here."

"No, Father," Terry replied, "I'm not homeless. Or actually, I am homeless but only temporarily. Have you seen the news? There was an explosion at a motel. The motel I was staying at."

"Oh, heavens," the priest replied. Terry detected a very faint hint of an Irish accent. "Are you hurt, son?" He opened the door wider and stood in it. The man couldn't have been more than five feet tall.

"No, Father," Terry replied, "but there were people who were. I helped get one of them out. A woman. They put her in an ambulance and took her over to the hospital." Terry pointed in the general direction of Kindred Hospital. "I just wanted to pray for her," he lied again. "And maybe clean up a little."

"Well, come on in," the old man said. "We can pray together and get you cleaned up."

## CHAPTER 30

Terry followed the man through the back door of the church and into the sacristy. The immaculate room gave Terry a massive feeling of déjà vu. When he was in Catholic School, the male students would rotate through altar boy duties on a regular basis for the weekly student masses. Terry never volunteered for the Sunday mass duty and certainly not for weddings or funerals; he never considered himself an actual altar boy. The two men moved through a door and out into the church itself. The inside of the building was cool and quiet. There were no parishioners occupying the pews at the moment.

"There is a men's latrine at the front," the priest said. "You can clean up there." Terry eyed the man.

"Latrine?" Terry asked with a smile.

"You're a soldier, aren't you?" the priest said. "From the base. You're a soldier. I can tell. I know a soldier when I see one."

"I am," Terry said. "Or, I was, at least. I'm retired now."

"Retired?" the man said with a smile. "That's good. A soldier's life is a hard one. Making it to retirement is something to be proud of."

"Thank you, Father." Terry could see the man was waiting for him to ask a question, "Were you a soldier?" The priest snapped into a British-style open-handed salute.

"Ceannaire O'Connor," he said. The old man stood straighter. He seemed taller. "That's a corporal. I served in the Irish Army for a bit. Before you were born, probably. Before *the troubles*. You know about the troubles?" Terry nodded his head.

As a kid, he had heard his Irish grandfather talk about what was going on in Ireland, especially amongst his countrymen. Most of those men, unlike like his grandfather, regarded what was happening in Ireland and Northern Ireland as something they should all be worried about. They spoke about the "damn Protestants" and would always contribute in the pubs when the hat was passed around for *the cause.* Terry's grandfather called the men "beer brave" or said they had "Stout courage," referring to the dark beer they all consumed by the pint. His grandfather never worried himself with the dealings in the old country. They had their problems and we had ours, he would tell his young grandson.

When Terry was a student at the US Army Command and General Staff College at Fort Leavenworth, counterinsurgency was all the rage. Iraq and Afghanistan were the focus and that was the fight the Army was in. Other students delved deep into the Russian writings about Afghanistan or the US experience in Vietnam. Terry spent time reading about Belfast and Algeria and how the Brits and French had fought the insurgencies in those locations. Terry knew about *the troubles.*

"I'm familiar," he told Father O'Connor. "I appreciate your help, Father." Terry turned and walked down one of the side aisles toward the front of the church and the latrine. Inside, he cleaned himself up, washing his face and his arms. The priest walked in with a clean shirt in his hands.

"Put this on and throw that other one away," O'Connor told him. He pointed to the medal on Terry's dog tags. "Saint Michael?" The old man's expression had changed as the priest turned and left. It wasn't the jovial smile Terry first encountered. Terry thought about putting on the shirt and leaving through the front door, but he was curious. He walked back into the church, finding Father O'Connor speaking to another man. Terry stood back to avoid interrupting the conversation. The other man turned and went back toward the sacristy, Father O'Connor gave Terry a beckoning wave. Terry felt in is gut, it was time to leave.

"Father," Terry said, "thanks for your help. I think I am going to go over to the hospital and check on that lady I helped."

"No, son," the little man said. "You can't go over to the hospital. You need to come with me." Terry froze. O'Connor looked at him. "Whatever trouble you're in, son, we need to talk about it. And not here where someone can see you. Follow me." Terry followed the priest out of the rear of the church and through the trees to a house next door. It was the clergy house where Terry assumed Father O'Connor lived, probably with another priest or two from the parish. Neither man spoke as they walked. Terry felt like he needed to trust the priest. Somewhere in his head there was a bad joke about an altar boy trusting a priest, but his tired brain couldn't piece it together. They walked through the side door of the clergy house and into the kitchen. Terry could hear a television coming from the next room. The man Terry saw speaking to O'Connor inside the church appeared.

"Hello," the man said. "I'm Father D'Ambrosio. Welcome," he held out his hand. Terry took it.

"Sit down," O'Connor said. "We will get you some food and then we will talk. All three of us." The two men busied themselves getting cold cuts, mayonnaise, and bread together for sandwiches. Father O'Connor pulled three Guinness bottles from the refrigerator. Terry looked at the Italian priest and then at the dark bottles of Irish Stout. "I'm converting him," O'Connor said.

"Yes," D'Ambrosio said. "He is trying to convince me this is better than wine." He laughed. "He is trying, but it isn't working."

"Thank you," Terry said as he took the paper plate with a ham sandwich from Father O'Connor. The old man sat next to him.

"Listen to me, son," O'Connor started, "that explosion you talked about is on the news. And so are you. And a woman." Terry hesitated while biting into the sandwich. "The news is saying she is a terrorist and they are looking for you." Terry set the sandwich down. He looked at both men.

"What else are they saying?" he asked.

"They said her car blew up accidentally," D'Ambrosio said, "at the hotel. That it was a car bomb meant for something else, but the police don't know what for. They said she was a terrorist." Terry was taking all this in. It was playing out almost like he predicted, except for the accidental detonation. "And they had a picture of a man that looks like you, but with a beard. They didn't give a name."

"And we don't want to know your name," O'Connor broke in. "Son, I believe you to be a God-fearing man. Maybe even a Catholic. I saw that medal around your neck. I don't believe you're a terrorist. You need to tell us what happened." Terry knew the priests had some kind of protection if this was a confession, like attorney-client privilege for a lawyer, but he wasn't sure what the parameters were.

"Father," Terry said, "it's probably better if you don't know everything. For your own sake."

"Dammit, son," O'Connor said. Terry was shocked by the curse coming from the old priest. "We are here to help you, but you have to be honest with us." The old man was stern. He was an old-school priest and had probably doled out some physical punishment in his life, especially to young men who stepped out of line.

"Okay, Father." Terry proceeded to recount the previous few days. He left out killing all the Smiths and even lessened the activities between him and the SEAL platoon at Peggy's farm. He didn't lie to the two men as much as he left out details. He was aware the more these two men knew, whether they were priests or not, the more they were at risk. Father D'Ambrosio had wide eyes at the end of the story. Father O'Connor never changed expression. Not once. Then he spoke.

"Anthony," he looked at the other priest. "Go to the hospital. See what the condition of the woman is. Before you go, get the truck from the church lot and put it in the garage." He turned to Terry. "Give him the keys. We don't have a car, so the garage is empty."

"Father," Terry said almost in shock, "why are you doing this?"

"Son," O'Connor said, "this is what we do. What the church does or is supposed to do. We help people in need." Father D'Ambrosio stood and held out his hand for the keys. Terry reached into his pocket and handed them over. "People lose their way, but not you. You are doing what you can to protect this woman. To protect all of us. If these men are doing what you say they are, and the government is involved, then our church and our religion is in danger as well." Terry was dumbfounded. That was a hell of a leap for this man to make, but he wasn't wrong.

"Thank you, Father," Terry said. O'Connor stood and walked into the room with the television. Father D'Ambrosio left with the keys and Terry heard Big Blue come up the drive in a couple of minutes. He was eating his sandwich alone in the kitchen when Father O'Connor returned.

"Anthony will walk over to the hospital and ask about the woman," he told Terry. "No one questions a priest when he asks about an injured person. We have been over there many times after car accidents, shootings, and even hurricanes. If it is on the news, no one asks." Terry nodded. "You can stay here as long as you need to." The old man turned and walked back into the TV room. Terry stood up and followed him. The news was on the television and the screen was showing live footage from a helicopter of the hotel explosion.

Terry stood there, drinking the Guinness. Father O'Connor was on the couch. The living room of the clergy house probably hadn't been updated in fifty years, except the television itself. The furniture and decorations reminded Terry of his Italian grandmother's living room, without the plastic on everything. O'Connor turned and looked at Terry.

"We will get you some clean pants," he said, then turned back to the news. Terry could see the charred Audi being loaded onto a flatbed truck. The hotel was still smoldering a little. The newscaster was describing the explosion as *devastating*. The only casualty being reported was Peggy. They flashed her picture on the screen and Terry felt sick. It was the photo from her military issued identification card. Clearly someone inside DoD had fed them the photo. She was being described as *the bomber*, a *domestic terrorist*, and a *radical Islamist sympathizer*. It made Terry sick to his stomach.

"They've convicted her already," Father O'Connor said.

"What?" Terry asked. He was confused. "What do you mean, Father?"

"You said she was unconscious, right?" O'Connor said, not taking his eyes from the TV. "No one has even spoken to her, yet. They've made her out to be all these things. How do they know?" Terry realized the old priest was right. Dawson and whoever he was working with were getting what they wanted. They had manufactured their own domestic terrorist.

"Because that is what they were told," Terry said. This had all the tentacles he assumed it had. The media message was being fed to them, even her picture. There was no mention made of her computer, the manifesto document, or even her dead Muslim husband. She was a doctor who focused on Middle Eastern studies, that was it. It was all being controlled. And Dawson knew where they were staying, he had said so on the phone. They had to have known to get the Audi there. And they had to have known in real time. No one knew they were headed to Tampa, so they were followed. One truck or the other was followed.

"What are you thinking, son?" Father O'Connor turned to look at Terry.

"I'm thinking that I've put you in danger, Father," Terry said. "And that I need to leave."

"Son," Father O'Connor stood up. "I've been in danger before. So has Anthony."

"Not like this, Father," Terry said. "Not with men like this." The old man laughed at him.

"Why are these men different?" O'Connor said with a smile.

"Anthony was a priest in Sicily, right from the seminary. There were dangerous men there. Then he was in Thailand. There are dangerous men there, too." Terry opened his mouth and the old man raised his hand to stop him. "I was a Catholic priest in the favelas in Brazil. And outside Juarez in Mexico. There are dangerous men there, too." Terry quickly gained even more admiration for these two men that had taken him in. "These men you've told us about, they are no different."

Father D'Ambrosio came in the kitchen door. Terry knew what he was going to say before the words came out of his mouth.

"I'm sorry, son," he said. "She's dead."

## CHAPTER 31

Terry Davis went cold. It was the same reaction he'd had a dozen or more times in his career. All emotion left him. There was no sadness. There was no anger. There was nothing. Whether it was a subconscious defense mechanism or not, it worked for him. He would grieve later, just like he had done in the past. At some point, in private, he would grieve. But not now. Now, he focused.

"Son," Anthony said. "Did you hear me?"

"Yes, Father," Terry responded, "I heard you. That doesn't change the situation."

"Young man," Father O'Connor said, touching his arm. "Why don't you sit. We can pray for her together."

"Father," Terry said, his voice level and cold, "I appreciate your concern, but really, I need to figure out how I'm going to get onto the base and get to the general." The two priests looked at each other. Father O'Connor had seen this reaction before, from the World War II veterans he served with in the Army. He knew there was emotion, somewhere deep inside the young man standing in front of him, but he knew it wasn't going to surface any time soon.

"Okay, okay," Father O'Connor said to Terry. He raised his hand to Father D'Ambrosio, softly shaking his head as if to say, "Let him be."

"What can we do to help?" Father D'Ambrosio asked, taking the hint from his elder.

"Right now, Father," Terry replied. "I need some sleep. Maybe an hour."

"Sleep, yes," Father O'Connor agreed, "that's a good idea. We have an empty room. The bed is made, and there are clean sheets. If you want to shower, we have that, too. Better than the sink in the men's room."

"The answer to this is probably no," Terry said. "but do you have anything stronger than this Guinness? Not a lot, just a mouthful to help my brain rest."

"I have just the thing," Father O'Connor said. He shuffled off to the kitchen and after opening and closing some cabinets, he returned with a bottle of Basil Hayden's whiskey and three glasses. The elder priest poured two fingers of the brown liquid into each glass. The three men stood there for a second until Father O'Connor raised his glass and then tipped it without saying a word. The other two followed suit.

"Thanks, Father," Terry said and started up the narrow stairs.

"The one on the right," Father D'Ambrosio called after him. Terry opened the door to find a spartan room. A bed, a chair, and a nightstand with a lamp was all the room contained. He didn't even turn on the light, he just fell backward onto the bed.

"Now, how the hell am I going to get onto the base?" he said quietly. His mind began to race. His thoughts would alternate between Peggy and MacDill AFB. How did they do this? All of this? He knew the why. He knew some of the who. He didn't know the how. How did they get the Audi there that quickly? How did they know where the four of them were staying? He could see Peggy chopping wood. Standing over the deputy she had just pistol whipped. Sleeping in the Jeep as he drove. Bloody and unconscious in the hotel. He faded into sleep.

When Terry awoke, it was dark. *Where am I? What time is it?* His mind started to clear. He was in the clergy house. He pushed the button on the side of his watch—2109. He sat up and turned on the lamp. There were clean pants and a new clean shirt at the foot of the bed. On the chair was a new pair of boxer shorts and a pair of socks, sitting on top of a towel. He stood up and stepped into the hallway. He could smell food cooking downstairs. It smelled like his grandmother's spaghetti sauce. She always called it *gravy*. The bathroom was opposite his room, on the other side of the staircase. The light was on, but no one was inside. Terry retreated into the bedroom, grabbed the clothes and the towel, and headed to the bathroom.

The shower water was hot and the exhaust fan in the bathroom didn't work, so the small space filled quickly with steam. Terry washed his body and his hair, taking special care to wash the little bit of Peggy's blood off his left forearm. He felt as if he was going to cry, but it never came. He stepped out of the shower and toweled off. It was tight, dressing in the small space. He almost fell over onto the white ceramic tile more than once. When he left the bathroom, he was fully dressed. He came down the stairs, turning left into the kitchen to find Father D'Ambrosio standing over the stove and stirring red sauce in a white apron.

"Just in time," the dark-featured man said. "We usually eat in front of the television. There is a plate there on the table. Serve yourself." Terry grabbed the plate and filled it with a moderate amount of pasta, then covered it in sauce, and grabbed a piece of Italian bread from the counter. The priest handed him a fork and a spoon. "For spinning the pasta," he said.

"My grandmother was Italian, Father," he said with a smile. "I'm familiar, thank you." The priest smiled back.

"Then you'll be having wine with your dinner?" Anthony said.

"Actually, Father," Terry said thinking of his tiny grandmother, "I never developed a taste for wine. At grandma's when she served pasta, you either drank wine or milk. No soda allowed. I always chose milk. Do you have any?" The priest smiled.

"Of course," he said. "Go sit. I'll bring you a glass. Father O'Connor is already eating." Terry walked into the TV room and sat at one of the armchairs with a wooden folding TV tray in front of it. Father

O'Connor was watching the news. There was still coverage of the explosion dominating the local channels.

"Did you sleep well, Mr. Davis?" Father O'Connor asked, staring at the TV. Terry stopped his fork halfway between the plate and his mouth.

"Father?" he said.

"They are talking about you on the news," he said. "Terry Davis, retired Army officer." Terry felt sick. He put the forkful of pasta back on his plate. "They said you saved that woman and the police are looking for you. You disappeared. They are calling you a good Samaritan." Terry thought for a moment.

"They want people to be looking for me, but not to raise an alarm," Terry guessed. "They don't want an entire city panicked about a terrorist on the loose."

"Have you considered turning yourself in?" O'Connor asked him.

"Father," Terry said, resuming his eating, "if I turn myself in, the FBI or someone else will have me in custody in less than an hour. And then I'm dead."

"That is what Anthony said," the old priest said. "So, what are you going to do?"

"It's probably better that you don't know, Father," Terry said around a mouthful of bread. Father D'Ambrosio joined them. He handed Terry a glass of milk. "Thank you," he said taking the glass.

"Are you going onto the base?" Antonio asked. Terry just looked at him, not giving any indication of his intentions. Father O'Connor turned and looked at him.

"Mr. Davis," he said, "we have taken you in. We have fed you. We have clothed you. We have done everything the church would expect us to do to help another man. I won't ask you for your confession because I don't think you will give it to me. Anthony and I will pray for you tonight. God will give you the clarity you need." Terry looked at the old man. Out of the corner of his eye, Terry saw the newscast flash to a commercial for a Gentleman's club in Tampa. His eyes lit up and the two men watched his reaction to the television.

"I don't think," Anthony said, "that is the satisfaction you are looking for Mr. Davis."

"You're absolutely right, Father," Terry said. His mind was spinning. That was it, a strip club. He needed a strip club. "Do either of you know how to cut hair?"

"I learned in seminary," Anthony said. The two priests shared a confused look. "We learned to cut each other's hair."

"He cuts my hair every other week," O'Connor added.

"Father," Terry said, finally breaking away from the TV, "I need you to cut my hair. A military style cut. Can you do that?" The priests shared another look.

"I can," Father D'Ambrosio responded. "I believe I can. Yes."

"Son," O'Connor said softly, "what are you getting at? Where is all of this headed? You cannot get onto the base. They will be looking for you."

"I know they will, Father," Terry said. "So, I won't be going as me." The confusion between the priests deepened. "I'll explain while Father D is cutting my hair."

"Go, Anthony," O'Connor said, "get your things. Cut his hair and we will listen." Father D'Ambrosio left and went upstairs. O'Connor grabbed Terry by the arm and lead him into the kitchen, leaving a plate full of pasta sitting in the TV room on the wooden tray. Terry stood in front of the refrigerator while Father O'Connor rearranged the table and pulled out a chair. They clearly had a system and Terry wasn't about to disturb it. The other priest returned with a leather shaving bag and a white sheet over his forearm like a waiter in a cartoon. He waved a hand at the chair and Terry sat.

Father O'Connor maneuvered a chair off to the side, close enough to listen to Terry but also giving the younger priest room to move around. The amateur barber draped the sheet over Terry, reaching into the leather bag for a clip to secure it tightly around his neck.

Father D'Ambrosio busied himself preparing his clippers and scissors.

"So, what are we doing here?" Father O'Connor asked. "Why the haircut?"

"You are right," Terry said. "I need to get onto the base. And they will be looking for me. I need an ID card to get through the gate."

"How do you want it cut?" Father D broke in. The two men looked up at him quizzically. "A military cut. Nevermind." He answered his own question and began to comb and snip the top of Terry's head.

"I need an ID card," Terry continued, "and a car. They probably know the truck and will be looking for that, too. You said the two of you don't have a car, so I need to get one."

"Do you have enough money for a car?" Anthony asked while he took snipped layers of hair from the top of Terry's head.

"Anthony," Father O'Connor spoke. He was getting impatient. "He is going to take a car. Steal one, right?" He looked at Terry. Terry suddenly became uncomfortable talking about stealing in front of two priests. "Cut his hair and let him talk. Please," he waved his hand for Terry to continue.

"Yes, Father," Terry said. "I am going to take a car, and an ID card, but I need to find someone who looks like me. A soldier who looks like me." Father D'Ambrosio stopped cutting hair, opening his mouth to ask a question. He was stopped by a glare from the older man. "All soldiers look generally the same with a short haircut. They are looking for a man with longer hair and a beard, right? That's what my picture looked like on TV?"

"Yes," Father O'Connor replied. "So, you get rid of the long hair and you shave. Now you look like a soldier. Then what?"

"Then I find a soldier who looks like me," Terry replied, "and I take his car and ID and I can get onto the base."

"At the club," Father O'Connor concluded, "with the dancing girls. You'll find a soldier there. You will find a drunk soldier there and you will take his ID and his keys."

Terry smiled. "You're pretty smart, Father," Terry said.

"And then what will you do?" the older man asked. "What will you do once you get onto the base?"

"One step at a time, Father," Terry said. He knew what he was going to do once he got onto the base, but he couldn't share that with the two priests. Terry sat quietly while Father D finished his haircut. He handed Terry a small mirror from the leather bag to look at himself. It was a high and tight military cut, just like the one Terry had worn for his entire career. He saw a much younger man in the mirror, someone he barely recognized. "That's great work, Father. If this priest thing doesn't work out, you can always become a barber." The three men smiled. Terry stood and brushed himself off.

*Keep moving, keep shooting,* he thought.

## CHAPTER 32

Terry didn't want to take Brian's truck, but he didn't want to walk on the street either. He knew the more people that saw him, the higher the possibility of him being recognized, even with his new haircut and fresh shave. He had never taken an Uber or Lyft before, but he knew taxi drivers didn't pay much attention to their customers so he would rather assume risk there. Chances of a cab driver making eye contact with him were slim and he was right. He stood on the corner a couple of blocks from the clergy house and hailed a cab. He had less than sixty dollars left in his pocket.

He hadn't been to a strip club in years. He chuckled to himself in the back of the cab. Brian still referred to them as *titty bars*. Terry assumed there would be a cover charge to get in the door and probably a drink minimum. He didn't know how long he would have to wait to find a soldier that resembled him enough to pass for, so he may have to tip some dancers to keep the bouncers off his back. He hoped tonight's little adventure was a one-time thing. He didn't think he had enough money left for a second night of this and he damn sure wasn't going to ask the priests for a stack of singles to go back to a titty bar.

The cab ride was short, but Terry saw all the familiarities of a military town. Even though this was Tampa, he still saw the used car lots, fast food places, tattoo parlors, bars, and pawn shops that existed in every military town in America. These places had been preying on young soldiers, sailors, marines, and airmen since the beginning of time. Maybe the wares had changed, but the victims remained. Terry always heard that prostitution was the oldest profession, but he was pretty sure the profession of arms came first and whores came as a result. Towns like this all had the same feel.

The cab pulled up in front of the club, the neon lights on the outside giving away any attempt at discretion. Terry paid the driver and walked to the door. The man standing there was massive. Like NFL defensive lineman big. Terry could see as he got closer, the man was a Pacific Islander. Hawaiian, or Samoan. Maybe from Guam. Terry quickly recalled the dozen or so soldiers he had served with from that part of the world throughout his career. To a man, they were all very good soldiers and all huge men with contagious smiles.

"Hey, boss," Terry said casually to the man.

"Twenty to get in," the big man said, holding out his hand. "Two drink minimum. Keep your fucking hands off the ladies."

"Yes, sir," Terry said as he fished a twenty-dollar bill from his pocket. He handed the man the money and began to walk through the door when he felt the huge paw grab his arm. Terry knew he couldn't take the man, even on his best day, and he wasn't looking for a fight. He froze and looked at the man.

"I know you," the big man said. "From Afghanistan. Back in two thousand and two." Terry couldn't place the man. He definitely wasn't a soldier in his infantry company. "You were a captain. I was on the Civil Affairs team." Terry had a decision to make. He could deny this man's recollection and potentially escalate the situation, or he could treat the man like an old friend.

"Damn, dude!" Terry had decided on the latter. "That was forever ago. You doing this on the side or is this a full-time gig?" The big man laughed.

"I got out in oh-three," he said. "Uniforms got too small for my big ass." That infectious smile came beaming through. There was a line forming behind him. "You have any issues in there, come get me." The big man shook his hand and Terry went inside. He had intended to keep a low profile and not draw any attention, but that was clearly out the window after the interaction with the big bouncer. Hopefully, there wouldn't be any incidents inside that would require the help of the big islander, but it wasn't a bad thing to have a man like that on your side in a fight.

Terry found a table off to the side and settled in. The vinyl chair wasn't even warm yet when a tall waitress came to him for his drink order. She wasn't a dancer; she didn't have the build for it. Standing over six feet tall in her heels and fishnet stockings, she was very skinny and didn't have the boobs or the ass most men wanted to see on stage. She wore boy shorts and a bikini top, showing off an impressive array of tattoos on her arms and torso. She smiled at Terry. It was a tired smile, but friendly. Terry decided that whatever cash he had at the end of the night was going to this woman.

"Whatever your cheapest beer is," he said. She scowled at him. A cheap drinker wasn't usually a great tipper. She returned with a bottle of Heineken. He looked up at her.

"It's a buck," she said. "I covered the rest. You going to run a tab?" She was trying to make nice with him, hoping for a better tip.

"No," he said. He pulled his remaining cash out of his pocket. After the cab ride and the cover, he had twenty-three dollars left. He kept the three singles and handed her the ten and two fives. She smiled at him. He waved her down to speak in her ear over the music. "When this one is gone, bring me one more. Keep the rest of the money for yourself." She stood up and smiled at him. Normally, the sober men didn't treat her like that, only the drunks.

Terry realized he was assuming a lot of risk. The bouncer already recognized him and now he was being overly friendly to the skinny waitress. He didn't know if he would need either or both of them tonight, but this operation of his had to work. He also knew, in the back of his head, that he wasn't likely to leave MacDill AFB alive so drawing just a little attention in the short term was a risk worth taking.

Terry sat back and watched the room. Men flowed in and out

over the next hour, but no one fit what he was looking for. Terry needed a man who looked like him. Build didn't matter because height and weight weren't on a military ID card. A white male, about his age who was a soldier, that was what he needed, but there was more. He needed a man that came into the club committed to getting drunk, drunk enough that Terry could steal his keys and ID card. It could be a loner, like him, or one of a group of men. He kept scanning the room. Ten minutes before, the skinny waitress had handed Terry his second and final beer and smiled as she walked away. Now she was back and plopped down into the chair next to him.

"What's your deal?" she said over the music. Terry looked at her suspiciously.

"My deal?" he asked her. "What do you mean?"

"You're clearly not interested in the dancers," she said. Terry just noticed she had black lipstick on. "Are you waiting for someone?"

"Yeah," he said. It wasn't a lie. He was waiting for someone; he just didn't know who it was yet. "A buddy. He comes here sometimes. He played a pretty bad joke on me. I'm going to pay him back." He was improvising and trying not to be a dick at the same time.

"What did he do?" she said. She put her heels up on the chair and tucked her legs into her chest.

"It's pretty bad," Terry said. He couldn't come up with anything on the fly. "I'd rather not say. Pretty embarrassing." A man walked into the room that may fit the bill for what Terry needed. He was short, but about the right age. Same hair color.

"Mister," she said, "I work in a strip joint where I couldn't get a job as a stripper." Terry took his eyes off the man and looked at her. "Not many things more embarrassing than that." She smiled. He smiled back. He realized Peggy would be furious right now. Even if he was doing it to accomplish something, flirting with this girl would piss her off. Then he realized it had been hours since she even crossed his mind. His expression visibly changed. She stood up. "Nevermind," she said. "I'll go waste my time on someone else."

"Wait," he said. "You still working?" She looked confused. "Waitressing, I mean. You can help me."

"I'm not on the clock, but I'll help you," she said. "But, you'll owe me." She smiled again. Terry guessed this was the most anyone had flirted with her, or maybe even talked to her, in a while and she was enjoying it. She sat back down. "What do you need me to do?"

Terry took a good look at the woman for the first time. Under the makeup and tattoos, she was probably very pretty. Built like she was, Terry assumed she never attracted many men and probably lacked self-confidence as a result. The outward persona masked in ink and eyeliner was full of confidence. Inside was a different story. He pointed to the man sitting by himself across the room.

"You see that guy over there?" She spotted the man across the room. "That's my buddy. I need you to get him shitfaced."

"That's not hard to do," she said. "He does that about every week in here. Why do you need him drunk?"

"Because I am going to take his ID card and his car," Terry said. Her eyes got wide. "He lives on the base and I want to get him stranded out here. Make him call his wife to come get him either here or at the gate."

"Damn," she said. "That's fucking cold." She smiled. The smile was sinister, not the same friendly smile she gave Terry earlier. There was something behind it that Terry couldn't put his finger on. "I can probably get his keys and his wallet for you." Terry snapped a look at her. He didn't expect that kind of help. He opened his mouth to stop her, but she was up and moving to the bar. After a brief conversation with the bartender, she walked toward Terry's target with two glasses in her hand. She sat down next to the man and handed him one of the glasses. There was a brief exchange and the two downed the drinks, the whole time she rubbed his thigh. She made her way back over to Terry.

"Two more of those," she said as she leaned forward and

whispered in his ear, "and he'll be wrecked." Terry motioned her back down.

"I don't want to know what's in it," he said, "but how come you can drink so many?" She laughed at him, leaning back.

"Because mine is water," she said. It was an old stripper's trick. Get a guy to buy you a shot, the bartender puts soda or water in the shot glass. You stay sober and keep the money instead. "I'll be back. And you are definitely going to owe me."

Terry thought about what that was going to mean for him. He assumed she wanted more than a ride home and he wasn't in the mood for fucking. At first glance, she wasn't his type. Not even close. He didn't mind the tattoos or even that she was thin as a rail, but there was something else about her that would have turned him off, probably like most other men. But, after talking to her and her willingness to help out, on most other nights Terry would have reconsidered and maybe even went home with her. Not tonight, though, and he would have to figure out how to get out of it.

The waitress made two more trips to sit with the other man and share a drink, not returning to talk to Terry between. He watched her. She had done this before, or something like it. Terry could see his "buddy" getting hit with the effect of the potent level of alcohol he was consuming. It was after midnight by Terry's watch. This needed to happen quickly. He intended on going straight onto the base once he got the ID and the car. If he waited until the next morning, the car and ID would likely be reported stolen and he would be back to square one. The waitress walked back over to his table.

"C'mon," she said. She grabbed Terry's hand and he followed. The two walked through the back of the club, past the dancer's dressing room and past an office where Terry caught a glimpse of one of the dancers giving a patron a blowjob. He assumed his waitress had something similar in mind when she pushed open the back door to the club. The lights in the parking lot were bright and Terry could see the woman clearly now. The lowlight of the strip club didn't do her justice, Terry was shocked at how attractive she was. She held out her other hand. "Here you go," she said. There was a set of keys, a wallet, and a cellphone. "Time to pay up."

"I don't know what you have in mind," Terry started. She cut him off.

"I'm not a fucking whore," she said. "Get that straight. I helped you because you were about as nice to me as anyone has been since I started working here." Terry stood there impatiently. He needed to get moving and this was eating into his time. "And because that guy attacked me a couple of months ago. Your buddy."

"He's not my buddy," Terry said. The waitress paused. She was confused. "I don't even know that guy. I just need his car and his ID," he said. "You can have his wallet and whatever is in it. I don't give a shit." He took the white military ID card out of the wallet and tossed her the leather billfold.

"You are stealing his car?" she asked. "That's what this is about? And you got me to do it for you? That's some kind of grift, mister."

"This isn't a grift," Terry said. "You don't want to know what this is. And I need to get going." Terry hit the unlock button on the key and looked around for which car beeped and flashed its lights. "What's your name?"

"Aimee," she said. "With two E's"

"Aimee," Terry said, walking toward a white convertible Mustang, "the best thing you can do is forget you ever met me. Forget about me, and this car, and this whole night." Terry climbed into the Mustang and fired the engine. He left her standing there and headed back to the church parking lot, tossing the cell phone out the window of the Mustang as he drove away. He didn't need someone else's phone tracking his movements all night.

He pulled the Mustang to the back of the lot and snuck through the trees to the garage behind the clergy house. Opening the door on the side of the garage, he found Big Blue still sitting there. He was moving quietly, trying not to make a sound and alert the priests or anyone else that he was inside. Terry fished the FNX out from behind his assault pack and then slid the Model 12 out from under the seat. He thought about the small arsenal sitting at the bottom of Larry's dry well in Nebraska and how useful that hardware would be right now. He threw the assault pack over his shoulder and peeked out the side door. The clergy house was dark and there was no one in sight. He moved quickly to the Mustang and put the guns in the trunk. Sitting in the driver's seat, he paused and thought through what he was about to do. His watch said 0104. Plenty of darkness to work with. He fired the engine and drove the stolen Mustang toward the main gate of MacDill Air Force Base.

## CHAPTER 33

Terry Davis pulled up to the main gate and slowed the Mustang to a stop. Only one lane was being manned since it was after 0100 and the amount of traffic was almost zero. These were Department of Defense security guards and not uniformed servicemembers or a contracted security company. Terry could see they were in black uniforms and full body armor before he even got to the gate. The area was well lit by overhead electric lighting and Terry was hoping the guard wouldn't look too closely at the ID card. There was a tense second as the guard flipped over the white plastic card and scanned the back. It took almost two full seconds before the scanner gun beeped acceptance of the ID card, clearing Terry to enter the base. It felt like an eternity.

Terry pulled away slowly, watching the guard in his sideview mirror as he gained distance from the gate. He drove slowly through the big military installation, knowing the Air Force Special Police were probably the only other cars on the road. The last thing he needed was to get pulled over. He had been here before, but never in the housing area where the military families lived and never driving around in the middle of the damn night. He knew about where the housing was for all the generals and hoped he could find it in the dark. Finding general officer housing on an Army base was pretty easy for the most part. Find the oldest, biggest houses and that's where the generals lived. Terry was hoping the Air Force operated the same way.

After a bit of searching, Terry found Dawson's quarters. It was a huge home, more than any two people needed. Terry had heard a number of generals complain over the years about the extravagance of their quarters. Most of them said the same thing: "I needed this when I was a major and had four kids at home!" Four-stars across the services were normally in their late fifties or early sixties and had few, if any, kids running around. Usually, it was just them and their spouse occupying the government quarters. Terry had never heard Boo-Boo or Tammy complain like that. Never. For the two of them, it had always been about their image and the big house was something they felt they deserved whether they needed it or not. Terry saw Tammy's Porsche in the driveway, along with Boo-Boo's big Chevy Suburban and two government sedans parked out front.

The Air Force police normally kept a car near the housing for the bigwigs, able to respond quickly to any call in a matter of moments. Most military police commanders learned early the quickest way to get on the general's shit list was to take too long responding to a complaint. Terry deliberately parked a few streets over, deciding it was best to walk his way in. He parked the Mustang and grabbed the suppressed pistol and the shotgun from the trunk. He shoved a spare pistol magazine and a handful of spare shells into the pockets of the pants provided through the goodness of the Catholic church. The irony wasn't lost on him.

Moving quickly in the darkness, Terry carried the FNX at the ready in his right hand, the Model 12 by the receiver in his left. He didn't anticipate having to use either before he got to Dawson's house, but if he needed to, it would certainly be the silenced pistol over the cannon-like sound of the scattergun. He found the back of the Dawson place and waited quietly in the trees, watching. His mind raced through the last few days. He remembered the deputies, George and Juanita, the hideout and the three men named Smith that came for them in the darkness. He thought about Larry covering his ass at the farmhouse with his lever-action Winchester and dumping the Suburban in the old strip mine. He could hear Brian laughing and cussing in his head and the sight of Emma and her ass cheek sticking out of her shorts. He wondered briefly where they were and if they were safe. He thought about the fight with the SEAL team and saying goodbye to Larry after he had saved his ass a second time. There was the hotel and the blast and Peggy in his arms. Peggy. He thought about the graciousness and safety offered to him by the two priests who owed him nothing and to whom he owed his safety when all of Tampa was looking for him. He thought about the lanky stripper named Aimee. And Peggy. He thought long and hard about Peggy and that she didn't deserve to die. But Dawson did. Dawson and everyone he was working with. They would pay tonight for Peggy. Peggy.

Terry took a deep breath and really smelled the salty air for the first time. He had forgotten how close the water was. There were still lights on in the house, but he couldn't see anyone moving. Dawson was allocated both an aide de camp—a lieutenant colonel—and an enlisted aide who handled the cooking for large events, the general's uniform, and a myriad of other tasks. Terry assumed both of them were long gone at this hour. Four people, maybe six. Dawson, Tammy, and maybe two people for each of the government sedans parked out front. He could manage six people.

As he stepped through the trees, a man came out the back door. *Bingo.* He wouldn't have to break into the house, the door was open. The man looked to be in his late twenties, wearing a suit. He reached into the suitcoat pocket and produced a pack of cigarettes, lighting one in the dark. The young man turned and looked back into the house, as if he were checking to see if anyone knew he had snuck away. Terry knew that once he left these bushes, there was no turning back. He committed, moving quickly from his concealed position. Terry closed the distance between him and the man in a flash. With his left hand, he swung the shotgun, hitting the man in the back of the neck with the barrel. The man crumpled to the ground, unconscious.

Terry quietly opened the back door and dragged the man inside by the collar of his gray suitcoat. Frisking him and checking his pockets, Terry found a Sig Sauer pistol in a waistband holster and a wallet with an ID card inside that only identified the man as a member of the State Department. His name was Jeffrey Johnson. If he was carrying a gun on a military installation, he was likely CIA. Terry unloaded the pistol and threw it and the magazine out in the grass then closed the door. Terry hadn't anticipated having to tie someone up. He grabbed the only thing he could find in the immaculate kitchen—a cell phone charging cord stuck in one of the outlets. It wasn't as long as he would have liked, but he didn't have another option. *Let's just hope this does the job*, he thought as he tied the man's wrists. Terry stopped to listen and heard nothing.

He moved slowly but deliberately through the kitchen and into the dining room. Light came from the open door that led to the basement. Terry knew the SCIF was down there and he likely just had to follow the light to find Dawson and whoever else was with him. He acted as if he were supposed to be there, like he was Jeffrey Johnson who was lying in the kitchen, out cold. He came down the stairs in a hurry, dropping the .45 pistol on the carpet as he opened the door to the secure room. Dawson froze as Terry entered the room, leading with the big barreled, pump action shotgun. It was only Dawson and the guy from the photos. The one they assumed was CIA. Dawson started to stand, as the man in the suit reached for the pistol at his waist.

"Don't fucking move," Terry said as he closed the door behind him. "Sit down, sir. And you," Terry said, pointing the business end of the shotgun at the nameless man, "slowly pull that pistol out and put it on the ground." The man did as he was instructed.

"Terry," Dawson said in a tone filled with disbelief, "what are you doing here?"

"Sir," Terry said talking with the shotgun stock still at his cheek, "I told you. I made you a promise. If she was hurt, I was coming to kill you. Now she's dead and I'm here to keep that promise."

"And who's fault is that, Mr. Davis?" the man in the suit asked.

"Really. Isn't it your fault she's dead?" The barrel of the shotgun was less than twelve inches from the man's face when Terry thrust it forward into his forehead, breaking the skin and knocking the man backward. There was a red, bleeding circle above the man's left eye. Dawson started to stand again.

"I said, sit the fuck down." Terry swung the shotgun at the general. Dawson put his ass back into the leather seat. "Now, who the fuck are *you?*" Terry asked the man in the suit. The man was trying to wipe the blood away from his forehead.

"He's an advisor," Dawson said.

"Advisor my ass," Terry said. "And I wasn't talking to you, sir." He focused back toward the bleeding man in the suit. "Now, answer my goddamn question."

"General Dawson is right," he said regaining his composure and standing erect. "I am an advisor. The people I work for are the same people that are going to insert him as the CIA director. The same people that sent the SEAL platoon after you. Nice work, by the way." He was avoiding the direct answer and starting to piss Terry off. "We watched the whole thing on the live feed. I thought they had you when the trucks came in, but you did well."

"Live feed?" Terry's pulse was up and his brain was moving quickly. "You guys had a fucking drone flying?" Dawson and his bleeding advisor were silent. "You watched that whole thing?"

"It actually was a stroke of luck that we had a Predator flying," the advisor said, referring to the MQ-1 Predator. The unmanned aerial vehicle can remain in flight for over twelve hours and can be armed with Hellfire missiles. "We kept eyes on you all night and into the next day. It helped us track you when you started moving. And then eventually to the hotel."

"You motherfucker," Terry had the answer to what had been eating him. "You tracked me and moved Peggy's car behind me."

"Well, yes," the suit said. "I told you before, it was your fault she was dead. We really didn't have any idea where she was until you drove right to her. Your nap in the state park gave us plenty of time to move it down here. Sacrificing those SEALs to find her was well worth it."

They let Terry kill that team of SEALs so they could track him. Whoever was watching the feed and controlling the drone would have known where both Terry and Larry were the entire time. It would have been easy to communicate to the SEALs and let them kill the two men, but they knew he would lead the way to Peggy. She was the most important piece in this game of chess. Worth two deputies. Worth the eight members of the National Guard. Worth an entire SEAL platoon.

Terry could feel the rage burning inside him. He felt guilt and regret and hate and rage. Above all, he felt the rage. His trigger finger moved forward of the trigger guard to the circular metal button, pushing the weapon off safe and into fire. It was an audible click that inside the small room may as well have been an explosion.

"Tell me who the fuck you are working for," Terry hissed. "You're not DoD. If you're not CIA, then who is it?"

"Let me guess," the suited man said calmly, "you're recording this? Broadcasting it? This is the big moment where the James Bond villain divulges his plan for world domination? It's your *get out of jail free* card, right?"

"Mister," Terry said, "I was dead the minute I walked into this room. I've got nothing to gain and nothing to lose. I'm doing this purely out of spite. I'm going to kill you and I'm going to kill him, period. Right now, you just need to decide how much pain you want to endure between now and then."

"You're just going to shoot us," Dawson said. "Right here in the house? You think no one is going to hear it?"

"I know no one is going to hear it," Terry responded. "You know, you're pretty goddamn dumb, sir. This is a SCIF. It is soundproofed so no one can listen, even right outside the door. Outside this room, it will sound like someone dropped a book." Dawson's face went pale. Terry turned back to the man in the suit. "I know whoever it is you're working for has an agenda, and he's a big part of it," Terry said as he motioned at Dawson. "So, after I kill him, it all comes apart."

"You really think so?" the man said with a laugh. "You think we can't get another four-star? The commander of USSOCOM is on this very same base." The United States Special Operations Command is located on MacDill AFB and is commanded by a four-star general like Dawson.

"Nice try," Terry said. "If he was a real operator, like a SEAL or a Delta guy or even an Air Force PJ, maybe. That fucking guy is a pilot. He flew Combat Talons. He's not a shooter." Terry was calling his bluff. The commander of USSOCOM was a career Air Force pilot that flew the Special Operations version of the C-130 cargo plane. While technically he had spent his entire career in the special operations community, he wasn't a trigger puller. "And as much as you'd like to believe it, not everyone is working toward whatever agenda you are. I'm done fucking around. Tell me who you are working for or that hole in your forehead is going to get a lot bigger."

"So, what happens when you kill me?" the suit asked. "And him. What happens then? You really think all this goes away? We had access to a SEAL Team, and a Predator. We handpicked a four-star general. You think power like this just goes away? And what happens to you?"

Terry shot the man in the left leg. The soundproofing in the room kept anyone outside from hearing it but it amplified the sound inside the room. It was deafening. Dawson fell out of his chair. The suited man screamed as he collapsed on the floor clutching the bloody stump below his knee.

"Yeah, that wasn't double-aught buck. That was bird shot. An old goose load, actually," Terry said as he regained his hearing. The man was screaming. "You know I'm not fucking around. Who did this? Who killed Peggy?"

The man took a breath and stopped screaming. "You killed her," he said. Terry hadn't pumped his grandfather's shotgun after he pulled the trigger. The only thing in the chamber was an empty shell. Terry pumped the Winchester, holding down the trigger as he jacked the action forward. The shotgun went off. The man's head erupted, plastering brains, hair, and blood on the wall. Modern pump shotguns have a disconnect that forces the shooter to release the trigger between pumps to reset the mechanism. Not the Model 12. It still had the capability to *slam fire,* where the trigger could be held down while the action was pumped, firing off a shell every time the shooter cycled one into the chamber.

Terry turned and pointed the big shotgun at Dawson. The former college football player cowered behind his desk, balled up in the fetal position. Terry moved to the side of the desk, giving himself a clear line of fire.

"Get up," he told the general. "I knew you were weak." Dawson uncurled himself and began to rise. "I knew that back in Paktia when you sat there doing nothing while I checked out that suicide bomber. You never moved. You never tried to protect yourself or anyone else. You fucking froze. And that's what you've been doing through this whole thing, you fucking coward." Dawson was getting angry, but Terry didn't care.

"You're going to kill me?" Dawson asked.

"You're goddamn right, sir," Terry said flatly.

## CHAPTER 34

"What if I tell you who's behind all this?" Dawson tried to bargain. "It may be enough to keep them from killing you."

"And if you tell me who it is," Terry said, "they kill you anyway. You really are stupid."

"Terry," Dawson said softly, "I can give you the bargaining chip you need. Maybe they would even bring you on board. You could work for me at CIA." The general was standing in front of Terry, right until Terry hit him in the balls with the butt of the old shotgun. He collapsed, wheezing.

"You know they are going to trace this to you," Dawson said trying to breathe. "The shotgun, they will know it's you." Terry smiled.

"Starting a war with a guy who knew every inch of your life," Terry said, "is probably not a good idea." Dawson looked up at him. "You remember, I was the one who taught you how to shoot clay targets, right? When you were trying to kiss up to the chief of staff of the Army? Yeah, I taught you how to shoot and even helped you pick out that nice Italian over and under shotgun. I'm guessing it is somewhere in this house. Probably in your bedroom closet or under the bed. It probably hasn't been cleaned either." Dawson looked confused. "It's a smoothbore. No rifling. They won't be able to tell the difference between yours and mine." It wasn't entirely true, but Dawson didn't know that.

"Get the fuck up," Terry said. "Is Tammy in the house?" Dawson shook his head.

"I sent her to DC after the bomb went off," he said trying to stand. The smell from the bloody corpse was starting to fill the room. It was the smell of death. Terry had smelled it hundreds of times in his life, everything from wild game he shot as a kid to dead humans. The smell of blood, internal organs, burned hair, shit, and piss. It was something one never forgot. Some men got used to it, others never did. Terry didn't know if it was that or the hit to the balls, but Dawson vomited all over the floor.

"Good," Terry said. "Then I won't have to kill her, too." Terry didn't mean it. He knew Dawson's wife had nothing to do with any of this, but he wanted to maintain the level of fear in Dawson. Terry pushed Dawson through the door, stopping to pick up the FNX he had dropped on the carpet. Terry heard the two shots before he felt the sting. Jeffrey Johnson was standing on the stairs holding a pistol in his hands. Terry dropped the Model 12 and fired two shots from his pistol as he fell.

Terry's improvised bindings had failed, and Johnson was now trying to kill him with a backup gun. In his haste to get to the basement, Terry had never searched the man, completely missing the tiny Glock strapped to his ankle.

Johnson had been trained well. He had fired a controlled pair from the small pistol to the center mass of his target. Fortunately for Terry, he had bent down to pick up the pistol just as Johnson had fired. The first round went through Terry's left shoulder, the impact twisting his body. The second round grazed the ribs on his left side, cracking two of them as it passed. Terry got lucky as he returned fire. The first .45 ACP round missed Johnson by about three feet, causing the man to move to his right, directly into the path of the second round. It struck his chest, just below his left nipple. The round pierced his heart and killed him almost instantly. *Luck counts.* Dawson made a run for it.

Terry was bleeding and trying to breathe with two cracked ribs. He mustered as much strength as he could and went after him. *Keep moving, keep shooting.* At the top of the stairs, Davis paused. Dawson was nowhere in sight. Terry scanned the rooms as he moved, looking through the red dot sight mounted on top of the big pistol. Nothing in the kitchen. Dining room clear. Living room clear. Davis heard footsteps coming down the stairs and paused. Dawson was a big man and although he was a college athlete, he wasn't exactly graceful, let alone stealthy. Terry moved slowly toward the staircase.

What came around the corner surprised Terry. He half expected to see the long, double barreled shotgun but what he saw was the barrel of what could only be Dawson's general officer pistol. These pistols were nicer, polished versions of the standard issue Beretta M9 troops had been carrying into combat for decades. When an officer pins on his first star, he is given a ceremonial black leather belt with a gold buckle. Along with the belt comes a matching leather holster and the pistol. As the general progressed, the pistol moved with him; it was *his* pistol. When the officer retired, he even had the option to purchase the pistol and keep it when he left the service.

Terry had to assume the pistol was loaded, even if he believed it wasn't. He closed the distance quickly, trying to time his movement. As Dawson's body came into view, Terry hit him as he was gaining speed, feeling his already cracked ribs break as he tackled the big man. The two men hit the wall opposite the bottom of the staircase and ended up in a heap, both pistols scattering away on the tile floor. Terry was quicker to his feet and kicked Dawson in the face, breaking his nose. The general may have been old, but he could still take a hit. He recovered quickly from the kick to the face and punched Terry straight in the balls. The big man was on him before Terry hit the floor.

"You're not going to beat me to death, you fucking punk" the general said. He kicked Terry in his broken ribs. "I'm going to break your fucking neck." Dawson grabbed Terry by the T-shirt the priests had given him and punched him in the face. Terry saw a flash of bright light behind his eyes as the big man's fist connected with his cheekbone. He fell on his back and kicked his legs out, striking Dawson in the knee and sending him to the floor shrieking in pain. Terry could barely breathe from the broken ribs and he could feel his eye swelling up. He spotted Dawson's pistol and crawled to it.

"You're right," Terry said as he turned and looked at Dawson. "I'm not going to beat you to death." Lying on his back Terry pulled the trigger, not knowing if the pistol was even going to go off. Dawson's head exploded, spraying blood on the wall like a Jackson Pollock painting. Terry fell back and laid there for a second, breathing heavily. He knew he had just ended his own life. The people Dawson was working with would come after him, but he would be damned if was going down without a fight. He got up and regained his senses, dropping Dawson's pistol. He found the FNX behind him on the floor, recovered it and moved quickly out the back door. He knew the sirens from the Air Force Special Police would be coming soon. He needed to get to the stolen Mustang and out the gate before the base was locked down.

Terry wasn't worried about stealth at this point, he was moving as fast as he could. He could barely open the door to the little sportscar when he got there. His broken ribs and bleeding shoulder made it almost impossible to use his left arm. Falling into the driver's seat, he didn't know what hurt more, the broken ribs or his balls after Dawson punched him. He threw up in the passenger seat. Terry tucked the pistol between the seat and the console and fired the engine.

He was a mess. Terry's right eye had swollen completely shut as he maneuvered through the streets of the base. Trying to operate the manual transmission and steer without the use of his left arm was difficult to say the least. He could see the brightly lit gate in front of him. *Just a little farther.* He drove the white Mustang out the gate and headed to the only place he could think of: the clergy house. The only thing keeping him going was adrenaline and Terry knew that wasn't going to last. He was fading quickly.

"Keep moving, keep shooting," he repeated to himself. He fought to stay awake as he navigated the streets of Tampa, finding the parking lot of the church just as the sky began to brighten before dawn. He coasted the car into the lot, parking next to the dumpsters in the back. Terry Davis, with his gunshot wound, swollen eye, broken ribs, and aching testicles, made a valiant effort to climb out of the sportscar. He failed. His body was finished. He passed out thinking only of Peggy.

## CHAPTER 35

Terry woke up, expecting to be in a prison cell. He was lying in the spare bedroom of the clergy house. He had no idea what time it was, or even what day it was. His ribs were taped, and his shoulder bandaged. Trying to blink, he could feel his right eye was still very swollen. He had a headache worse than any hangover he had ever had. He was naked under the sheets and could feel the ache between his legs. He passed out again.

When he awoke the second time, the room was dark. His body still ached, especially his shoulder and ribs, but the swelling in his eye had gone down and his balls weren't as tender. He knew it was after sunset but had no idea what time it was. Terry saw another white T-shirt on the back of the chair and what looked like a pair of athletic shorts. He gingerly hauled himself out of bed and put the clothing on. The bandage on his shoulder had bled through. He would need to change it soon. The shoulder hurt like hell as he tried to maneuver the T-shirt over his head.

He moved slowly into the hallway and put a lot of weight on the railing as he came down the steps. He could smell food again. Father D'Ambrosio was in the kitchen, standing over the stove in his apron. Terry looked right to see Father O'Connor watching the TV. The two priests looked at him.

"Thank you, gentlemen," Terry said. Neither priest said a word. Terry moved slowly to the TV room and sat down. "Who patched me up?" he asked.

"I did," Father O'Connor said. "Corporal O'Connor was a medic." Father D brought Terry a bowl containing some sort of red vegetable soup and set it on the coffee table with a spoon. Terry nodded at him. "Son," O'Connor continued, "we helped you because that is our duty to God. I don't know what happened or how you got into that condition, but as soon as you are able, you need to leave." The old man got up and went into the kitchen. Anthony sat down in his spot and looked at Terry.

"I found you in the car when I took the trash out," he started quietly. "Luckily, it was before the garbage men came to empty the dumpsters." He looked over his shoulder into the kitchen. "That car is gone now. It showed up on the news this afternoon. Look." He pointed at the TV. Terry could see the outside of the strip club where he had stolen the car and the words *murder-suicide* on the screen. Terry's heart hurt as he saw two faces appear on the screen. It was the man he stole the car from and Aimee, the tattoo-covered waitress. They were both dead. The Mustang was back in the parking lot where he had left Aimee standing as he drove off in the stolen car.

"And there is a dead general," O'Connor said as he came back into the room. "On the base. A four-star general. Shot to death." Terry looked over his shoulder at the older priest. Father D'Ambrosio began to stand, vacating the seat normally occupied by O'Connor. The Irishman waved at him to stay sitting. "I am guessing this was your general?" Terry didn't say a word. He didn't need to implicate these two men any more than he already had. "The news said there were two other men with him. That was you, too." Terry only looked at the old priest. "They say it was the man who killed the waitress girl. They say he killed the general and those other men, not you." Terry's eyes narrowed. O'Connor turned and went back to the kitchen.

"A package was left on the doorstep this afternoon," Father D'Ambrosio said. "We think it is yours." The priest with the gentle nature got up from the couch and went to the doorway. He returned with a long box, placing it on Terry's lap. Terry leaned back and opened the box. Inside was his grandfather's shotgun. The Model 12 was separated into two major components, the barrel and magazine tube and the receiver and buttstock. That's how the gun was placed in the box. It was clean. There were no marks or smears on the blued steel. There was no note of any kind.

"Let me guess," Terry said, "there was no address and you have no idea who delivered it."

"Yes," Anthony said. "It was just on the doorstep, wrapped in brown paper." It was a message. They knew where he was. They knew he was here with the two priests. But why didn't they come get him? Why wasn't he dead already? The phone rang. Father O'Connor answered it in the kitchen.

"It's for you," the old priest said as he came into the TV room. He was holding the phone receiver and pointing it at Terry. Terry got up slowly, putting the box with the shotgun onto the floor. He moved gingerly around the couch and took the phone from Father O'Connor. The old man beckoned to his younger counterpart to follow him into the kitchen and give Terry some privacy. When the two men were out of the room, Terry put the phone to his face.

"Yes?" Terry said into the receiver.

"Mr. Davis." It was a man's voice, older, gravely, and not one he recognized. "Mr. Davis, I wanted to call and say thank you. You cleaned up a mess for us. General Dawson was not the man we assumed he was. Thank you for taking care of that problem for us." Terry stood silently. "I trust you have your grandfather's shotgun by now. I'm glad we could return that to you as a token of our appreciation." This man was part of whatever organization Dawson and the man in the suit were working for. "The other man was a valuable asset to us. I wish you hadn't dispatched him the way you did, but we understand. He will be replaced. We have others."

"Collateral damage, I guess," Terry said. The man chuckled.

"Yes, collateral damage. Mr. Davis," the man continued, "we need to come to an understanding. You are alive because we have allowed it. This is a *live and let live* scenario. Do you understand that?"

"Explain it to me," Terry said.

"Mr. Davis," the voice said, "we are powerful people. We aren't Democrats or Republicans. We aren't politicians or soldiers. We are Americans and we are doing what we think is best for America. We are the media. We are the government. We are the people that can move mountains. We are going to get our way whether we allow you to live or not. We would even be happy to let you join our cause." The voice paused. Terry was taking all of this in. "You've proven yourself to be quite capable. We are impressed."

"I'm not here to impress you," Terry said. "I did what needed to be done—for Peggy."

"Yes, Ms. Baron," the voice said. "She'd like to speak to you."

Terry went cold.

"Terry," Peggy said. She was alive. "Terry, you made this more difficult than it should have been."

"You're alive," Terry said. He was overcome by more emotions than he could process—relief, shock, disbelief, anger.

"Yes, I'm alive," she said. "But you shouldn't be. Terry, this is bigger than you or me. Just like Dawson told you. This is the right thing for our country."

"What do you mean, I shouldn't be alive?" he interrupted her.

"You should have been dead a long time ago." He could hear frustration in her voice. "I should have let the deputy kill you like he wanted. All those men, Terry, they were there to kill you and take me so I could finish all of this."

"You?" he said. "You're part of this?"

"Yes," she said. "You weren't supposed to be part of the call with Dawson. And those men, the men at the house, the men at George's hideout, even the SEALs. I was part of that. Then you got Brian and Emma involved and it all fell apart. And you got Larry killed." She was rambling.

"What are you saying?" Terry was putting the pieces together. "You led those men to us? To kill me?"

"Yes," she said. She was angry now. Angry at him. "You're so fucking smart. Damn you. Now do what they are asking, Terry. Walk away from this." She had betrayed him. It was all a lie from the start. From the minute he found her chopping wood, it was a lie. Even before that. He had killed men and was almost killed himself because of her.

"Mr. Davis," the gravely man was back on the phone. "Listen to Ms. Baron, walk away from this. Live and let live. Stay out of our business, Mr. Davis. We've cleaned up all the messes. It's clean. You are free to walk away, but don't disrupt our dealings again. Do we understand each other?"

"Yes," Terry said. "Live and let live."

"Thank you, Mr. Davis," the man's voice said quietly. "And make sure your friends understand that, too. That nice couple with the German Shepherd." The line went dead. Terry stood for a long minute, staring at the phone.

Terry said goodbye to the two priests, thanking them again for everything. For all his goodness, Father O'Connor wasn't upset to see Terry leave. The church was tolerant, but Terry's activities of the last few days were definitely pushing the limits. When he got to the garage, he found Big Blue still sitting there. Moving slowly to the passenger side of the truck, he put the box containing the shotgun behind the bench seat. He found the FNX lying on the floor. Father D'Ambrosio must have put it there after he found Terry passed out in the Mustang. Terry stashed that behind the bench seat as well. After the phone call with Peggy and the mystery man, he didn't expect a fight between here and Kansas. Even if he did, he wasn't in any shape to take it on.

Terry sat behind the steering wheel and took an assessment of himself. He looked in the mirror, finally seeing his face after the beating he took from Dawson. His eye was swollen and bruised, but he could open it a little. His left arm was still sore and bleeding, as well as the broken ribs. He was thankful Big Blue wasn't a manual transmission like the little Mustang had been. Mostly, he was happy his nuts didn't hurt as much as when he woke up. It was a long drive to return the big Chevy to Brian and he knew sitting on sore testicles would have made it almost unbearable.

Terry headed north. He was reluctant to use his credit cards after everything that had happened in the last week. Was it a week? Maybe two? But he was out of cash thanks to the tip he had given poor Aimee and didn't have any other choice. The first time he stopped for gas and swiped his card, he almost expected a Hellfire missile to kill him where he stood. It seemed the mystery man on the phone wasn't lying when he said he was free to go. Terry was paranoid as he moved north, waiting to be followed or even be recognized at a fast-food restaurant or gas station. By the time he reached the Missouri state line a day later, he was convinced that if anyone was watching him, it was through the feed on a Predator and he couldn't do anything about that.

It was late afternoon when he pulled into Brian and Emma's drive with Big Blue. He was met by Jumper coming to greet him as he opened the door. Brian and Emma only stood on the porch. Terry was still in the T-shirt and athletic shorts the priests had given him. He knew he still looked like hell. Emma kissed him softly when he reached the top of the steps. The three walked inside without saying a word. It was a very different feel than when he was here just a few days ago. The couple had no idea what had happened since the explosion, except that Dawson was dead. Terry sat at the kitchen island and Brian handed him a beer. Terry took a long pull off the bottle of Michelob Ultra.

"So, what the fuck happened?" Brian asked. Emma gave him a look.

"Listen," Terry started, "you need to understand one thing before I tell you." Emma touched his leg, Brian handed Terry a can of Copenhagen. "The three of us are only alive because they are allowing it."

"They?" Brian said. "Who the fuck are *they*?"

"That's the million-dollar question, brother." Terry tipped the bottle back, finishing the beer. He could feel it in his eye when he did. He put a dip of snuff in his lip and spit into the bottle. Emma was being patient. Brian was not.

"Quit talkin' in fuckin' code," Brian said. Terry recounted everything from the explosion to the phone call at the clergy house. He told them about the phone call, but not about Peggy.

"That's the quietest I think you've ever been since I met you," he said to Brian, who sat silently. Terry turned to Emma. "Why did you leave the hotel? Right before the blast."

"Peggy told me she was hungry," she said with a tear welling up in the corner of her eye. "She said she would be fine and that I should take Jumper with me."

"Was her car there when you left?" Terry asked. "The Audi. Was it there in front of the room?" Emma shook her head. Terry nodded. "I'm not kidding. You two can't breathe a word of this. Ever."

"Who the fuck would believe us?" Brian said. "Some dark, magical organization tryin' to take over the government. No one would believe that shit anyway."

"It's real," Terry said.

"We believe you," Emma stood up and hugged him.

"I need some sleep," he said.

"Stay as long as you like," the little redhead said softly. "You're safe here."

Terry went down to the spare bedroom and stood in the doorway. In his mind's eye, he could see Peggy there. He went into the bathroom and looked at himself in the mirror. There were still hairs from his beard in the sink. He splashed some water on his face, then turned and walked out to the bed. He slept until the next morning.

## CHAPTER 36

The farmhouse was dark when Peggy unlocked the front door. The place was immaculate. The glass next to the door had been replaced, the blood from the deputy scrubbed completely off the floor. There was no trace that anything had happened at the house, inside or out. It had been a week since she talked to Terry on the phone, almost three weeks since they had left in a rush. It seemed like an eternity. His presence had been erased. She walked down into the basement. His things were gone. Guns, gun safe, his gear—all of it gone. These people she was working with were thorough.

Back upstairs, she looked in the garage. An Audi Q5 just like hers was sitting in the garage. It even had the same license plate. Back in the kitchen she opened the refrigerator to find it full. Bottles of water, food, even condiments, all new and all neatly placed inside. It was as if her life returned to what it was before Terry came stay. It was eerie and comforting at the same time. She dropped her bag as she went up the stairs, moving quietly without trying. She walked into the bedroom and turned on the lamp next to the bed. She jumped when she saw him sitting in the chair against the wall.

"Why?" Terry asked her.

"You scared the shit out of me," Peggy said, holding her chest. "What are you doing here? How did you know I would come back?"

"Your horses, Peggy," he said. "And this house. I knew you couldn't leave it. Couldn't leave them. Now answer the question." There was no anger in his voice. There was nothing.

"Why?" she repeated the question. "You want to know why." He nodded. She realized his beard was growing back. "Because, Terry. Because this is the future. Governments don't control anything anymore. It's all a fallacy. A dream that people like you cling to. You're a fool."

"Peggy," he interrupted her, "I don't care what your beliefs are. Or what kind of bullshit you've bought into. I want to know why you were willing to let me die, to sacrifice me to accomplish it. To put Brian and Emma at risk. All of it. Why?"

"You're smart Terry," she said with a bit of anger in her voice. "But you still don't get it. We are willing to sacrifice everything and everyone we know to get this done. That includes you."

"We?" he said. "You really are one of them. You're even talking like that guy on the phone. You manipulated this whole thing. You manipulated me. You called someone from the gas station, right? George and Juanita's place. You never called Larry." She stared at him. "Between that and the beacon, that's how they found us. Then you put it in my pack at the farm. That's how they found me there." He could see the surprise in her face. "I've had a lot of time to think about this. It was a long drive back from Tampa.

"You controlled all of this," he continued. "Every conversation. Every lead we had. You kept it moving where you wanted it to go, right? I fucking missed it because I trusted you. And I loved you, Peggy."

"I needed you, Terry. You could have been part of all of this. A contributor. You still can," she said. Her voice was different now. There was an edge to it he had never heard before. "But, make no mistake—this is the future. This is *my future.*"

"There is one thing that has been eating at me. You could have killed me. I can't even guess how many times you could have killed me along the way. You're smart, Peggy. At some point, you had to know I wasn't going to buy into this shit. You had to know." She was staring at him. "So, why didn't you? Why didn't you just kill me and get it over with?"

"I was hoping . . ." she said.

"No. Bullshit," he snapped at her. "You knew I wouldn't. So, why didn't you?"

"Because I'm not *you*, Terry," she said. There was anger in her voice. "I can't just go around killing people. I'm not a killer like you."

"That's right. You're not. And I am." Peggy's eyes widened as Terry stood. She started to speak but the words were cut short as he shot her twice in the chest.

He stepped over her body and down the stairs, the old house creaking at every step. Terry walked casually out the front door, around the house, and behind the barn where he had stashed the Jeep. He looked in the backseat as he strapped himself in, the interior lights revealing the weapons and gear he had recovered from Larry's dry well just hours before. Davis fired the engine on the Jeep and pulled out onto the blacktop. He headed east, back to his native Chicago. Back to family and friends. Back to ground he knew he could fight on because he knew a fight was coming. He hit the button on the CD player and sang along to Led Zeppelin and Robert Plant, wailing the lyrics to "Ramble On" with only one thought on his mind.

*Keep moving, keep shooting.*

# ACKNOWLEDGMENTS

To my family and friends, thank you for standing behind me throughout this process, the support was more important than you know. To Pop, thanks for teaching me to love to read by tossing me a book and saying, "read this." To Mick, thanks for convincing me to take this chance. Like so many others throughout our lives, this would not have happened without that push. Thank you to my wife and kids who said, "you have to try." To Abi, thank you for being a solid rock for me for the last six years. And to You, the reader, . . . thank you.